UFUOMAEE

Who Killed Nnamdi?!

First published by Ufuomaee 2025

Copyright © 2025 by Ufuomaee

All rights reserved. No part of this publication may be reproduced, stored or transmitted in any form or by any means, electronic, mechanical, photocopying, recording, scanning, or otherwise without written permission from the publisher. It is illegal to copy this book, post it to a website, or distribute it by any other means without permission.

This novel is entirely a work of fiction. The names, characters and incidents portrayed in it are the work of the author's imagination. Any resemblance to actual persons, living or dead, events or localities is entirely coincidental.

Ufuomaee asserts the moral right to be identified as the author of this work.

Photo credit: www.canva.com

Unless otherwise stated, all scriptures referenced are from www.blueletterbible.org.

Trigger Warning: Though not explicit, this book contains frequent references to sex and sexuality, anger and violence, with occasional bad language. Themes of hypersexuality, infidelity, and revenge are explored. Parental guidance is advised.

First edition

ISBN: 9798313435626

This book was professionally typeset on Reedsy. Find out more at reedsy.com

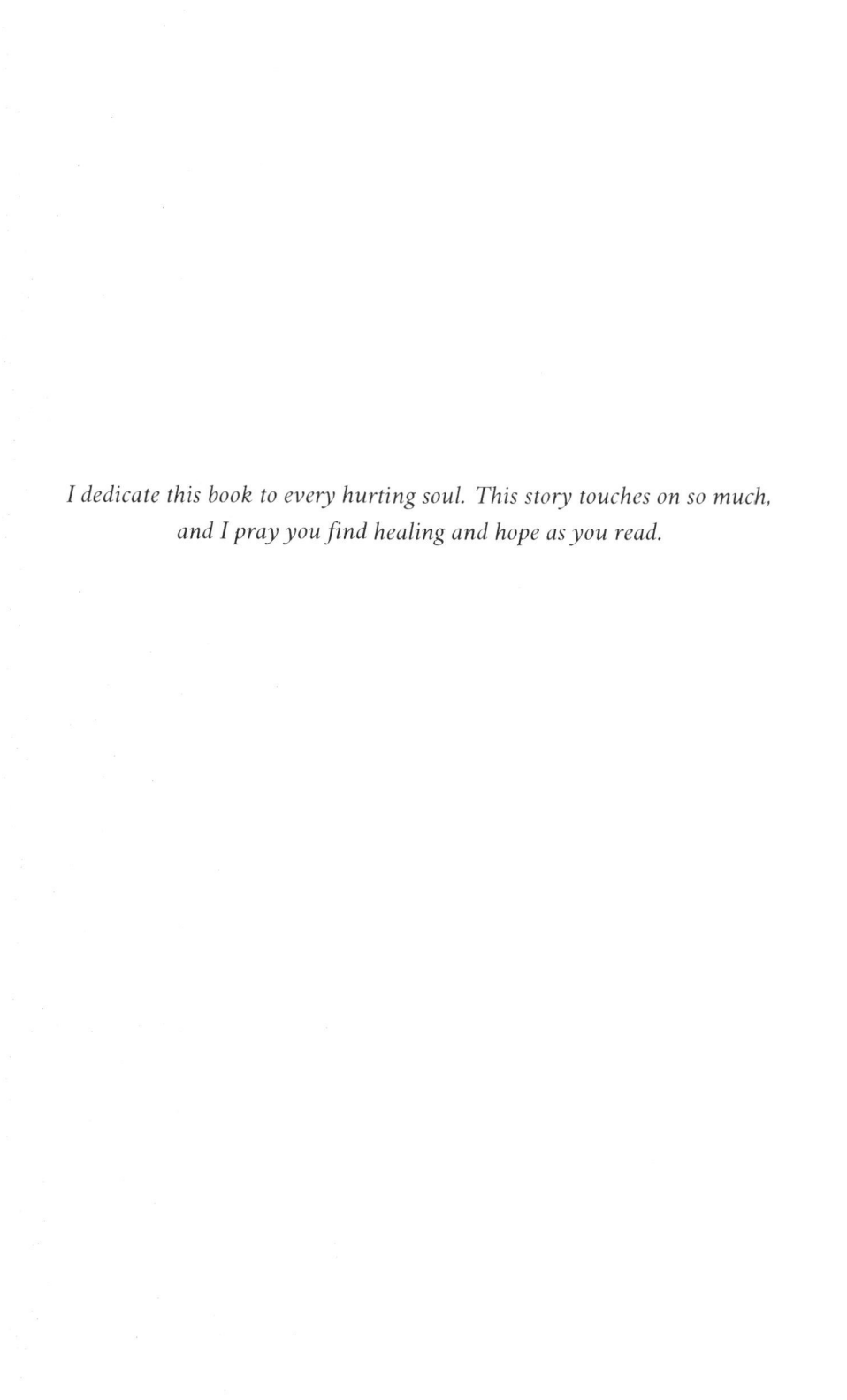

I dedicate this book to every hurting soul. This story touches on so much, and I pray you find healing and hope as you read.

Contents

Preface   iii
Praise for Who Killed Nnamdi?!   v
THE PROLOGUE - SUSPECT #1   vi

I   ADA'S STORY

CHAPTER ONE - THE DAY MY LIFE CHANGED   3
CHAPTER TWO - THE SUMMON   11
CHAPTER THREE - DANGEROUSLY IN LOVE   18
CHAPTER FOUR - MR AND MRS NNAMDI UKWUEZE   26
CHAPTER FIVE - A LOVE MATCH?   34
CHAPTER SIX - ENTRAPMENT   42
CHAPTER SEVEN - BLEEDING LOVE   49
CHAPTER EIGHT - NO MORE "I LOVE YOU"S   56
CHAPTER NINE - OUR MARRIAGE   64
CHAPTER TEN - THE LAST INSULT   72

II   THE INVESTIGATION

CHAPTER ELEVEN - THE LAWYER   81
CHAPTER TWELVE - THE USUAL SUSPECTS   89
CHAPTER THIRTEEN - MATTERS ARISING   99
CHAPTER FOURTEEN - SUSPECT #2   108
CHAPTER FIFTEEN - REVELATIONS   115

CHAPTER SIXTEEN - SUSPECT #3	123
CHAPTER SEVENTEEN - AN ARREST	131
CHAPTER EIGHTEEN - MYSTERIOUS WAYS	140
CHAPTER NINETEEN - A WOMAN SCORNED	148
CHAPTER TWENTY - ONE NIGHT IN DECEMBER	155

III THE AFTERMATH

CHAPTER TWENTY-ONE - THE MIND OF A KILLER	165
CHAPTER TWENTY-TWO - BETRAYED	173
CHAPTER TWENTY-THREE - BEREAVED	180
CHAPTER TWENTY-FOUR - THE ARRAIGNMENT	188
CHAPTER TWENTY-FIVE - THE WIDOW	196
CHAPTER TWENTY-SIX - THE REDEEMER	205
CHAPTER TWENTY-SEVEN - THE AWAKENING	212
CHAPTER TWENTY-EIGHT - MAKING PEACE	219
CHAPTER TWENTY-NINE - FORGIVENESS	227
CHAPTER THIRTY - LIFE AFTER DEATH	235
CHAPTER THIRTY-ONE - TRUE LOVE	242
THE EPILOGUE - THE LAST WILL AND TESTAMENT OF NNAMDI GERALD...	250
BONUS CHAPTER - A WOMAN'S SECRET	252
Acknowledgements	261
About the Author	262

Preface

The idea for this book came to me in September 2022, a year after I had released the last book of **The Naive Wife Trilogy.** But I wasn't in the right frame of mind to start on it. Honestly, I was tired of writing about marriage and infidelity. I wrote a short synopsis, with sufficient detail for me to develop the story later, and forgot about it. In February 2025, I was looking for a story to write, I came across it, and it was perfect!

This book was so much fun to write! Even though I was afraid to, especially as I have never written a murder mystery before, I knew that if I put in the work to write this story, it would be explosive. 'Who Killed Nnamdi?!' isn't just a murder mystery, it is an exposition of humanity and relationships. There are so many themes I explored in this story, but for the sake of suspense, I will leave you to discover them all.

The only way I could do justice to the story was to inhabit the minds of my characters as I let them narrate their experiences. Because there were so many perspectives, I was tempted to write from an author's perspective, but I think the story is richer this way. I allowed my characters full expression, using their preferred language to communicate their experiences, thoughts, and feelings. So, you will see some profanity as you read, but every word I left in this book was intentional. I hope that as you read through, you will appreciate the authenticity this brought to the narrative.

Please be advised that this book is not for a young or immature audience. Even though the scenes are not explicit, there are frequent references to sex and sexuality, thoughts of aggression and violence, and the act of violence itself, as seen in the murder of two people. All of these are captured not because I believe they are justified but to communicate the experiences of my characters effectively. So, you may be triggered as you read.

Ultimately, I pray that the story blesses you. I hope you will come away with many lessons you will keep close to your heart and with wisdom that will guide and uplift you.

The story has an accompanying multi-genre playlist available on YouTube Music - https://bit.ly/WKNPlaylist. I enjoyed listening to these songs as I wrote the book.

Thank you for getting my book. I would greatly appreciate it if you would leave a review for me on **Goodreads** or **Amazon** or on my website at **www.ufuomaee.com**.

God bless you, and enjoy the book!

Love, *Ufuomaee*

Praise for Who Killed Nnamdi?!

"The excitement with which I dived into the book didn't douse one bit while I read through the chapters. Ufuomaee drew me in with such beautiful writing, keeping me at the edge of my seat with each turn of the page. I kept wondering who really killed Nnamdi with how well she kept the suspense. I also liked that she infused some strong themes in a subtle way drawing up lessons as we read on. I would highly recommend this book as it was a beautiful read. I rate it a 5☆"
   - Temitope Adeniran

"I wasn't expecting the plot twists in this book at all; I was on the edge of my seat all through. If you think you are so good at guessing, this book will show you otherwise!"
   - Gloria Elemide

"Ufuomaee has written another spellbinding book, a story that might seem unbelievable but occurs even more than we can imagine in today's world. It is a book that enlightens and encourages one to believe that even from the midst of pain, hope and love can still rise again..."
   - Oruare Ojimadu

THE PROLOGUE - SUSPECT #1

Looking at the pictures of my husband sprawled over his mistress in a bed soaked with blood, I struggle to choose an emotion. Like a legion of demons, they wash over me… Anger, jealousy, hatred, bitterness, sadness, disgust…vengeance, and more that I can't put names to.

I look away, but the images are seared in my mind, and I can't seem to unsee them. The only consolation is that they are dead, which is a pity, only because I have no idea of how it came to be nor joy from knowing that it was I who ended their lives! If I could kill them again, I would. Nnamdi especially!

"You need to answer the question, Mrs Ukwueze."

I look up at the investigating officer, and a sneaky emotion wants to get the best of me as a smile tickles my lips. I can't deny that I'm happy he's dead, but God forbid that I should rot in prison for a crime I didn't have the pleasure of committing. I suppress the smile and swallow.

I cannot cry. I'm a terrible actress and a worse liar. Any attempt to pretend to care would make me more of a suspect than I already am. If it were possible. Besides, he doesn't deserve my pretence. Everyone, and I mean everyone, knows now, even if they didn't before, what an awful husband he was to me.

"Where were you last night at 8:45 pm?"

I heave a sigh as I try to relax. They are only going through due process, and it's not my fault that I don't have an alibi. But isn't that the best alibi of all?

Confidently, I look the officer in his eyes as I respond. "I was at home in bed."

"So, you do not have an alibi for the night your husband and his girlfriend were murdered?"

"I didn't know I needed one."

A smirk crosses the officer's face. "But you wanted him dead, didn't you? It must have eaten you up to know that he would rather be with someone else…"

I have a good mind to yell at this officer and affirm his thoughts, but hell will freeze over before I allow Nnamdi's abhorrent existence ruin my life even more than it has. His death is supposed to set me free!

"What I want, sir, is a lawyer."

I fold my arms and watch as the officers walk out of my interrogation room. I swallow as I consider my situation. *How the hell did I get here?*

I

ADA'S STORY

What a vile man! I married a wicked man! A lying, manipulative monster of a man! I fumed, getting angrier by the second as I waited for him to come out of the bathroom.

Eventually, he did, with a towel around his waist and another that he used to pat his body dry. He looked at me, and there was no trace of remorse. He wanted me to find out today. He put on a show for me, I realised.

Enraged, I ran towards him and began to hit him as I cried, "You bastard! You wicked bastard! How could you?!"

CHAPTER ONE - THE DAY MY LIFE CHANGED

I remember it was raining that day. I stopped over at the bank to resolve a failed transaction issue on my corporate account. I was next to be called when I heard someone call me from behind. "Ada?"

I was not prepared to see him at all, but I thanked God that I was dressed smartly for work and looked moderately attractive. He, on the other hand, was dressed in joggers, with a vest that showed off his well-built frame. Obviously, he had stopped over from the gym. His fair skin glowed like he had smeared baby oil all over it, but it wasn't excessive. Just enough to make a woman look again.

"Nnamdi... Hi," I greeted backwards and returned his smile.

There was just one man between us in the line, and he spoke over his head as he said, "Wow, you haven't aged one bit."

I should have known he was a liar then because, at 34, I looked nothing like I did at 16, which was how old I was when I last saw him. Yes, it's true that I have a babyface, and my boobs that came in late decided they were done growing at a size B-cup, but I had since grown in stature and weight, the latter of which I had a constant battle.

Nonetheless, I smiled and looked down, not wanting him to notice the things I was insecure about, like the excessive hair above my nose, which got plucked daily. Before I could return the compliment, a cashier called, "Next!"

Knowing I was being watched, I sucked my tummy in, put my shoulders up, and strutted the small distance to the counter to meet the cashier, making sure to stick my butt out a bit more than usual. It is the one part of my figure that I am absolutely proud of, and I flaunt it every chance I get.

My complaint took longer to resolve than I anticipated, and I was disappointed when he waved at me as he left the banking hall. It was my turn to admire his body, and I swooned on seeing his tight behind, visible as he walked in his joggers. From the back, he looked even more delicious than from the front, if you can imagine it. Broad shoulders, taut muscles, narrow waist, and long legs!

I looked back at the cashier when he was out of view and exhaled, thinking it was a good thing he left without getting my number. In my heart, I knew the heartbreak from a man like Nnamdi Ukwueze would be fatal. But though I knew I wasn't his type, it didn't stop me from crushing on him. I collected my new token from the cashier and made my way out of the bank.

The light drizzle I had met when I entered had turned into a downpour that trapped many customers in the shaded areas around the bank. I saw Nnamdi as he looked around, as if he was going to brave it and run through the rain to his car. He kept looking at his watch and looking up at the sky.

Someone bumped me - I didn't know I'd been blocking the exit - causing me to bump someone else, who didn't find it funny.

"Excuse you!" he yelled, causing Nnamdi to turn in my direction.

"Hey, hey. I'm sure it was a mistake," Nnamdi said in my defence, causing the man to hiss and walk away. I don't blame him for wanting to leave Nnamdi's towering stature. Compared to him, that man was a munchkin! "You're alright?"

I nodded and swallowed as I saw care in his eyes. "Yes, thanks," I

CHAPTER ONE - THE DAY MY LIFE CHANGED

muttered at last.

I walked away from the exit and closer to where he stood at the edge of the awning, when the rain kept pounding. He was a full head and shoulders taller than me, meaning he had grown significantly since we were at High School together. Back then, I think he was only a head taller.

My phone rang, distracting me from my reminiscing. On seeing the caller ID, I picked up.

"Hi, Victor. No, I'm still at the bank. It's pouring here. Okay, don't worry. I will be there soon. Okay. Thanks."

"Boyfriend?"

The question took me by surprise, and I had to look at Nnamdi in a daze, wondering why he would ask me that. I shook my head.

"My younger brother."

"Oh!" Nnamdi said, nodding.

I put my phone away smiling. Now, I wanted to know if he had a girlfriend…or a wife. From where I stood, I couldn't see his ring finger.

"Well, I figured you're not married, since you're not wearing a ring," Nnamdi continued, and I just looked up at him, wondering again why he was interested in my relationship status.

He smiled down at me, and I almost fainted because the man was too fine! God was having a good day when He sculpted him. Even his teeth were still white and perfectly aligned. I bit down on my lips, hoping he hadn't noticed the small gap between my front teeth. I had worn braces throughout university to straighten out my crooked teeth, and that was the best I got.

"Seeing anyone?"

By now, my heart was doing a mile a minute, wondering where his questions were leading. All I could do was shake my head. And I saw him swallow! Like, seriously… Nnamdi Ukwueze was nervous about asking me out?! If that was what he was doing. I didn't get asked out a lot, so this whole interaction was strange to me.

He finally got quiet, and we both listened as the rain kept on pouring down. Some people braved the rain and ran for their cars, but I just wished it would rain forever. Anything to keep standing beside Nnamdi and feeling like someone finally saw me.

He brought his hands forward, placing the left on top of the right, and at last, I saw that he was not married. There wasn't even the impression of a ring. I drew in a sigh as hope arose in me. Dangerous hope! Stupid hope!

The sound of his phone ringing broke the companionable silence between us, and he rifled in his pocket to bring it out. I watched the muscles in his arm contract as he raised the phone to his right ear. Smooth and hairless skin held me in a trance, making me yearn to touch them, until he returned his phone to his pocket, drawing my eyes to notice he was gifted below also. Immediately, I looked away, not wanting to be caught staring. His hands returned to rest in front of him.

He looked up again at the sky, and I followed his gaze. The sun was coming out. *Damn it!*

"You live around here?"

"Yeah, off Admiralty Road."

"Oh, cool," he said, turning slightly and looking at me with a side eye. "Maybe we can meet up for drinks sometime."

No way! What?! I did not see that coming.

Smiling, I nodded up at him. "Sounds good."

He brought out his phone again and unlocked it. "What's your number?"

I called it out for him, and he called me. "Miss Independent," by Neyo, the ring tone I used for unknown callers, began to play as my phone rang. Nnamdi chuckled as he watched me rush to quickly end

CHAPTER ONE - THE DAY MY LIFE CHANGED

the call.

"Really? You're Miss Independent?"

I giggled. "I just like the song."

"Nice. Me too," he beamed at me.

With the rain still falling, though it was down to a drizzle, he stepped out of the protection of the awning and waved at me, as he rushed towards a black, Lexus jeep and got into the driver's side.

I watched him drive away and then looked up at the heavens. The rain had stopped, the clouds had disappeared, and the sun stood high in the sky, with what I imagine was a big grin on its face.

*****

My brief stop at the bank took a whole hour, so I didn't get to my office until 9:45 am.

Back then, AdVi Grand, the architectural firm I run with my brother, was still quite small, and we had an office in a mini complex along Admiralty Way. The office was divided into three cubicles. One for me, the CEO, one for Victor, the Architect, and another for the Executive Assistant we shared, Tamara.

I stopped by Tamara's cubicle on my way to mine. "Have you confirmed our presentation time for this morning?"

"Yes, ma," Tamara replied, looking up from her laptop. "They said 10:30 am."

"Okay, then."

I continued walking to my cubicle. Behind my desk, I went through the presentation Victor had sent the day before, which Tamara had printed and left on my desk. I remembered that I was supposed to send the model designer money so Victor could pick up the model he had built for the presentation.

With the new token, the payment went through, and I heaved a sigh of relief. My trip to the bank wasn't wasted. I shut my eyes as the memory of Nnamdi looking down at me cheekily as he said, *"Maybe we can meet up for drinks sometime,"* replayed in my mind and filled my heart with warmth. I would have loved to spend more time fantasizing about the hunk, but I had a business to run. Knowing the traffic situation in Lagos, I didn't want to risk arriving late, so I hurried back out with the proposal in hand, once I was assured that I had everything prepared for the presentation.

*****

Victor was in the reception of the real estate firm when I got there at 10:15 am.

"Hey, sis," he said, smiling at me as I walked towards him. He rose for a brief hug, and we sat down together. I could tell he was nervous. Going after this contract was a big deal! It would be the biggest project we had ever done, but it had been his dream since he was little. I rubbed his back, knowing he would make me proud today.

We were eventually let into the boardroom to prepare, about 20 minutes later. Two men walked in, followed by a woman, and they took their seats at the board table, leaving the prominent space unoccupied.

"Will someone else be joining us?" I asked just as he walked in, his phone to his ear.

Nnamdi ended the call and looked at me. He seemed like he wanted to say something but thought better of it and took his seat and joined the others in looking expectantly at me and my brother.

"Good morning, everyone," Victor began in a confident voice. "We are thrilled to present our design proposal for the new shopping complex on Freedom Way…"

I looked from Victor to Nnamdi, then the lady sitting beside him, to Nnamdi, then Victor, to the two older men, then to Nnamdi, to Victor, and back again. The whole time, Nnamdi's gaze was fixed on the screen or the model, as Victor expounded on the design details,

CHAPTER ONE - THE DAY MY LIFE CHANGED

which included the parking lot, the small stores, the megastores, a huge supermarket, a food court, and even a children's playground. I hoped he would look at me and smile, but he didn't, which was strange.

At last, I looked down at myself, wondering if there was something out of place. Was my tummy sticking out again? I should have gone to the bathroom to check my appearance, I thought. Who knows what damage the rain had done to my hair and make-up. I swallowed as Victor rounded up. It was my turn to present on the project's timeline and budget.

He looked directly at me, a curious expression on his face, but I didn't let it sway me. I moved my gaze from one member of the board to another, using the slides I had prepared to give what I knew was an excellent presentation. The man immediately to his right clapped first, then the man on the far end, followed by the woman. At last, Nnamdi bobbed his head.

"Not bad," he said softly.

"Thank you," I replied with a smile. "Any questions?"

A lot of the questions they had were directed at Victor, and he did a good job assuaging their concerns. Nnamdi wanted to know if our design was based on primarily using locally sourced materials, and I answered in the affirmative.

"This not only minimizes costs, but it also builds our local economy, which is something AdVi Grand Architecture is committed to doing."

"Okay, we will get back to you," Nnamdi said, putting an end to the meeting.

My legs felt like jelly as I walked out of that boardroom. As much as I wanted the job for us, and I believed we did our best, I couldn't fight the feeling that it was just too good to be true. Even though Nnamdi was being nice, he didn't look all that impressed nor convinced. Maybe, it was that 'familiarity breeds contempt' thing, but it left me with a sour feeling as I walked towards the elevator with Victor.

I was just at my car when my phone rang. It was the secretary at LionsGate Properties, who I had only spoken to once before.

"The ED would like to see you in his office."

CHAPTER TWO - THE SUMMON

"The ED would like to see you in his office…"

The words kept replaying in my head as I made my way back up to the fifth floor, where Nnamdi's real estate company had their offices, in a prestigious building at Victoria Island.

Had it really come to that? One minute we were mates and old friends, and he saw me as someone he could date. The next, he was summoning me like a common secretary. Had he lost my number already? Or he didn't want to pass across the wrong message? These were the thoughts in my mind as I waited outside his office with my brother, Victor.

My only hope was that he would give us the contract, not that I could even dream of more.

We had been waiting five minutes before his secretary said we could go in. I let Victor lead the way.

"Oh," he said, rising as Victor and I approached his desk. "My secretary must have been confused. I only asked for you to come."

His secretary must have been confused? *You're the one who is confused!* I ground my teeth to keep from speaking.

"Okay, sorry," Victor said, turning around to leave, still carrying the six-storey model of a shopping mall in his hands. *Poor guy!*

"I'll see you back at the office," I said, not wanting him to waste any more time waiting for me. After he left, I turned my gaze back to

Nnamdi, ignoring his offer of a seat. "I'm fine, thanks."

Rather than sit down, he decided to come over to my side of his desk and rest on it, his hands folded across his chest as he looked at me, amusement in his eyes.

"So, you're the one behind AdVi Grand. Miss Independent..."

I forced back a smile and took a deep breath. Was his plan to humiliate me and make me beg?

"I'm sorry, I was taken by surprise in there," he said, exhaling. "You don't have to be so nervous. It's still me."

That helped, and I relaxed the shoulders I didn't know I'd set at attention. Not knowing what to say in response, I simply nodded.

"Or did you know you would be presenting to me today?"

I met his eyes. "Of course not."

He shrugged, probably not sure if I was lying or not. "It was a good presentation, if I'm being honest... But..."

Here it is... Come on, spit it out!

"It sort of muddies things for me, *'cos,*" he looked from my eyes to my waist and up again, "I don't like to mix business with pleasure."

What?! Thank God I took my dad's complexion because the heat that ran to my cheeks burned. Suddenly, I felt like meat under his gaze.

I swallowed, flattered but not deterred. "That's fine. We'll take the business."

Nnamdi threw his head back and laughed, causing me to relax a little more and chuckle.

"You're funny! I like that," he said, rising to return to his seat. "Oh, dear," he muttered when he sat down again. "Please, sit down."

I did as I was told.

"How big is your team?"

I swallowed. "Three of us."

"Hmmm... Do you have other organisations you partner with?"

I nodded. "Yes, we are part of an association of Architects, and we

CHAPTER TWO - THE SUMMON

also have a network of reliable contractors we work with."

"So, will you be doing other projects while working on mine?"

"Not anything as big…"

"Hmmm… I'd prefer if you didn't. Would you be willing to give us the focus we need."

"Yes, we can do that. We just have one project that should be completed next week, and we will be free to focus on yours."

He nodded. "Okay. We have another presentation tomorrow, but I'd like to give you guys a shot."

I beamed and gasped. "Oh, thank you! That means a lot."

"We still have to see them… And I can't promise anything until we do."

I nodded. "I understand. Thank you."

I stood up to leave, and he rose too. He was behind me when I reached to open the door.

"So, you really would rather take the contract?" he asked with mock hurt, his hand on his chest and a cheeky smile on his face.

For a moment there, I had a second thought. Looking into his eyes as they danced, I knew this guy would eat me alive, and I'd have nothing to show for it tomorrow. I was not deluded enough to think he would want to marry me.

"I'm not one to gamble. I don't play with my heart."

"We'll see…" he grinned, shutting the door after me.

I hesitated at the door, wanting to turn around and say I changed my mind. Even if all we had was a fling, I would take it over the contract. But AdVi Grand wasn't just my dream. It was my brother's too.

I swallowed and carried my heavy legs to the elevator.

*****

The next day at the office, I got a bouquet of 24 red roses on my desk! I didn't need to see the card to know who they were from. I swallowed as I looked at them. *What if this is love?*

I was no fool. I had googled Nnamdi Gerald Ukwueze. First son to Chief Chinonso Christopher Ukwueze and heir to a conglomerate fortune. As his wife, I need not work a day in my life! In fact, some women would have considered it a full-time job to be his girlfriend, not to mention his wife. I wasn't sure I was one of them, though.

Jokes apart, I liked my independence. I liked the fact that I could look after myself, and I could say that everything I had, I had worked for. It was what made up for not being the prettiest girl in the room. I knew I was smart, and I didn't want anyone to take that away from me.

But I also knew I wanted love. I used to hear about how successful women drove good men away because they chose business success over love. I didn't want to be one of them. But I still didn't understand one thing.

Why me? He could be with any woman he wanted. Why was he knocking on my door?

Eventually, I sat behind my desk and opened the card.

"Miss Independent, will you dine with me tonight?"

The guy was really hanging on to this independent woman thing, *sha!* It made me wonder if it was the hook. Maybe he loved the chase and the challenge. Well, no one else was on my case. Maybe I could play his game and win both. *"You can't win if you don't play"* is something my dad used to say a lot. So, I decided it wouldn't hurt to entertain his advances.

I sent him the first text message. *"Yes."*

His response came almost immediately. *"I'll pick you up at 8."*

*****

He sent a message later requesting my full address, which I sent to him. By then, Tamara had gotten a response from his office that we

CHAPTER TWO - THE SUMMON

were good to go, and we would be signing the contracts the following Monday. I was beyond elated!

Because of me, he was breaking his rule of mixing business with pleasure. I'd never felt so good in my life. Even though the thought came to me that I wasn't his type, I pushed it aside.

I had seen many pictures of him with other women. Skinny, light-skinned, and beautiful were adjectives that they had in common. I even recalled that he and my younger sister, Nneka, had dated back in High School. I thought to ask her how she felt about me dating her ex, but it was *sooo* long ago, and she had gotten married two years ago. She was even pregnant with their first child!

I decided that if tonight went well, then I would have to 'let her know,' because no way was I going to ask for permission to fall in love. At 34, I was ready, *over-ready sef*, to fall in love!

At 8 pm on the dot, my doorbell rang. I took another appraisal of my outfit, turning to look at my butt from different angles. Satisfied that I looked my best, I went to open the door in a black, high-waisted pencil skirt, with a magenta, loose, spaghetti-strap, blouse, and a pair of black heels that made my legs look longer. My hair was braided, so it didn't need much work. I rubbed some olive oil in it and was satisfied with the sheen.

The smile on Nnamdi's face, when I opened the door, was all the compliment I needed. Still, he said, "You look beautiful."

I blushed. "Thank you. You look great."

He beamed then stuck his elbow out for me to put my hand through. And that's how we walked to his car. After he let me in, he walked to the other side and got in too. I was so relaxed and happy. The night was already off to a great start.

*****

I will say this for Nnamdi; he was romantic. At least at the beginning.

He took me to Eko Hotel and Suites for our first date, and they had set up a special candlelight buffet table just for us by the pool. It took my breath away seeing that, and I couldn't believe the effort he was going through to woo little ol' me.

When we were escorted to our seats and the waiter left us with the menus, I couldn't keep my insecurities to myself anymore.

"I want you to try—"

"Why are you doing this?" I whispered, interrupting him.

He looked at me, apparently confused, and I swallowed. Was I just about to ruin a good thing? But I was too afraid to allow myself fall in love with a lie.

"Why did you bring me here?"

"Because I'm attracted to you," he said at last.

"Really?"

He gave a small chuckle. "Is it so hard to believe?"

"I know your type…" I said, looking away.

Nnamdi reached out his hand to hold mine on the table. "My type has evolved over the years. I got tired of the pretty airheads…"

So, he didn't think I was pretty?

"I now find beautiful, intelligent, *independent* women far more sexy…"

I swallowed. *Smooth talker! Who are you lying to, calling me beautiful,* I thought? But I swallowed it, hook, line, and sinker.

Still, I wasn't satisfied.

"What about Nneka?"

"Who?" He raised a brow as he looked at me.

"Your High School girlfriend…? My sister…? Nneka?"

To that he laughed. "Are you serious? Is that an issue?"

I just looked at him, surprised that he apparently hadn't given it a thought. After what felt like a minute, I swallowed and said, "Well, it could be. For *her*…"

CHAPTER TWO - THE SUMMON

He shook his head, as if completely confused. "Isn't she married?"

I nodded and held his stare.

"Wow… I didn't think it would be an issue," Nnamdi said. "That was like…20 years ago? Is it a deal breaker?"

I looked at him as he looked back at me, and I knew it was all up to me. If I said yes, we would call off the whole thing and just stick to our business deal. But if I said no, then there was a chance I could get to have my happily ever after. It was so long ago; what did it matter?

I swallowed. "No," I breathed and smiled at him. "Of course not."

He breathed a sigh of relief. "I'm so happy you said that because I've been looking a long time for someone like you…and if we couldn't be together because of your sister, well… That would suck."

That speech! That did it for me. He just told me I was the one he had been looking for. I, who thought no one was looking for me, had the most eligible bachelor in Nigeria checking for me. It was a no-brainer after that. In fact, I think I actually lost my brain!

CHAPTER THREE - DANGEROUSLY IN LOVE

Falling in love with Nnamdi was too easy. *Abeg*, the guy was a pro!

After that initial emotional hitch, the rest of our first date went swimmingly well. We talked a bit about our school days. Even back then, he was voted 'Most Likely to Succeed.' Yes, his family was rich, but he also had a good head on his shoulders, and all the teachers loved him. Even with that, he enjoyed the non-stop attention of the girls and popularity among the boys. I teased him that he was 'God's favourite,' because why should one person be so blessed?!

He then told me of all the bad luck he had had relationship-wise, which was why he had never married. After two broken engagements, one from a woman who cheated on him, and another from a gold-digger, he decided he wasn't going to choose by popular standards anymore. He was looking for the 'Diamond in the Rough,' and you guessed it, that was me!

That night, he kissed me at the door when he dropped me off at home. I didn't want him to stop. Up to that point, I had never been kissed. I didn't know what I was missing!

Every day afterwards, I received something sent to my office. Anything I told him I liked, I got. Be it jewellery, bags, phones, laptops, books, food, treats, you name it. He even upgraded my ride! After the first couple of weeks, when I realised what he was doing, I learned that saying how much I loved muffins was a bad idea. I got good at telling him my preference for the expensive, hard to come by things, as opposed to food and chocolates because I could get those myself, and well, I wasn't trying to get fat!

It was a couple of months before the issue of sex came up. Nnamdi had been a real gentleman, and he always kept our make out sessions PG 13. I was the one who got tired of waiting. So, one day, I planned to seduce him. I invited him over to my place with an offer to cook for him.

When he came, I opened the door in my lingerie and walked straight into the kitchen. The look on his face when he strolled in after me was almost enough satisfaction. He gaped at me as I acted as if I wasn't half-naked.

"What you trying to do to me, baby?" he cried.

I just wiggled my butt as if to music.

"Nah, nah, nah. You can't do this," he said, walking into the living room, away from me.

"What's wrong, baby?" I followed him.

"I told you… I want us to be different."

I swallowed as I looked at him, perplexed. *"Asexual*? Oh my God! You don't find me sexually attractive!" I gasped as I ran to my room to find a robe.

He came in after me and sat on the bed beside me, where I was already covered in a white bathrobe. "Ada, I made a promise to God…"

"God?" I looked at him, thinking *"this nigga must be playing me!"*

He nodded. "I promised that the next woman I sleep with would be my wife. I don't want to play around. I'm looking for the real deal."

I swallowed. "So, what does that mean?" I didn't know what to think. I just watched him.

"It means, if we are going to sleep together, then we're going to have to get married first..."

Oh. So, am I waiting for your proposal or what? I didn't know how to say the words to him. I knew men didn't like to be pressured to marry, so I certainly wasn't going to force it. But I loved him, and I wanted to be with him.

"Will you marry me?" he asked after a while, looking at me with puppy-dog eyes.

What?!!! After two months?!

I swallowed and looked at him. "Stop playing me, Nnamdi. Please don't play with me," I cried.

He walked over to my side of the bed and got down on one knee. The man had actually purchased a ring! And he presented it to me, saying, "Marry me, Adaeze Stella Okpara. Make me the happiest man in the world."

I didn't need to think about it anymore. If he was all in, so was I! I threw my arms around him and shouted, "Yes!!!"

That night, we didn't make love, but he pleased me in a way I have never been pleased before. He used his tongue to bring me to ecstasy, and I cried like a baby from my first sexual release. He stayed with me through the night, holding me in his arms. If anyone had told me that man didn't love me, I would never have believed it. Never, ever.

*****

Now that we had decided that we were going to get married, it was time to tell our families. I was scared because, up to that point, I still hadn't told my sister that I was dating her ex!

I didn't know what to expect when I told her, but it wasn't the easy acceptance I received.

"Why are you worried? Ada, I'm fine," Nneka said, smiling. "That was so long ago... Like a lifetime, *sef*!"

"Oh, wow. Really? You're not angry that I didn't come to you first?"

CHAPTER THREE - DANGEROUSLY IN LOVE

"Ada, do you love him?"

I nodded. "With all my heart."

"Then it doesn't matter because I want you to have love too. Even if it's with my ex."

At that, I threw my arms around her and hugged her as tightly as one could hug a six months pregnant woman.

"Thank you, sis! I love you!"

Nnamdi introduced me to his family by hosting a dinner party in my honour. His mother was so happy to see me and showed me all his baby photos and birthday albums. His dad was nice too, though he was a man of few words. Nnamdi's younger brother, Uzo, came with his wife and two kids, they were all friendly. It was only his elder sister, Adaora, who seemed a bit unimpressed by me. I guess she expected him to bring home a Victoria's Secret model. *LOL!*

Anyway, it was a lovely dinner.

Nnamdi charmed his way into my parents' heart at first meeting. A graduate of Harvard University no less. I think the only reservation they had was that he wasn't a Churchgoing, Bible-believing Christian, but I wasn't particularly religious either, so that wasn't an issue for me.

After meeting each other's families, we took the fast track to get married. With sex on hold till marriage, I was ready to even go to Vegas to elope! I could hardly believe how lucky I was to be marrying the most popular boy from my school, the most eligible bachelor in Lagos, and the most remarkable man I had ever known.

When I looked at him, I just wanted to be in his arms, kissing him; in his bed, loving him. I got so wet thinking about him; I got used to changing my pantyliners at least three times a day!

Our make-out sessions got more heated. We did everything but penetration, as we strove to pleasure ourselves in every way. But after we did the Introduction Ceremony about a month later, Nnamdi didn't hold back anymore. That very night, I lost my virginity to him.

"You're mine, now," he said, as we lay in bed together, spent from making love.

"I have been yours since I was born," I confessed to the only man I had ever been with, the only man I have ever loved. I had loved him since I first met him, but I never believed he would love me back.

"Ada," he shouted at my confession, raising me to look at him. "What are you saying?"

I had tears in my eyes as I told him, "I have always loved you, Nnamdi."

Nnamdi looked at me and devoured me with open eyes. He didn't take his eyes off mine as he made love to me again that night. "Tell me you love me," he whispered.

"I love you," I cried.

"Again..."

"I love you..."

"Again..."

That was my chant until he came inside of me with a guttural cry. Looking back, I think my devotion to him was the greatest turn on.

*****

The wedding date was set. We would be married in December, before Christmas, just two months after our Introduction Ceremony. But we were both satiated sexually, though still living apart. However, to honour his agreement with God, we had to get married as soon as possible, and I had no problem with that.

Business-wise, our collaboration was still going on, and with the money LionsGate Properties was paying, I was able to hire two new staff, one of them an assistant Architect, to help us fulfil the demand for the project. We were also able to afford a bigger office within the same mini complex.

I worked as hard as Nnamdi allowed me to. There were weeks

when I didn't even show up at the office. Tamara did a good job of running things now that we had a secretary. All my attention was on the wedding and making Nnamdi happy, which I loved to do.

But then the rumours started. Somebody said they saw my Nnamdi in one club with one skank. Another said he was seen in a compromising position with his secretary. Yet, another reported that he was flirting with her friend at the gym!

Nnamdi denied all of it. He said it was bound to happen because nobody but our families wanted us to get married. "They are haters… Ignore them," he said.

And that was what I did. Nnamdi had waited for me, and he would have waited longer if I hadn't tried to seduce him. He was a good and faithful man, who loved me. Anything he did before was in the past. With me, he was a new man. That was what I told myself any time someone tried to tell me otherwise.

My anthem back then was "Dangerously in Love" by Beyoncé, and I sang it almost daily. I loved how much I loved my soon-to-be husband. What a fool I was!

*****

In mid-November, Nnamdi took me for a weekend getaway in Dubai. It was in his nature to spring trips on me or treat me to spa days. I was getting very accustomed to living the life of an heiress, and it was all good because I knew he knew I could take care of myself. He just wanted to be the one to take care of me, and I loved him for that.

When we returned, he got very busy at work. He said it was because of the end of year consolidations and meetings. Plus, with our wedding and honeymoon coming up, there were things he had to attend to before he could take two weeks off at Christmas.

I understood perfectly well and used the opportunity to get things sorted out at my firm too. The construction project was coming along well, and it seemed I wasn't needed as much in the office. I started feeling lonely and missing my boo, and I decided I'd pay him a surprise visit at the office one Tuesday in December.

It was almost lunchtime when I arrived, and I expected that he would still be busy at his desk. His secretary was not on seat when I got to the reception, and I figured she had stepped out for lunch or for a bathroom break.

I did a little tap on the door before I opened it, but Nnamdi was so lost in his climax he didn't see me until Sophie shrieked and rose from where she was kneeling on the floor, giving him a blow job.

When he finally saw me at the door, he stood up hastily and pulled his pants up. I couldn't believe it. The rumours were true! I turned around and rushed back to the reception to request the elevator, but Nnamdi ran to stand in front of me just as it opened.

"I'm sorry. I'm sorry," was all he could say. "Please forgive me. I'm sorry."

"The wedding is off!" I shouted.

"No, please. God, no," he cried as he rubbed my arms. "I love you, please, I'm sorry. It was a weak moment. It will never happen again!"

I shrugged his hands off me. "Get out of my way, Nnamdi."

"I can't live without you, Ada," he put his hands on either side of my face. "I will die. I made a mistake. Please forgive me."

"Fire her!"

"It's done." He threw his arms around me. "Do you forgive me?"

I swallowed. I thought of what I'd just seen, and my heart broke. I cried.

"Say you forgive me, please."

"Why did you do this to me? Nnamdi, why?"

He took hold of my hand as the elevator closed again and led me back to his office, now devoid of his whore.

"I'm sorry you had to see that, baby. But I'm a man with needs…" he said looking into my eyes. "And you're not a very experienced woman."

I swallowed. Was he blaming me?

"It's not your fault that I was your first. I love that I was your first… But sometimes, I need more."

It was all true, the realisation came.

"But you're the one I want. The only one I want. Do you understand that?"

I shook my head. "Are you telling me you're going to keep cheating on me?"

"No, no… I'm saying I need more from you. If you'll let me teach you…"

I swallowed. So, I wasn't good enough. All he had to do was say this before. I was ready to learn. He didn't have to cheat on me. I told him as much.

"That's why I said I'm sorry. I was wrong. Forgive me?"

I nodded.

"Tell me…"

"I forgive you."

He smiled and then kissed me. But my heart was bleeding.

CHAPTER FOUR - MR AND MRS NNAMDI UKWUEZE

After trying some of the new positions Nnamdi wanted us to try in bed, by myself, I carried my two legs to the gym! It was that serious. One time after sex, I actually walked around with a limp for hours! I didn't even know I was so out of shape. And I wanted to be more confident and appealing to him. I didn't want anyone replacing me because, even though he said he would never do it again, I feared he would if I made no changes.

I also hoped joining him at his gym would dissuade any temptress thinking they could entrap my man. Still, I knew it was really up to him to keep his promise to me. I prayed that he loved me enough because I loved him too much.

In mid-December, just a week before my wedding, my sister gave birth to a bouncy baby boy! I received the call from my mum while I was at the hair salon, and I got there as soon as I could. I sent a quick message to Nnamdi to let him know, so he could join us.

"*Oh, wow! Congratulations to her! I'm sorry I won't be able to make it. In meetings all day. Will stop by in the evening.*"

But he didn't stop by in the evening, and when I tried calling, his phone kept sending me to voicemail. I decided to go over to his place. His housekeeper let me in, seeing as he wasn't around, and I didn't have my own keys yet.

CHAPTER FOUR - MR AND MRS NNAMDI UKWUEZE

It was the sun that woke me up in the morning, and I realised I had slept on his sofa all night, and he hadn't returned home. When I still couldn't get across to him, I called his brother, Uzo.

"Hey, Ada," he greeted jovially. "What's up?"

"Hi, Uzo. I haven't been able to get across to Nnamdi. Do you know where he is?"

"Ummm, he didn't make it home last night?"

"No. I was here, but he didn't come home."

"I guess he stayed at the hotel then. We threw him a surprise bachelor's party at Eko Hotel. He didn't tell you?"

"Oh, okay. I must have forgotten. Thank you."

I swallowed after the call ended. Something did not feel right. Why didn't Nnamdi tell me? Why was his phone still off? When was he going to come home?

Just when I thought I would go and meet him at the hotel, I heard his horn at the gate, and I peered out of the window as he drove into the compound. I sat up when I heard his key in the door, and I looked at the entrance expectantly.

"Hey, babe," he said when he saw me. He was still dressed in the executive suite he wore yesterday. "What are you doing here?"

I stood up and walked towards him. I didn't know what I was looking for, but I was scanning him for any evidence of foul play. "I came to see you. You didn't come to the hospital as promised."

He palmed his forehead. "Oh, yeah. I knew there was something I had forgotten. How's she? Baby okay?"

"She's fine. They are both fine." I reached him and touched his arm. "What happened last night?"

He turned around and took the stairs up, mumbling as he climbed, "The guys threw me a surprise party. They came to drag me from work."

I followed him up the stairs, carrying the briefcase he had left at the bottom. "I tried calling, but your phone was off."

"Don't mind them. Someone took my phone. I just got it back this morning."

He sat on his bed and pulled off his shoes one by one, and I saw that he was tired. If anything happened last night, I had no way of knowing. I felt so vulnerable.

"Baby… What are you thinking about?" he asked as he watched me watch him.

I went to place his briefcase on his desk. A lump had formed in my throat, and I couldn't speak for the tears I held at bay.

He came up behind me, placing a hand on my butt. "You worried about me, baby?"

I just swallowed as he undressed me. The tears fell from my eyes, and I made no effort to wipe them.

I felt his erection against my butt as he whispered in my ear, "You see how I missed you? You're the only one I want."

He turned me around to face him and wiped my tears. "Ada, my love, don't allow one mistake to tear us apart. You have to trust me again…"

I looked into his dark eyes, and all reason went to hell. I leaned into him, and he claimed my mouth with his and slipped between my lips below with a single move. I cast my fear aside and let him own and please me, as I did him.

*****

Six days later, it was the day of our traditional wedding, and I was elated. The church wedding followed the next day. I had made up my mind that I would forgive Nnamdi and trust him because I could not and did not want to live without him. He was right that my fears and distrust would tear us apart, and I couldn't do that to us.

He loved me. I knew it in my soul. I knew it in the way he looked at me, held me, spoke to me, and made love to me. He was as close to a perfect man one could get, and I loved him *die*!

"Do you take this man to be your lawfully wedded husband, for better or for worse, in sickness and in health, for richer or poorer, until death do you part?"

I looked into Nnamdi's eyes and beamed as I made my promise, "I do." He had just done the same for me, and his eyes hadn't left my face at all.

"I now pronounce you husband and wife. You may now kiss your bride…"

Nnamdi didn't wait for the minister to finish the second sentence before he grabbed me, lifted my veil, and ravished my lips in the presence of an adoring congregation. *Wow!* I felt wonderful at that moment.

In the background, the minister continued, "What God has joined together, let not man separate."

In my heart, I said, "Amen," even as Nnamdi kissed me like he had been starved kisses for years. When he eventually let me go, we both turned to the congregation and raised our hands together to a loud applause!

The reception was mad! It was such a huge affair, and so many of our friends from High School came to celebrate with us. Nneka couldn't make it because she was still recovering from her delivery, but Victor took it upon himself to share photos and videos to our family WhatsApp group so that she didn't miss a thing.

From the reception, we went to the Oriental Hotel to spend the night before we left the next day for our honeymoon in Hawaii. And it was perfect. Nnamdi was fully present with me and doted on me for the two weeks we spent in Hawaii. It was the best time of my life; still the best Christmas I have ever had.

*****

When we returned in January, I had four weeks to plan a party for my husband to celebrate his 35th birthday! It was more than enough time really, even though I had lots of work to catch up on. I was going to need help, though, because I still wasn't well acquainted with Nnamdi's friends.

I reached out to his elder sister, Adaora, and she was happy to help. She shared some contacts she thought I should call to invite to the bash, and I got across to most on WhatsApp. There were a couple I decided to call because the messages I'd sent via WhatsApp weren't delivering.

"Hi, Ada!" one guy called Wahaab said when he picked up. "Hey, I've been meaning to call. I'm sorry I couldn't make it to the wedding."

I smiled, surprised that he knew who I was already. I guess he had Truecaller. I had already changed my name to Ada Ukwueze.

"No worries. How are you?"

"I'm great! That your brother is one lucky bastard, though… I didn't think he could do it."

"Do what?"

"You know, get married before his 35th birthday! And to a woman who loves him!" he chuckled. "Anyway, how are you doing?"

I was stunned for a minute. What was he talking about? I wanted to see what more I could get from him.

"That's my brother. The lucky one!"

Wahaab giggled again. "You can say that again. Anyway, what's going on?"

"Please check your WhatsApp for your invite to his 35th birthday party on the 5th of February."

"Okay, will do."

I cut the call, not sure what exactly I'd just learned. Obviously, Nnamdi had an ulterior motive for wanting to get married by his 35th birthday…which meant, what we had wasn't love.

CHAPTER FOUR - MR AND MRS NNAMDI UKWUEZE

I swallowed. It couldn't be true. It had to be a misunderstanding. But I needed to know. I needed to find out the truth.

I invited Adaora over for a cake tasting, and though she said she would be happy with my judgement, I insisted that I wanted her input, and it was a chance for us to get to know each other better.

When she came the next morning, I acted distressed and tearful when I opened the door to her. I guess my acting wasn't very good because she didn't even ask me if I was okay or anything. Or maybe she just didn't care. Was it really that bad that they didn't give a damn about me?

As she sampled the cakes that had been delivered just that morning, and ummed and ahhed, I looked at her and realised she hadn't made eye contact with me since she entered my home, the one I shared with her brother as his wife.

"Did you know?" I ended up blurting out.

She looked up briefly and back to her plate.

"That Nnamdi didn't marry me for love…"

"What are you talking about?" She looked at me then, holding my gaze.

"I know already. You don't have to pretend. I know he needed to marry before his 35th birthday."

She shrugged. "So, if you know, what's the problem?"

I just looked at her, jaw dropped. "The problem is I didn't know before I married him. Don't you get how wrong that is?"

Adaora smiled. "I honestly don't know why you're complaining. Are you not also benefitting?"

"What?"

She looked at me with wide eyes as if she had just goofed. "Talk to your husband, honey," she said before she shut down, and I knew I couldn't get more from her.

What benefits? Was my husband withholding more from me than

the truth about why he married me? I suddenly felt sick to my stomach.

Adaora indicated the two cakes she liked and then left. And I realised that I didn't even know the man I married nor the family I married into.

*****

That night, I decided that I'd do exactly that. I'd talk to my husband. I had confirmed enough to know how to angle my questions to get to the bottom of it. At least, that's what I thought.

However, when he arrived home at 9 pm, he said he had a headache and headed straight for our bedroom. My first thought was Adaora had told him of my confrontation this morning. My second was maybe he had had a really bad day and needed me. But one thing was clear; he didn't want to talk to me.

Regardless, I boiled some water and carried it in a jug with a selection of teas and other beverages, milk, and honey too. He was still my husband, and I still loved him.

He smiled as I came in carrying the tray and sat up in bed. I brought a stool close, made him a cup of Earl Grey tea at his request, and sat on the bed as he sipped it.

"Thank you, baby. I needed this," he said, leaning to peck my lips.

I swallowed. "I need something from you too, baby."

He sipped his tea. "What's that?"

"Do you love me?"

"Of course, I love you…"

"So, we didn't get married because you needed a wife by your 35th birthday?"

"Uh? Where did you get that from?"

"That doesn't matter… Tell me the truth."

"You need to stop listening to these rumours, honey…"

I couldn't help the tears that escaped my eyes. "If you care about me at all, you will tell me the truth! I deserve to know! It's my life too."

He swallowed. "Look, honey. I have a headache. Let's talk about this in the morning."

He put down his cup and returned to lie down on the bed. It was true; that much I knew. The question was, 'why the deception?' I had no choice but to wait till the morning to find out.

CHAPTER FIVE - A LOVE MATCH?

After a couple more days of his excuses and absolute refusal to talk about it, I decided to do the only thing within my power to do. I packed out of his house, while he was at work, and returned to my apartment. It was so painful, but for my own sanity, I had to leave that house, and ultimately, I had to leave Nnamdi.

I had been so stupid. I was right to have been suspicious of his motives, but he had deceived me into believing that he truly loved me. But he made a mistake if he thought I needed him or his money. I knew how to take care of myself. It would hurt, but I would get over him.

I had just drawn myself a hot bath and had gone to take a bottle of wine and a glass from my minibar, when my doorbell rang. I wasn't expecting anyone, and if it was Nnamdi coming to beg, he was too late! How dare he play me for a fool!

"Ada! Ada! Open the door!"

Yup, too little too late!

"I know you are there... Open the door!"

I couldn't help myself. "Go to hell!"

There was silence for a moment, then he tried the door handle before banging on the door again. "Please, let's talk."

"Get lost, Nnamdi! You're going to hear from my lawyers!"

"Ada, please! Please open up. I'm sorry."

CHAPTER FIVE - A LOVE MATCH?

Yeah, whatever.

As tempted as I was to open up, I knew I couldn't. He held all the cards in our relationship. He held too much power over me, and I needed to get some control of my life back. I ignored him and went up to enjoy my soak, happy that at least I'd gotten a response from him.

The next thing was my phone ringing non-stop. *Now, he wants to talk!* I didn't care anymore. I had enough truth to know I wasn't in the relationship I wanted. I switched off my phone.

The next day, as I got ready for work, I realised that my phone was still off, so I switched it back on. I enjoyed a little peace before it started ringing again. I was surprised that it was still Nnamdi calling. My anger had cooled somewhat, so I picked up.

"Hello."

"Baby, open the door."

My mouth dropped open. He was still outside?!

Curiously, I looked out of the window and saw his Lexus jeep on my driveway. A warmth filled me, but I was so confused. What was this really about?

I opened the door, and he got out of his car. I left it ajar as I went to sit on my sofa. He entered and shut the door behind him. He just stood there looking at me in unbelief, pissing me off because I wanted answers.

"You really want to divorce me?" he asked with accusation and hurt.

"You deceived me! That's grounds for a divorce."

"How did I deceive you?"

"You pretended to love me instead of telling me that you needed a wife by your 35th birthday!"

"I was not pretending…"

I rose up, now completely pissed off. "Stop lying for God's sake. Just tell me the truth."

He swallowed. "You want to know the truth?"

"YES!"

"Yes, I had a requirement to marry before I turned 35. All that did was intensify my search and help me be decisive about what I wanted. I didn't expect to find it! I didn't expect to fall in love with you! But I did! I didn't marry you because I had to... I married you because I wanted to. I want you!"

I didn't have anything to say to that. He just stood where he was by the entrance, while the weight of his revelation made me sit down.

"I can't believe you were going to divorce me," he said again.

"You were not talking to me, Nnamdi. I'm not in your head. You need to talk to me!"

"How many times do I need to tell you that I'm crazy about you? Do you still not believe me?"

I swallowed. He had a point. I didn't want to drive him away with my insecurities. I stood up and walked to him. I hugged him, but he just stood there, not hugging me back.

"I was scared, Nnamdi. I hate secrets. You should have told me about your need to marry by your 35th..."

He removed my hands from his back. "And how do you think that would have gone? Do you think you would believe I loved you then? Would you not have run from me like you are doing now?"

I looked up at him and saw that his eyes glistened with unshed tears. *Oh, God. I hurt him*, I thought. I knew he was right too. I would never have believed his decision to marry me was from love if I had thought there was another motivation. I swallowed.

"I'm sorry, Nnamdi." I felt the sudden need to beg him. I got down on my knees. "I love you, Nnamdi. I don't want to leave you...ever."

He held my hands and pulled me up. "Don't do this again," he said emphatically.

"I won't."

"In fact, I'm going to put your apartment up for sale..."

CHAPTER FIVE - A LOVE MATCH?

"I'm renting."

"Well, I'm going to put in a bad word for you with your landlord! That you're a naughty, married woman who likes to escape from her husband."

I laughed. "I deserve it."

He smiled, and I swooned. *I'm screwed*, I thought. He lifted me off the floor and carried me to my bedroom to deliver my punishment for being a naughty wife.

*****

"So, how did you discover my secret?" Nnamdi asked as I stroked the few hairs on his chest, my head on his shoulder.

"One of your friends thought I was your sister when I called to invite them to your party?"

"Who?"

"Like I will tell you!"

"So, you want to keep secrets now?"

"This one is allowed," I smiled up at him.

"So, you're planning a party for me…"

"Hm hmm."

"Was it supposed to be a surprise?"

I shrugged. "Not really. Do you want a surprise party?"

"It's too late for that now…"

I looked up at him and beamed. *What a sweetheart*, I thought. "Don't worry, babe. It's my first party for you. Now I know you like surprises, I'll do better next time."

Nnamdi kissed the top of my head. "Where have you been all my life?"

I chuckled. "I was there; you just didn't notice me."

Nnamdi ran his hand down my back to grab my butt. "Believe me, I noticed."

I giggled, thrilled that he loved my favourite part too. I turned to lay on top of him, my big butt sticking in the air.

"Baby... Why did you have to marry before turning 35?"

"It's a condition for my inheritance from my grandfather. It legally passes my inheritance to me when I am 35 years old, as long as I am married to the woman I love, who loves me too."

"Anything about kids?" I asked with a brow raised.

"No. It just has to be a genuine love-match, not any type of arrangement."

"But I thought you were already rich?"

Nnamdi chuckled. "There's rich, and there's wealthy. This allows me to inherit my grandfather's estate from my father, who currently owns it through inheritance. So, if I didn't meet the condition, then it would have been passed to my younger brother, Uzo, who's already married with kids!"

"Doesn't your father have to die first, though?"

"No. The inheritance I receive from my father is different. This is from my grandfather. So, it's like my dad has been keeping it in trust for me. But it's only up to my generation. I am not obligated to pass it on the same way to my children."

"Oh, okay. What about your sister? What does she inherit?"

Nnamdi sighed. "What her husband has... Or whatever I choose to give her."

I gasped.

"I know it's not fair, but that was the condition my grandfather made in his will."

"No wonder she doesn't like me!"

Nnamdi squeezed me to himself. "Why do you say that?"

"She wasn't very nice to me when I asked her about it... Even when I asked her to come for the cake tasting."

"I guess she probably doubts that our love is genuine..."

CHAPTER FIVE - A LOVE MATCH?

I lay my head on his chest, fulfilled. Ours was a genuine love was the thought that carried me to sleep in his arms that morning.

I woke up a couple of hours later to find Nnamdi still sleeping, and I watched him for a bit. I couldn't believe he had slept in his car the night before. For the first time ever, I got on my knees and prayed for our love to last. There was nothing I wanted more.

*****

We were meant to be.

That's what I believed with all my heart by the time my husband's 35th birthday came around. If not for his 35th birthday coming up, he might not have thought to try his luck with me. He might have continued with his lifestyle and not given me a second glance. But he had looked, and he had seen, and he had desired me... And we had fallen in love.

I was on cloud nine!

That evening, as we got dressed for his dinner party, I sang in front of the mirror as I did my make-up. "I love my baby, yep, yep, I love my baby..."

Nnamdi laughed as he watched me. He was sitting on the edge of the bed putting on his socks.

"And he can get it," I sang, sticking my butt out and doing a little bounce.

"Oh, he wants to get it!" Nnamdi said as he walked towards me, the protrusion in his trousers letting me know I was causing damage. "He's gonna hit it," Nnamdi sang as he came up behind me.

"Baby... We're gonna be late."

"It's my birthday..." he muttered in my ear as he lifted my dress up and took possession of what was already his.

We arrived at his dinner party fashionably late, and by the looks we received, I knew everyone knew what had kept us. Ours was clearly a love match.

We could hardly keep our hands or eyes off each other the whole night. If it wasn't me looking for him, it was him looking for me. Halfway through the dinner, Nnamdi stood up and clinked his glass, putting a pause on all conversation.

"I want to give a toast to the woman of my heart, the one I didn't know I was missing, Adaeze Stella Ukwueze. I love you, baby. Yup, yup. I love that chick!"

He winked at me, and everyone laughed and clapped as he pulled me up for a kiss. It was the most beautiful feeling in the world to have our love so affirmed.

And it was a wonderful party. I got to meet some of his friends I hadn't met before, even the loud-mouthed Wahaab.

"Hi, Ada," he said when he came up beside me at the chocolate and marshmallow fountain. "I'm Wahaab."

I recognized his voice and was happy to put a face to it. He was tall, dark, and handsome, with a footballer's build.

"You were the one who called me, right?"

I nodded, smiling sheepishly.

"Oh, boy! What a goof! I'm sorry about what I said."

"What did you say?" I feigned ignorance.

He shook his head and chuckled. "Hmmm. Nnamdi did find his match, after all. Don't break his heart."

"I wouldn't dream of it."

"It's nice to meet you," he said, walking away with his chocolate covered marshmallows on a stick.

I smiled and returned to my seat with my chocolate marshmallows in a bowl. For a moment, I was happy just to watch everyone having a good time while enjoying my treat. I was glad to see Victor and Uzo sitting together and chatting animatedly. Nneka had also come with her husband, Dotun, and their baby boy, Demilade. They looked

CHAPTER FIVE - A LOVE MATCH?

picture-perfect with his arm around her and her arms cradling their infant.

"You did good tonight," Adaora said, taking the vacant seat beside me. "Nnamdi is really happy."

I turned to her and smiled before looking at him, where he stood laughing with a couple of his friends.

"I'm sorry about the mix-up before. I didn't know it was real."

I looked at her, and she met my gaze. "It's okay. You didn't do anything wrong."

"I'm really happy for you both," she said, opening her arms for an embrace, which I happily gave.

Nnamdi looked in our direction at that moment and gave me a knowing smile. I let out a happy sigh.

CHAPTER SIX - ENTRAPMENT

Valentine's Day came around, and Nnamdi whisked me away to Venice. We arrived in the afternoon and enjoyed lunch at the Impronpta Restaurant at the heart of Venice. It was exquisite. There, he presented me with my Valentine's gift, a Valentino Garavani purse; a clutch bag made of calfskin. I gasped as I took it from him and thanked him profusely. I hadn't even hinted that I wanted it!

I rose from my seat to hug and kiss him, and he chuckled. I just gushed over the purse until the waiter returned with our last course, Tiramisu and hot tea. I actually hadn't gotten him anything for Val's. After the big bash we held on his birthday, I hadn't expected anything fancy for Valentine's. I told him as much.

"It's okay, baby. You can make it up to me tonight…"

At that, I beamed and fluttered my lashes at him.

I did make it up to him; three times that night. We started in the bed, then in the shower as we bathed afterwards, then on the balcony of our hotel, overlooking the ocean. My husband was insatiable, and I'd learned to please him on demand.

*****

A month later, Nnamdi presented me with another gift; a home he had built for me in Banana Island, designed by my brother, Victor! It was a redesign of an original plan I had drawn when I was a teenager.

CHAPTER SIX - ENTRAPMENT

It was so thoughtful, so personal, so romantic that I cried as I beheld it and the man I had married who had gifted it to me.

My life was a fairytale, and I lived the life of a princess. Yes, I still worked, but it was more of a hobby those days. It wasn't what provided for my needs, which had somehow grown beyond what my salary could provide. I became used to buying expensive wigs, having a different hairstyle every week, wearing only designer clothes and accessories, and being pampered at the spa at least twice a week.

One day, I came home from a day of shopping and saw that Nnamdi's car was still in the compound. I smiled because I had bought him some new shirts, and I couldn't wait to show him. For a man who had everything, he was very hard to shop for, but I still looked out for clothes and shoes I thought he would like whenever I shopped.

He wasn't in the living room when I let myself in. I called for the housekeeper, expecting that she would come to the door to help me with my shopping, but no one came. She wasn't in the kitchen either. I figured Nnamdi had sent her out on an errand, so I carried a few bags with me upstairs, leaving the rest by the doorway.

"Nnamdi," I called as I climbed the stairs to the master bedroom. "Baby, you—"

The words were caught in my throat as I opened the door to see my husband on our bed and Marie, the housekeeper, bent over before him as he humped her. The bags fell from my hands, and I stood there, pinned in position by his stare. He didn't even stop.

He pushed Marie's head further into the mattress, pinning her in position as he started groaning, "I'm coming, I'm coming, I'm coming…" all the while keeping his eyes on me. Eventually, he attained his climax and shivered, shutting his eyes for a moment and freeing me to escape the room.

I didn't go far, though. I could hardly move. I just left the doorway to our bedroom and rested my back against the wall as I tried to unsee what I had just witnessed. He couldn't have just done that to me. I was imagining things!

But my heart was shattered, and tears ran unbidden down my cheeks. Eventually, Marie crept out of the room, her head bowed as she scurried past me on the landing and hurried down the stairs.

It had happened. I didn't dream it. Nnamdi had broken our marriage vows on our bed. And I wanted to kill him!

But before that, I crumbled to the floor and cried like a wounded animal. It was then I heard the shower running. The bastard was acting as if he hadn't just rammed a knife into my heart. I found the strength to pick myself off the floor and enter our bedroom.

I looked at the bed that he had defiled, the white sheets scattered, with parts of our bedding even touching the ground. I picked up the things I had bought and threw the bags into the closet, knowing I wasn't in the right frame of mind to put them away. I just sat on the armchair in our bedroom and waited for my husband to come out of the bathroom. Clearly, he had no plans to beg me today.

What a vile man! I married a wicked man! A lying, manipulative monster of a man! I fumed, getting angrier by the second as I waited for him to come out of the bathroom.

Eventually, he did, with a towel around his waist and another that he used to pat his body dry. He looked at me, and there was no trace of remorse. He wanted me to find out today. He put on a show for me, I realised.

Enraged, I ran towards him and began to hit him as I cried, "You bastard! You wicked bastard! How could you?! How could you?!"

He took my hits at first, then restrained me with his hands before he pushed me onto the bed. But I jumped away as if it was diseased, remembering what he had just done on it.

I looked at Nnamdi as he held my gaze. "You're not even going to apologise?!"

CHAPTER SIX - ENTRAPMENT

"I'm waiting for you to calm down," he said calmly.

My God! This man is a psychopath, I thought.

I went to the closet and brought out a suitcase. I began to throw in my clothes and shoes, as much as I could fit into the suitcase. I had money to buy everything else I needed. I opened the drawer that contained my jewels and threw as much as I could into my purse, then made for the door.

The bastard didn't stop me. I guess he had no need for a wife anymore. He had gotten his inheritance! I cried as I opened the front door and carried the suitcase to my car. I didn't even bother taking any of the things I had bought while shopping that day. I just got into my car and reversed out of my spot.

I pressed the horn for the gate to be opened, but nothing happened. Again, I pressed my horn, but the security guard didn't open the gate. Realizing that he had probably received instructions from the beast not to let me go, I got out of the car and went to push the gate open by myself. Though electric, it had a manual handle that allowed it to open with physical force, but either I wasn't strong enough, or they had actually locked it because it refused to budge.

I looked up at what had been my dream home to see my husband looking down at me from our bedroom window, and I cursed!

God punish him! "God punish you, Nnamdi!!!"

I went back to my car and pulled out my suitcase. With it and my handbag strewn over my shoulder, I decided I'd walk out.

"Open the gate!" I shouted at the security when I saw that the pedestrian entrance had been padlocked. "Open the fucking gate!"

"Madam, please calm down," Isaac, the gateman, had the nerve to say to me.

How humiliating! I seethed with hatred for Nnamdi as I returned to the house, leaving my suitcase by the gatehouse.

"Let me out of this hellhole, you bastard!" I cried out to my husband.

"You can do what you want, I don't give a fuck! Just let me out!"

I couldn't cry anymore. I was too angry, too afraid of what this man was capable of. Obviously, he had lied to me! If he really wanted a wife just for show, couldn't he have found a more willing victim?! Why me?!

I went into the kitchen, and Marie ran from me, escaping through the back door. *Stupid girl!* I picked up a big knife. *This shit ends today,* I thought.

I started bounding up the stairs with it when I heard my husband behind me.

"What do you plan on doing with that?" he asked calmly, startling me. He took hold of the hand that wielded the knife and bent it to my back, peeling the knife from my grip. He threw it to the ground. "It has not come to this, Ada."

"Fuck you!" I spat at him.

"Will you, please?" he smiled.

The bastard. I was so disgusted, I slapped him. But he just pulled me close to him, and I saw to my horror that he was aroused!

Oh my God!!! I suddenly remembered how he had used his arousal to convince me that he hadn't been with anyone the night of his bachelor party! This man was insatiable! He was diabolical!

"Ada, what do you want from me?" he asked, his breath on my neck, where he had me pinned to the wall.

"I want to be free of you!"

"I'm sorry I can't give you that. What else do you want?"

I looked at him as the tears returned. What was this?! A game?! Why was he doing this?

"I want to know why you are doing this to me."

He nodded. "Let's go upstairs."

He freed me enough to climb the remaining steps. When I got to our bedroom, I sat on the armchair, while he sat on the edge of the

CHAPTER SIX - ENTRAPMENT

bed, looking at me.

"I'm sorry you had to find out like this…"

"No, you're not!"

He swallowed. "Like I told you before, I have needs, and I can't depend on you to fulfil all of them…"

It was the same pathetic speech. "You promised me it wouldn't happen again."

He nodded. "Look, baby, I lied. But I don't want to lie to you anymore," he said, looking into my eyes. "This is who I am."

I shivered. He wasn't going to stop cheating on me! "I can't accept that."

"You promised to accept me for better or for worse."

"Fuck you! You promised to forsake all others! This is bullshit!"

Nnamdi shrugged. "It's just sex, Ada." He rose from his position to come and kneel in front of me. "It's like eating. It doesn't mean I don't love you."

Was he still trying to claim he loved me?! "I thought you said you wanted to stop lying to me. Can you stop with the love crap?!"

"I love you, Ada. I do," he stroked my face, and I squirmed away in disgust. "It's you I want to live my life with, whom I want to share my bed with. Just once in a while, I desire to sleep with another woman. Don't let it be a big deal."

I couldn't believe what I was hearing. I pushed him away and stood up. "You are mad! Nnamdi, you are actually insane! I will never accept this type of marriage. I want out!"

"Think about it, Ada. Monogamy isn't natural. That's the lie, and that is what hurts. If you can accept me as I am, we are going to be really happy together. I promise you that."

I just looked at him, unable to believe my ears. This guy actually believed he was right.

I swallowed. "So, what about me? Can I take another lover?"

A grimace crossed his face. "Nah, baby." He shook his head. "It doesn't work like that. And besides, you will never need another lover. I will satisfy you."

I didn't know when I sat on the bed. My heart was thumping. Was I really reasoning with this fool?!

"Get out of my house!" I didn't know where I got the nerve to, but I remembered that the house belonged to me. He had shown me the deed in my name. I had more power than I realised. "Get out of my house, Nnamdi."

"Okay, baby. I'll give you some space. I'll be at the Pearl Tower for a few days. If you miss me, just come over."

He said it with so much confidence, sure that I would go to him of my own free will. He didn't even pack a bag. He just left the room, and the next sound I heard was the gate opening, and he was gone. *What the hell?!*

CHAPTER SEVEN - BLEEDING LOVE

After he left, I looked for the skank. Marie was hiding in the boys' quarters. She cried that it wasn't her fault; she was just doing her job. I could hardly look at her face. I didn't want to think of the horrible possibility that it hadn't even been consensual. I just asked her to pack her things and leave my house. Even the security guard, after he showed me how to unlock the gate and gave me the remote control, was thrown out, and I locked them out of my home.

But even I couldn't stay in the house. I locked up, carried my suitcase back into my car and drove out of the compound. I couldn't go back to my old apartment because my lease expired in February, and the place was already rented out. I just drove, not knowing where I was going.

My phone rang, and I saw it was Nneka calling. *Perfect!* Just who I needed to see.

"Hi, Nneka," I answered handsfree. "You home?"

"Yes, sis. How are you?"

"I'm okay. I'm coming over... Did you want to talk to me about something?"

"No, I just wanted to invite you and Nnamdi over for Dotun's birthday dinner."

"Oh, I forgot. Is today his birthday?"

"No, next Saturday."

"Okay, sis. I'll see you when I get there."

"Cool," she said before I cut the call.

I was already in Lekki. It was just a short drive to her home in Ikate.

She was sitting on the sofa, breastfeeding, when their house help, Nina, let me in.

"Wow, what happened?" Nneka asked the moment she saw my face. I had been crying intermittently and must have looked like a mess. Her question brought on the waterworks again.

I didn't have words, I just sobbed on her sofa. Nnamdi had built me a castle in the sand, and now the ocean waves had washed it away...

After a while, she came to me and just hugged me.

"What happened?" she asked again.

"He wants to sleep with other women!"

"What?! He told you that?"

"I caught him humping our housekeeper," I spat out. "In fact, I don't think I caught him. I think he meant for me to see him doing it! He was so cold!"

"Oh no. This is terrible."

I bawled. "How can he be so cruel?! What did I do to deserve this?"

"No, you don't deserve this. I can't believe he did that to you. I'm so sorry, Ada."

I just cried and let her comfort me.

"What do you want to do now?"

"I don't know. I don't think he will let me go easily... But I can't stay with a cheater. I just can't."

"Do you know where he is now?"

"He said he was going to stay at the Pearl Tower for a few days..."

"You mean the new Eko Pearl Towel at Eko Atlantic?"

I nodded.

"Hmmm."

"What?"

CHAPTER SEVEN - BLEEDING LOVE

"He's loaded!"

"I don't care about that! I didn't want that from him. The one thing I wanted was real love, and he has denied me of it."

"Look," Nneka said. "Sis, at least he is being honest with you. There are many guys in his shoes who do the same but keep lying to their wives…"

"What are you saying?"

"Didn't he buy you a house?"

"So what?!"

"And wasn't he the one that gave Victor his big break?"

"Wait, Nneka… Are you saying I should just go along with it?"

Nneka swallowed and looked away. "I'm saying you could do a lot worse than him."

I looked at her and wondered what she wasn't telling me. "Are you and Dotun happy?"

She let out a sigh and looked at me. "All marriages have problems. The way I see it, it's about choosing your hard…"

I was quiet for a moment.

"I don't know a man who has never stepped out on his wife. You remember that Dad used to have a mistress?"

"And I'll never forget what it did to Mum."

"But she stayed with him, and he worked it out of his system. They are pretty happy now. Do you see what I mean?"

I swallowed. I didn't know how to be that kind of woman. I told her as much.

"Well, you can fight him for your freedom, lose his money and influence…and still end up broke and alone. Will you be happy then?"

I looked at her, confused. "Why are you defending him?"

"I'm not defending him. I'm on your side. I'm just trying to be real with you. It's your decision."

Clearly, it wasn't as black and white as I thought it was. Maybe I could let go of my need to be loved the way I want and let Nnamdi have the marriage he wants. Maybe we could be happy if I could just forsake my belief in monogamy. I swallowed.

I spent the night in Nneka's guest room and went back to my home the next day. I got a cleaning service to clean the whole house and bought a new queen-sized bed for my room. God forbid that I should lie in a bed he had defiled.

I hired a new matron, an older woman who I believed could do the job without enticing my husband. I also got a security company to dispatch a new security guard to me. It was my house, after all. Maybe Nnamdi knew that all along. Maybe he planned to buy another house for another wife. I swallowed. I didn't care what he did anymore. He had denied me the only thing I ever wanted.

*****

I cried myself to sleep every night because I missed my husband. The cruel twist was that he had indeed trained my body to long for him, and I did, every night. But all I had to do was think of the scene I had walked in on, and I would feel sick to my stomach.

I knew, even as I was alone in bed, he was not alone. He had never been alone, I realised. All the while we dated, he probably satisfied himself with his maid! How was I to know…? And that bullshit about promising God that the next woman he slept with would be his wife was clearly part of the entrapment. He was a mastermind!

And I remembered his friend, Wahaab, who had been laughing at how lucky he was to not only find a wife, but one who loved him also, and I realised that he must have boasted to his friends about how devoted I was to him! He played me *good*!

No way was I going to leave this a victim! I would find my way out of this marriage on my own terms. I just had to bid my time. But I knew now that the love was gone. I hated Nnamdi Ukwueze. I hated

CHAPTER SEVEN - BLEEDING LOVE

him with every fibre of my being!

*****

When I got tired of feeling sorry for myself, I decided two could play that game. I called up an old friend, Omi, who was also one of my bridesmaids, and told her I wanted to go clubbing. I was going to dance like I was single, and if it came down to it, I was ready to let another man have his way with me. Let Nnamdi deal with that!

I smiled as I admired myself in the mirror. The workouts I'd gotten used to and the many spa treatments I took made sure my body was firm, fresh, and glowing in the black, cowl neck, minidress I chose for the night. Maybe Nnamdi would be forced to divorce me when rumours start spreading about my promiscuity. I laughed. I didn't mind how I got free, I just had to break free!

I picked up my girl, Omi, from the 1004 apartments in VI at 11 pm, then headed to the club. I guess we were early because it wasn't buzzing yet, but I was determined to stay and get buck wild up in there!

We sat at a table and asked for a menu. When the waiter came back, he presented us with two cocktails, compliments of two guys seated across the room. They wiggled their fingers at us, and we giggled. *Gosh, that was too easy.* I hadn't even had the chance to shake my butt yet.

We sipped the margaritas but decided we would wage higher bets. I didn't like my drink, so I ordered something sweeter.

Eventually, by midnight, the place got crowded and the dancefloor was packed. We were relaxed enough, after downing a couple of drinks, to hit the dancefloor.

The DJ was on point when he played "Cheap Thrills," by Sia and Sean Paul. Omi screamed and started twerking her way into the dancefloor. I followed her, twerking and winding. The men who had bought us drinks decided to come and dance with us, and I was ready. I held on to the taller one and started twisting and rolling on his junk, loving his responsiveness to my tease. When Christina Aguilera and Pitbull came on next with "Feel this Moment," the atmosphere shifted again, and Omi and I started jumping up and singing along. We were having so much fun.

When our dance partners left and returned with more drinks for us, I decided I didn't trust them enough to take another drink from them. I shook my head when Omi looked at me, about to take hers. I grabbed her hand, and we went to the bar, where we ordered our own drinks. *Mama didn't raise no fool.*

The music had taken a turn for the worse, so we were happy to sit out the next few songs. But when Eve's "Tambourine" came on, no one could stop me. I loved that jam!

I didn't know when I decided to climb on the bar and start twerking, shaking my tambourine for all to see. Omi was just laughing at me, while others watched. Another girl decided to climb on the bar too, and the crowd went wild. Omi joined us, and they started copying my moves as if we had rehearsed them.

Suddenly, the music changed, and Neyo's "Miss Independent" started playing. Annoyed by the abrupt switch, I turned in the direction of the DJ station, and that was when I saw him. Nnamdi was seated across the club watching me. *Mtcheew,* I hissed.

I got down from the bar, letting a man standing in front of me to help me down.

"You're a good dancer," he said.

He was handsome and looked available, so I kissed him. He kissed me back, and it felt good until he was suddenly pulled away from me.

"*Oh, shit,*" I heard Omi say.

Nnamdi's towering presence was before me, but I pretended I didn't notice and returned my attention to the bartender.

CHAPTER SEVEN - BLEEDING LOVE

"I'll have another one," I said.

"She's done!" Nnamdi countered, and the bartender turned away to serve another customer.

"What are you doing here, Nnamdi?" I finally asked. Turning to him, I added, "Shouldn't you be fucking somebody else?"

The vein in his temple twitched, and he grabbed my hand. "Let go of me!" I struggled to be free, but his grip was impossible.

Nnamdi carried me over his shoulder and out of the club, though I kicked, screamed, and swore at him. I pulled at his shirt, hoping it would rip, but the beast wore expensive shirts. He finally threw me in the backseat of his jeep and locked me in the car before going back to the club.

He came back with Omi moments later, and she got in the front seat beside him. For a moment, I wondered if she had been the one to tell him, but I didn't want to believe it. He probably had friends who had seen me at the club and told him.

But I had lost the will to fight. *I will fight again tomorrow*, I thought. I sat back and closed my eyes, happy that no one said anything as we drove. Even after dropping off Omi, Nnamdi didn't say anything at all, and I fell asleep in the back of his car.

CHAPTER EIGHT - NO MORE "I LOVE YOU"S

I woke up to find Nnamdi in my bed, his arm around me, fully clothed. I had actually been snuggling in the arms of the monster. He didn't look like a monster in the light of a new day. The handsome demon looked completely harmless, but I knew better now.

I removed his hand from my waist and slipped out of the bed. I could kill him now, I thought. Did I have time to go down and get the knife and kill him before he woke up? If I succeeded, what would I do with the body? Where would I run to?

He opened his eyes and looked at me as if he could read my thoughts.

"Good morning, my love," he muttered.

I swallowed. *What good morning? Who is your love?* I ignored him and went into the bathroom. If I was going to kill him, I'd need a better plan, one that wouldn't land me in prison!

When I returned to the bedroom after easing myself and covering my body with a robe, he was propped up on his elbow, watching me.

"Interesting stunt you pulled last night…"

I had no words for him. He was a snake, and I was the mouse in his cage. I walked out of the room before he could strike.

I went into the kitchen and fetched some water to boil in the kettle.

"You know, things could get a whole lot worse for you. Is this how you want to play it?"

CHAPTER EIGHT - NO MORE "I LOVE YOU"S

I looked at him. I would have asked what he wanted, but I was pretty sure I already knew. Was there any point talking to this fool?! I continued to ignore him.

"So, you're going with the silent treatment then?"

The silence was broken only by the whistling of the kettle. I made a mug of tea for myself and walked past him into the living room.

He followed me and watched me as I sipped my drink. "Hmmm..." he muttered. "I guess it was too soon for you to find out," he swallowed and shook his head, "and for that, I'm sorry."

For that? For that?! Where is a gun when you need one?! God, this man was going to turn me into a criminal! I chuckled.

"What's so funny?"

"Just get over yourself, will you?" I finally said.

"Look, I want to have kids..."

Eh hen? I just looked at him, like *"this dude is smoking something!"*

"I was hoping you'd like to be the mother of my children...unless you'd like me to delegate the responsibility?"

I suddenly gagged. Then bile came out of my mouth! It would have been funny in a different circumstance.

"Are you okay?"

He came close to sit beside me. I flinched and moved away from him. How dare he pretend to care?!

"Divorce me, nigga! I'm not trying to be your wife," I spewed as I went to the kitchen to find something to clean up the mess.

I didn't see his expression nor notice when he got up. All I heard was the front door slamming.

*****

Later that day, I decided I'd go and visit my mum. I needed a second opinion. Nneka's advice didn't sit well with me at all. I liked the good life like anybody else, but the hatred that was building in me for my husband was murderous. I couldn't live like that.

Nnamdi had his driver drive my car back with us last night, and I saw that he'd left the keys in plain sight on the dining table. I took them and drove to Obalende, in Ikoyi, where my parents lived.

"Hey, Ada, how are you?" she asked with a big grin when she saw me. "You're looking very sweet," she added before I could even answer.

I walked into her arms and hugged her tight. She hugged me back.

"Are you okay, dear?" she asked after a while.

I nodded, but the treacherous tears betrayed me.

"What's going on?" she asked, holding my hand. "Let's go to the patio and talk."

From the beginning, I told my mum everything, all that I knew about my husband and our marriage.

"Oh, dear. This is not good," she said.

I just sighed, happy to hear her voice of reason.

"Nneka has a point, but we are not all the same. It seems to me that Nnamdi picked the wrong woman to mess with."

I smiled at that vote of confidence.

"But she's right that the choice is really up to you. It is good that he is being honest, but it seems very cruel after the fact. He should have laid out his cards upfront instead of tricking you into accepting this type of marriage. I'm not happy with him at all."

"Can we not annul it?"

Mum shook her head. "I don't think so. But you can push for a divorce. Of course, you also have to consider the baby that's growing inside of you."

I looked at my mum. "What baby? I'm not pregnant..."

Mum raised her brow. "Are you sure? When last did you see your period?"

I put my head down in my hands. I knew I was late, but I hadn't thought anything of it. I had been experiencing some cramps, and I

CHAPTER EIGHT - NO MORE "I LOVE YOU"S

figured it was my period coming. Perhaps it was my pregnancy taking form.

"I need to see a doctor."

"You should take a pregnancy test," my mum said at the same time as me.

"Crap!" I didn't want to carry the beast's baby! "But I can still divorce him, pregnant or not."

"You could. But he also has more reason to fight you. Be careful, baby."

Mum reached for me and hugged me. I drew in a sigh. "You know you can pray, right? Prayer helped me and your father." She released me, holding me at arm's length to look into my eyes. "Talk to God about what's happening. He wants to help you."

I swallowed and nodded. I didn't want to tell her that I had already prayed, and God hadn't answered me. I guess I could pray again, but did He even listen to people like me?

On the way home, I stopped by a pharmacy and bought a pack of six tests. When I got home, I peed on all six sticks. They all said the same thing. Positive! *Crap!*

*****

A trip to the doctor's office revealed that I was already eight weeks pregnant. I figured it must have happened when we were christening all the rooms in my new house in mid-March!

I didn't want to tell Nnamdi that I was carrying his baby. He would find out sooner or later.

But with my sucky luck, it turned out to be sooner. He called me that night. After ignoring his call the first two times, I picked up.

"What?"

"I know you're pregnant."

Silence. "Who told you?" I doubted my mother would have said a word to him.

"It doesn't matter. I'm coming home."

"This is not your home."

"You're very funny, Ada. You are my home. I'm coming for you."

I swallowed. My mum was right! I had to play this one smart.

*****

When Nnamdi rang the bell, I let my matron open the door for him and remained in my room. I had bought a lock for the door. He would have to sleep in the guestroom downstairs.

After trying the handle to my room, he knocked on the door. I chose that moment to run a bath. I sat on my bed while the tub filled with water, and Nnamdi kept knocking.

"Ada... Ada, baby. Open up," he said.

Eventually, my tub filled, and I went in for my soak, this time without wine. The knocking had stopped, and I could hear music playing in the hallway. It sounded like Nnamdi was listening to "Stuck on You," by Lionel Richie. I guess he was feeling romantic.

I decided to connect my speakers to my phone and played the anthem that had been ringing in my head since I found him humping my housekeeper.

I smiled when the sound of Kelis shouting, "I hate you so much right now!" drowned out his sappy love song. *Eat shit, nigga!*

Rihanna's "Cold Case Love" played immediately after, and I shut my eyes as I bathed in the lyrics. Yes, what Nnamdi did to me was a crime!

But my enjoyment was cut short when the door to the room opened. It turned out he could pick a lock! *Thug!*

He barged into the bathroom and looked at me as if he was scared something bad had happened.

"Get out!" I shouted.

"I thought you were trying to hurt yourself," he said.

CHAPTER EIGHT - NO MORE "I LOVE YOU"S

"Because of you?!" I hissed.

He really had an over-inflated ego!

"Baby, you know you're emotional. These songs you are listening to. I don't want you to do something stupid."

He found my phone on top of the laundry basket, where I had kept it, and paused the music.

"Can you get out?"

"Let me help you out of the tub."

"I can do it my damn self," I shouted at him.

But still, he hung around and watched me as I stepped out of the tub and wrapped my towel around my body. I flinched when he tried to hold me. *Nigga, please!*

He followed me into the bedroom and sat on my bed, clearly not getting the message that he wasn't wanted.

"I need to change."

"Need my help?" he asked with a smile.

"Get out."

"No."

I hissed.

I used the towel to cover my body as I turned my back to him and creamed myself. I got a nightgown and wore it before I discarded the towel. I took it back to the bathroom and returned, my phone in hand.

"I hope you don't think you're sleeping here…"

"Ada, baby. You can *vex, sha*…"

"You think this is a joke?"

He swallowed. "We have to get past this. You're still my wife."

"Wife or prisoner?"

He swallowed again and looked at me. "Wife." He rose from the bed and came to where I stood. "I know I'm a bad husband because I like…other women. But you know, I'm also a very good husband. We can come to a reasonable compromise."

"What? You're gonna drop dead?"

"That's not funny, Ada. I'm the father of your child."

"That's what you think!" I spat at him.

He looked at me and shook his head. "You can't make me jealous, Ada. I know you love me. I know I'm the only one you've been with. I know you, Ada."

He put his right hand around my waist and drew me into him. "Can you let go of your anger and forgive that I am not perfect?"

He seemed so sincere that I wasn't revolted when he brought his face close to mine and kissed me again. My body betrayed me as my nipples pressed against my nightgown, just as his other hand cupped my breast. He took full advantage. With both his hands, he played with my nipples as he kissed me, inching closer and closer to the bed.

"Nnamdi," I wanted to protest.

His head came down to my neck where he kissed, sucked, and nibbled, before carrying me off my feet and placing me on the bed. It had been so long.

"Nnamdi, no," I offered a weak protest.

He brought his hand down to my haven below, which was moist and aching to be touched. I gasped when he did just that.

"Please, Nnamdi…"

But I might as well have been begging him to continue the way my body did the opposite of what I commanded it. My legs wrapped themselves around his neck as he decided to treat himself to my juices, which kept flowing for him until I cried out in contentment.

I shut my eyes, satiated. After a while, Nnamdi carried me and repositioned me on the bed, so my head was on the pillow, then lay beside me, his arm around me, just like the first night I had spent in his arms, the night he proposed to me.

"I love you," he whispered. "We can make this work, Ada. Please love me too."

CHAPTER EIGHT - NO MORE "I LOVE YOU"S

"Please, Nnamdi," I turned in his arms to look at his face. "No more 'I love you's, please. My heart can't take it."

He shut his eyes and swallowed. He squeezed me and kissed my shoulder. I turned again in his arms and let him spoon me as we slept.

CHAPTER NINE - OUR MARRIAGE

Nnamdi and I attended Dotun's birthday dinner together the next night. Victor brought a new girl he was seeing, Amber. She was cute, with a round, fair face and low-cut hair dyed blonde. Three other couples joined us to make it a party of 12.

I hadn't had a chance to talk to Nneka before then, but when we packed up the plates together and took them to the kitchen, she asked how things were going.

"Have you decided to stay?"

I wasn't happy about it, but I'd decided I could accept it. I had nothing more to lose. I nodded.

"Really?"

I looked at her. Wasn't she the one saying how better off I was? I shrugged. "It's unconventional. And we won't be the first. He has promised to be discreet, though."

"It's the least he can do..." Nneka said. "Hmmm. Congrats on the baby, though!"

"Oh, how did you know? I only just found out on Thursday."

"Mum told me..."

"Oh, okay... Thanks."

"Awww, come here," she said, reaching to hug me. Sometimes, Nneka behaved like she was the older sister. Maybe because she had married first. But right then, I didn't mind. I allowed her to baby me because,

CHAPTER NINE - OUR MARRIAGE

even though I was putting up a brave front, I was so scared of what my life in marriage would become.

*****

That first week of my acceptance, Nnamdi took me on a second honeymoon, "to celebrate," he said. He was so excited as we packed for the Mediterranean cruise, leaving from Egypt. He was like a kid who had just learned that he would be going to Disneyland for Christmas.

Our first night was wonderful. Nnamdi had booked us a corner suite on the top deck of the cruise liner, and the views were breathtaking. After we returned from clubbing in the big dome in the middle of the ship, Nnamdi ravished me in our bed, literally all night long! It was an amazing, unforgettable night.

On our second night on the cruise, Nnamdi made a special request. There was a lady he wanted to sleep with, and he wanted me to invite her for a threesome with us. He said doing it together would make me appreciate it for exactly what it was - just sex. Fun, exciting, pleasurable sex. I hated the idea, but I went along with it.

Nnamdi had me watch him as he had sex with a young girl, who couldn't have been a day older than 20! Then he wanted to watch us play with ourselves. It was while we were doing that that he came for me. It was not the same as when it was just us. It wasn't better, though Nnamdi seemed to be on overdrive. It was just different. There was no emotion to the act that was meant to build our intimacy.

He asked me how I felt afterwards, and I told him I found it repulsive and disappointing. He said it was because I wasn't used to it yet. He said we should try again the next night. After three nights of orgies, I knew it wasn't for me and doing it for him would hurt me more than it would help our marriage, so I told him to keep me out of it. If he wanted to do two women at a time, he was free.

And so, that was how I grew accustomed to my husband having

multiple sexual partners. I got used to knocking and waiting for a response before trying to enter any room, except in my house. He didn't bring anyone to my home. It was the only place I felt safe to make love to him whenever he 'missed me' as he liked to say.

Apart from that, we were friends. I gave up my anger and jealousy because they got me nowhere. He came often to check on me and our baby, and he still took me on vacations, even though I actually preferred to holiday on my own because there were times I would return from the spa or a shopping trip to find a sign on the door, indicating he was with someone, and I should come back.

I used to cry. I cried a lot in the first few years of my marriage because it seemed unbelievable that someone would think this way of living was more natural or fulfilling than committing to be faithful to one person that you love and choose to build a life with.

My mum used to invite me to pray and join online prayer meetings, but all the yabba dabba do speak they were doing was off putting. Even the one where they just spoke in English, I attended once but didn't go again. I didn't see how that was going to change anything.

There were times I wanted to leave. I was constantly asking him for a divorce, especially as he called on me less and less, sometimes even going a whole month without seeing me.

My joy at giving birth to our daughter, Osinachi, was short-lived when I found out a month later that he was expecting a child - a boy actually - from another woman. A younger woman in her 20s; slim, fair, and beautiful, like the spec he said he had outgrown. Even though he had promised to be discreet, I was disgraced. I wanted to die!

I tried to leave then, but again, he wouldn't let me. I got a lawyer, and I started divorce proceedings, but he actually paid my lawyer to drop the case. I felt so powerless.

One day, I barged into his office to confront him. "Why do you want me to stay? What do you need me for?" I cried.

CHAPTER NINE - OUR MARRIAGE

"You are my rock, Ada," he said. "Every man needs a rock. You're the one I want to come home to."

"So, why are you fathering babies up and down?!"

"It's not intentional, baby. These things happen. But I promise you, my heir will come from you. You are my only wife."

Like a fool, I held on to that promise, as though Nnamdi could be trusted to keep his word.

My parents were not happy about the situation at all. They said any time I was ready, I could pack out of the house and return home. They would gladly return Nnamdi's bride price. But I chose to stay. I was glad that at least Nnamdi cared enough to fight for me to stay.

I gave birth to Chinedu in our fourth year of marriage. We hadn't been trying. It just happened, like with his other women. But unlike their babies, mine were celebrated. My son was the heir. My children were my gift, my benefit. Their heritage was my consolation prize for abiding in my marriage to Nnamdi.

I didn't expect or demand anything from him after that. I lived my life, focused on my children and my business and enjoyed the luxuries his wealth afforded us. Like Nneka said, it could have been worse, though I couldn't imagine it then.

*****

Then on my 44th birthday, 14th June 2025, the last wave hit my castle in the sand to complete its destruction.

Nnamdi took me to Las Vegas to celebrate. I organized a weekend getaway with my old friends from High School and College, just six of us, including Omi. Nneka couldn't come because she was still nursing Sade, her fourth child who was only four months old. Nnamdi covered our travel and accommodation costs. He accompanied me to enjoy himself in Vegas, but I planned to do my own thing with my friends.

However, we all had breakfast on our first morning, my actual birthday, and that was when he met Rita.

Rita Osineye was my best friend from UNILAG. She had gone to study her Masters in the States and had lived there ever since, but we stayed connected. She knew all about my hellish marriage to Nnamdi Ukwueze, and she told me about her vibrant, sometimes lonely, single life in the US. We had met up a few times during my vacations to the US, but she and Nnamdi had never met.

After our breakfast, when I went to the bathroom to freshen up before going shopping with my girls, Nnamdi came to ask me about Rita. I looked at him through the mirror, wondering where his questions were leading to. Finally, in the name of honesty, he told me that he wanted to have one night with her!

I freaked!

"You cannot do that, Nnamdi! You can't sleep with my friend!"

"Come on, Ada. It's just sex. Just one night."

"I'll never forgive you, Nnamdi, if you do that. There are boundaries that cannot be crossed, and this is one of them. Take your eyes off my friends! You have a whole city filled with young, beautiful women. I beg you, leave my friends alone."

"Okay, baby. If it means that much to you."

I was so appalled, I wanted to call off the whole trip. I probably should have.

When I went out with the girls later, I kept looking at Rita, wondering what it was he saw in her. She was the only one of my friends that was still single and without kids. Was that it? Yes, she was also very successful... Was that also a factor? Okay, so she was gorgeous with a well-rounded figure and looked 20 years younger than her 43 years. *God!* Why could my husband not keep his vermin away from me and my friends?

I tried to be cheerful, but it felt like someone had died. Every part of me wanted to cry. It was like a dark cloud had taken over my holiday,

CHAPTER NINE - OUR MARRIAGE

and I just felt miserable. I had to tell my friends I was feeling sick and wanted to have an early night.

Later that night, my husband crawled into bed beside me, not to apologise, not to comfort me, take care of me, or make love to me, but to say, "Baby, please. If I had met her on my own and we had fucked, you wouldn't have known about it, and it wouldn't even be an issue because I wouldn't see her again! But this one that you're saying I can't have her… I can't think of anything else but her. Please, baby. Can Rita be the exception?!"

I could not believe the campaign he was going through for one night with my friend. I turned to look at him and saw him for what he was; a selfish infant of a man, a spoiled child who had never been denied anything he wanted.

"Can you not see that I am hurting here?" I asked him. "It's my birthday! It's only 9 o'clock, and I'm in bed because you want to fuck my best friend! Are you so cruel?"

He swallowed and seemed repentant. "I'm sorry, baby," he muttered.

But he didn't stop. The next day, at breakfast, he flirted with all my friends, somehow always finding a way to get Rita to talk to him. I had to leave the table because I was so humiliated. Rita followed me out onto the balcony of the penthouse Nnamdi had booked for both of us.

"Hey, girl. What's going on? Why are you so upset?"

I looked at her and didn't know how to tell her. I didn't want her to be offended. I couldn't have been more wrong.

"Really?" she asked, smiling and looking mighty interested when I told her my husband had been on my case about sleeping with her. Then, as if realizing my own offence, she reigned in her enthusiasm and tried to keep a serious expression. "But you know that's how he is. Why are you so worked up?"

"Because you're my friend! Isn't it bad enough that he does it with strangers? How can you be so cool about it?"

She shrugged, and that was when I saw the attraction. She was hypersexual like him. "It's just sex."

All the time I had been crying to her about my husband, Miss Single, Sexy, and Free had thought me a prude!

"So, you want to fuck him?" I asked outrightly.

She swallowed. "You have to admit, he is very fuckable."

I couldn't believe what I was hearing. Nnamdi was right. If they had met on their own terms, even knowing he was my husband, Rita would have had sex with him and thought nothing of it. I just gawked at her, and she looked away.

"Look, I'm not saying I will…"

"Why don't you?" I asked. She looked at me wide-eyed. "Why don't you put him out of his misery and get it out of your system…"

"You think? No, Ada. You think?"

I turned around and walked away from her. *Fuck them both!*

For the rest of my birthday weekend, Nnamdi and Rita were noticeably absent.

Nnamdi returned the following morning, just before I had to check out of our penthouse. I knew he had been with Rita. He was so happy, and I wanted to die. He actually came to thank me as I was packing up my things.

"Thank you for being such an understanding wife," he beamed.

"One night, you said," I said, lifting my right index finger for emphasis.

"I want to stay with her a little longer. You don't mind, do you?"

I was crushed! "I hate you! I hate you, Nnamdi! I hate you!!!" I cried.

In all the years I'd thought it, I had never said it to his face before. I had all sorts of curse words for him, but this was the first time all I could say was how much I hated him.

He just stood there, head bowed, as I carried my suitcase and left our penthouse. I prayed his plane would crash! I prayed they would

CHAPTER NINE - OUR MARRIAGE

get into a horrible accident and die miserable deaths. All I could think of as I left that room was how they would perish together for the humiliation they had caused me.

CHAPTER TEN - THE LAST INSULT

Rita changed everything.
Nnamdi did not miss me anymore. He didn't come for me anymore. He stayed in the States with her for three months before he returned to check on his children. Yes, he remained a part of their lives, but I was no longer his home.

In November, a month to our 10-year anniversary, I heard that he was building Rita her own mansion in Eko Atlantic! I wanted to die! Nnamdi had done me dirty!

As for Rita, I had no words for her. She never reached out to me after our conversation on the balcony. It was a triple loss because she was the one I used to confide in, and now, she was the one I hated the most. Well, second to Nnamdi!

I was in a very bad place in the weeks leading up to our anniversary. Not only had Nnamdi not made any plans, but I was also hearing through the grapevine that he was planning to take a second wife!

He had wasted ten years of my life, and I could not stand for him to treat me like I did not matter. How do you do this to someone you claim to love?! How do you do this to another human being?!

I decided I needed to speak with Nnamdi. I didn't know what good it would do, but it felt so much worse not being able to say how I felt about everything that was happening in my life. He used to be my friend.

CHAPTER TEN - THE LAST INSULT

"Hi, Ada," he answered the call jovially. "How are the kids?"
"They are fine, Nnamdi. How are you?"
"I'm great. About to step into a meeting. What's up?"
"Can I see you tonight?"
"Hmmm… Tonight isn't looking good. Is it urgent."
"Yes, very urgent."
"I'll check on you in the morning, okay?"
"Okay. Thank you."
"Bye!"

He sounded like he was in a noisy place, not in his office. But I didn't want to worry about that. He said he would come in the morning, so I prepared myself for what I wanted to say to him.

*****

In the morning, I waited for his car horn, but it didn't come. I waited for his call, but my phone did not ring. I called and called, but my calls went unanswered. Was he ignoring me or had something happened to prevent him from coming, calling, or even picking my calls?

The first call I received that day was from my brother, Victor. He was calling to check on me. There was something in the news about Nnamdi and Rita. He asked if I had seen it, but I hadn't.

"I'm so sorry, Ada. That man did not deserve you. If you want to talk, I'm here."

I opened my Instagram app, and the trending story was of Billionaire Nnamdi Ukwueze's engagement to Engr. Rita Osineye. He had proposed to her last night in Paris, and they were set to marry in the new year.

My heart sank all the way to my feet. He never had any plans to see me that morning. He had nothing to say to me. After ten years, he let me find out that our marriage was over in the news!

It was strange to me how there was no mention of the fact that he was already married with children. Most commentaries were on what a beautiful couple they made, how the wedding was going to be the biggest affair of the year, and what a power couple they would be.

In all the pictures posted, Rita looked the epitome of beauty, and Nnamdi looked absolutely smitten. Did Nnamdi not even think about what this would do to his kids? How could he do this without even giving us a warning?! He had managed to keep his other affairs out of the press, why was this different?

A part of me said it was better for me that he had decided to marry another wife. Let him be her problem. But the part of me that still remembered how much I had loved him and all he had caused me to go through was not ready to let it go.

On one hand, I thought maybe he would finally give me the divorce I wanted, but on the other hand, I was livid! He said I was his rock! Now he was building a life with someone I had considered my best friend. Was I supposed to roll over and die?!

The truth was, I knew they wouldn't care if I did. Everything they had done from the moment they met showed that they didn't regard me as worthy of consideration, let alone respect. I had suffered an injustice, and oh, how I needed it to be righted!

*****

It was the day after that Nnamdi came to see me, but I was no longer in the frame of mind to have a heart to heart with him. I beheld him with contempt when he walked through the door, dressed in a dark grey native suit and reeking of cologne. He was still on the phone as he walked into the house. He lingered in the hallway, finishing his call before he strolled into the living room like he owned the place. I remained where I was on the sofa, watching him.

"Hey, Ada. Sorry, I couldn't come yesterday. What's up?"

Wow, I thought. That *'sorry'* really came out of his mouth, *sha*. I just

CHAPTER TEN - THE LAST INSULT

looked at him, like, *"Is that all you have to say to me?"*

"What is it? You said it was urgent..."

He continued to act ignorant.

"Was this your plan all along, Nnamdi? Did you plot how you would kill me with humiliation?"

He swallowed as he looked at me. "I'm sorry, Ada. I don't know what you are talking about."

I stood up then. "Have you not announced your engagement to Rita to the whole world?! Did you not think to talk to me - your one and only wife - before you did such a thing?"

"Oh... That." He sighed and sat down. "Is this what you said was urgent? You had me scared thinking it was something serious."

I looked down at him, livid. "What am I to you? *Furniture?!* Nnamdi, I have been *begging* you for years for a divorce, but you said you needed me. Well, you have not needed me in months, and you did not care to tell me."

"Please, can you calm down, Ada? There's really no need to be so worked up."

The nerve of the man! I wanted to strangle him, but I knew what a wasted effort it would be. I took deep breaths as I looked at him sitting so calmly, watching me. This man didn't have one ounce of love for me. Not one. I was wasting my breath.

I eventually returned to my seat on the sofa, across from the armchair he had settled on.

"You're right. I should have given you a heads up. I'm sorry," he said, leaning forward and looking me in the eyes. "I'm happy, Ada. I'm in a good place, and I want you to be too."

This man is mad!

"If you still want a divorce, I won't stop you. In fact, Rita would prefer not to be a second wife..."

Rita would prefer?

"I don't give a damn what Rita prefers!" I shouted. "How can you treat me this way, Nnamdi? You said you loved me!" I cried.

He was quiet for a moment.

"Look, I'm sorry, okay?" he said, rising, signalling the end of our conversation. "You can have whatever you want in the divorce. I have to go now."

And that was how Nnamdi walked out of my life. That was the last time I set my eyes on him.

*****

That night, I dreamed of 1000 ways to kill Nnamdi Ukwueze and the bitch he left me for! I tossed and turned over how I would get rid of the evidence and dispose of their bodies. I created a timeline of things I had to do in advance to ensure that I wasn't a suspect or to make sure the deaths looked accidental. I couldn't sleep a wink as I cooked up my payback.

"I'm happy, Ada. I'm in a good place..." his words taunted me.

He should be in hell! He should burn for all the pain he had caused me! How dare he be happy while I was miserable, my best years gone?! *Oh, God, that Nnamdi should die by my hand!*

At one point, I decided to stop pretending to sleep and opened my eyes. I gazed up at the ceiling as I assessed my thoughts and the emotions that were denying rest to my eyes.

I was sure Nnamdi was sleeping peacefully. Or maybe he was fucking his whore. But he certainly wasn't wasting his life thinking about me. And there I was, consumed with thoughts of him. Who was the fool?!

I cried silent tears on my pillow. He wasn't worth it. I had wasted enough time. It was time I let him go. At least he'd had the decency to visit and apologise. I'll take that as closure. It wasn't enough, but it had to be. I had to make the most of the life I had left, and living to payback Nnamdi was a poor way to live.

CHAPTER TEN - THE LAST INSULT

I heaved a sigh and shivered as a residual sob passed. I shut my eyes again. I let it go, and somehow, I eventually slept off.

*****

I woke up to the news that Nnamdi was dead. Pictures had not been released, but the story went that he and his fiancée had been shot several times and had their throats slit in their hotel room yesterday evening.

While I had been losing sleep dreaming of how to end their lives, someone else had spared me the trouble. Now that I had gotten what I had wanted, retribution, I had nothing else to feel. I felt like a ghost as I walked through my house, devoid of tears to shed for the two people who knew me the most and who hurt me the most.

My doorbell rang while I was in the kitchen, still trying to get accustomed to the reality that the world was now devoid of Nnamdi Ukwueze. Then I thought of my children… That was when a lonesome tear found its way out of my left eye. From nowhere at all, as I thought more about my children being fatherless, the other children Nnamdi had fathered being fatherless, and the mess he left behind, my body was racked with sobs as I cried.

"Madam, the police are here," Mrs Abike, my matron said, causing me to look up with a face soaked with tears at two officers who had come to question me about the murders of my husband and his mistress.

I thank God they found me crying because I have looked for tears to cry since but cannot find them.

*****

Thankfully, they let me go after a brief interrogation, with a promise to visit again or invite me in for more questioning as their investigation produces more evidence.

How does one go about finding a good defence lawyer? I don't have any friends who have been accused of murder but acquitted to provide recommendations. The few lawyers I know specialise in corporate law or family law. I guess I could start my search from there. Perhaps one of them could point me to a trustworthy firm to represent me.

Second to my decision to marry Nnamdi in the first place, I know this will be the most important decision I make to protect my future. I also know it's going to take a miracle for me not to be hanged as a scapegoat for this crime.

For the second time in my life, I shut my eyes and get down on my knees to make a sincere prayer to God.

"Please God, You know I didn't do this, even though I wanted them dead - forgive me. Please, do not let my children be motherless as well as fatherless. Help me find the right lawyer to clear my name. Amen."

I don't know if I really believe there's a God out there who hears prayers, but right now, I am hoping that there is, and He will answer this prayer, even though He didn't give me the love I once prayed earnestly for.

II

THE INVESTIGATION

"There is nothing hidden that will not be disclosed, and nothing concealed that will not be known or brought out into the open..."
(Luke 8:17, NIV).

CHAPTER ELEVEN - THE LAWYER

A DAEZE

It's funny how life just goes on, no matter what happens to you or those around you. When Nnamdi walked out of my home the morning he died, I remember being amazed that nothing stopped. The world didn't stop spinning, my heart didn't stop beating... Nothing stood still to acknowledge the monumental heartbreak I was experiencing.

And now it is with his death. Life just keeps going on. Today being Thursday, I didn't want to disrupt my children's routine by making them stay home to mourn their father. At nine years and five and a half, they really don't have a clue what has happened, and I don't know how I will even begin to have the conversation about their father's passing. They hardly even saw him for his death to have a significant impact on their lives. However, I plan to sit down with Osinachi on Saturday and let her know what has happened and why she will never see her father again.

After dropping the children at school, my usual routine would have been to go to the gym, but I am in desperate need of a lawyer. Ideally, as Nnamdi's widow, I should have been hosting mourners at our - *my* - house, but being the primary suspect in a double-homicide, and my estranged relationship with his family, seeing as Nnamdi and I were practically separated for nine and a half years as he went off on a shagging spree, I know that's not going to happen.

Besides, my house wasn't Nnamdi's home. Anyone wishing to mourn his death will have to find their way to his parents' home in Victoria Island. I probably should go there now, but I am not ready. I have no more tears for Nnamdi, even though the wound of his betrayal is still so raw. Though I have prayed for forgiveness, thinking of him makes me want to stomp on his corpse until he is just a puddle of blood and guts!

I realise it will take a long while before I overcome my feelings of hatred and anger towards him, so being around people who love him and are weeping for him is abhorrent. It would be like pouring gasoline on my fire. By extension, I hate the whole bloody lot of them! I suspect they knew he was rotten but chose to look the other way as I married the bastard.

No, nothing, no custom nor law, will make me mourn his death! In fact, I am seriously thinking of treating myself to a spa day.

But I know I am being watched. It will look even more suspicious if I go about as though his death hasn't impacted my life in any way. Deciding that a visit to the gym or the spa is probably not the best idea, I drive to my mum's place.

As I approach the turning for Keffi Street on Awolowo Road, the light turns yellow, but I figure I still have time to turn, only to hit the bumper of the car in front of me that has stopped. I curse. If he wasn't going to turn, he should have been on the other lane, for God's sake!

The man, decent-looking except for the frown on his face, steps out of the car to inspect the damage. Annoyed, I switch off my engine and step out too.

SEGUN

The light turns red just as I am about to turn into Keffi Street, and I step on my brakes, only to be rammed in the back by what I now see

CHAPTER ELEVEN - THE LAWYER

is a lady driver in a Mercedes-Benz SL-Class. Obviously, she thought I would turn at the red, like many drivers do, but I don't like to take such chances.

I switch off my engine to examine the damage to my Acura TLX. It takes her a moment to join me. She looks stressed and irritated as she walks towards me, a pout on her full lips. She looks somehow familiar, but I can't figure out where I might have seen her before. She stops and sighs when she sees the damage she has done to my right taillight. Apart from that, there are just a few scratches to my bumper and negligible damage to her more expensive ride.

"I'm sorry," she offers without prompting, softening me. I was sure she was going to make me beg for it.

"Are you okay?" I don't know why that's the question I ask, but there's something about her that makes me think all's not right in her world.

She looks at me for a moment, as though shocked and moved by my question. "My husband just died."

"Oh, I'm sorry, ma'am," I reply, not at all expecting that response. She could be lying, but I'm willing to give her the benefit of the doubt. I slip my hand into my inner suit pocket and hand her my business card. "May I have your contact?"

She collects my card and begins to call out her phone number. I bring out my mobile phone to record it and call it back to her.

"You're a lawyer?"

It doesn't sound like a question as much as it sounds like an observation. "Yes, ma'am."

The driver in the car behind hers honks his horn. I guess we are holding up traffic. And I also need to get going to my interview. I begin to walk to the driver's seat of my car.

"Wait, what type of lawyer?" she asks.

"Call me," I reply as I enter my car. She turns to enter her car as I drive away.

I arrive just in time at Classic 97.3 FM to share my thoughts on the top story this week, the Nnamdi Ukwueze murder. The news has everyone shook, and the investigating officers have their work cut out for them figuring out who killed the billionaire and his girlfriend. I understand that his widow has already been brought for questioning as a primary suspect. I wonder who's representing her.

ADAEZE

Wow, he is a lawyer, I think as I return to my car at the honks of other impatient road users. I get in my car and switch on the engine.

Immediately, I hear, "Stay tuned on The Morning Show with Bukola and Ifeanyi. After the break, our next guest, Barrister Olusegun Adetokunbo (SAN) will be here to share his expert opinion on The Roles of Investigation, Prosecution, and Advocacy in Criminal Justice, in light of the murder of Billionaire Nnamdi Ukwueze and his girlfriend. Don't touch that dial."

What? I look at the card the man gave me again, and for sure, he is the Barr. Olusegun Adetokunbo. *Wait, hold up...* I did not have the radio on when I was driving before... And if I had, it would have been set to 93.7 Rhythm FM because of my love for RnB.

How strange that my radio should come on at this exact time and to this specific station? Even stranger is that I just bumped into the person - the *lawyer* - that is being interviewed in view of my husband's murder investigation. In my heart, I know something mysterious just happened.

The driver behind me manoeuvres past me and shouts at me before cutting in front and making the turn. I get in gear and take the turn after him to continue to my parents' place, my ears tingling as I listen to the radio show, waiting for the promised guest.

The Barrister arrives on the show just as I get to my mum's place.

CHAPTER ELEVEN - THE LAWYER

I keep the engine running as I listen to the radio, parked in the large compound. Using my phone, I send a message to my mum that I've arrived, and I'm outside.

"Tune in to Classic 97.3 FM," I tell her via WhatsApp.

After 15 minutes, they take another break, and I switch off the engine to enter the house, now listening on my phone.

"Good morning, Mum and Dad," I say when I enter the living room, where they are both seated listening. I remove my headphones.

My mum rises to hug me, and we stand like that for a whole minute. When we separate, I go over to hug my dad. My mum wipes tears from her eyes as she returns to sit next to my dad. I take a seat on the armchair across from them.

"How are you coping with all of this, Ada?" my father asks.

The weak emotions, as though summoned, bubble to the surface again, causing my eyes to water. I thought I had run out of tears. I shrug. "I just want it to be over. I should have left him years ago."

"You should never have married that monster!" my mum says, wiping her eyes.

The advertisement break is over, and the female presenter gives a recap of what they discussed in the first half, which looked at similar cases in the last decade and the challenges faced during investigation, prosecution, and defence.

"Do you know I just met this man?" I say as the male presenter welcomes Barr. Segun.

"Ifeanyi?" my mum asks, with raised brows.

"No, the Barrister. I hit his car on my way here…"

"Really?"

We all get quiet again as Barr. Segun starts talking.

"When things like this happen, it is easy for investigation and prosecution to be led by emotions, especially when the people involved are influential. A good defence for those accused in such cases cannot be overestimated. As awful as it is for a criminal to be set free, I find it far more repugnant when an innocent person is convicted or denied their rights because of a scapegoat culture or inadequate representation…"

"Maybe he can represent you," my mum says, distracting me from his speech.

I swallow. I have thought of it, and I intend to call him to ask for his help. I hope he will be able to take my case.

"Do you know they have taken your brother in for questioning too?" Mum continues, speaking over Barr. Segun.

"What?! When?"

"Just this morning. He called when they were at his house."

"Wow… What do they want with him?" I ask, more to myself than anyone else.

We continue listening to the show.

"Are you going to go to his parents' house?" my mum suddenly asks.

"Why in the world will she do that?" my dad retorts, surprising me. "These people owe my daughter an apology! Now, they want to accuse her of murder!"

My dad bows his head and rests it on his left hand. He shakes as he sobs. I go to him and put my arm around his shoulder.

"It's okay, Dad. I'm okay. Everything is going to be fine."

Dad nods and wipes his eyes. He looks me in the eyes. "You don't owe that family anything."

I hug him, and my tears fall. "Thank you, Dad."

"So, what do you think? Will justice be served in this case?" Bukola asks Barr. Segun.

"I believe we are at the stage that we can expect justice from our legal system, as long as we remember that every one of us is innocent until proven guilty."

"It was great having you with us, Barrister Olusegun Adetokunbo,"

CHAPTER ELEVEN - THE LAWYER

Ifeanyi says before announcing that they will be taking a musical interlude.

SEGUN

I'm just heading to my car when my phone rings. I see that it is the woman who ran into me today. I really wasn't expecting her to call, but I'm glad she did. I answer as I open my car door.

"Hello, madam."

"Hello. I'm the lady from this morning. I just listened to you on the radio."

"Oh, wonderful. Thanks," I beam. "May I know your name, please? I currently have you saved as 'Sad Widow Driver.'"

I hear a slight chuckle from her end, which makes me smile. "I am Adaeze Ukwueze. Nnamdi's widow."

I'm stunned into silence.

"Are you still there?"

"Yes, ma'am, I am." I swallow. *How uncanny!*

"So, umm, well... I am actually looking for representation, and I was hoping—"

"No, problem, madam. It would be my pleasure."

She breathes an audible sigh of relief. "Thank you. Thank you so much."

My heart is thumping because this is so unreal. I had been secretly wishing I could represent her, but I hadn't even voiced it in prayer to God. He must have known, I think as my heart is gladdened at the thoughtfulness of my God.

"Where are you now? Would you like to meet today?" I ask.

"Oh, wow, would that be okay? I figured you would be busy."

I smile at her humility. I didn't imagine the billionaire's wife would be so considerate. "I actually cleared the morning for my interview," I say, leaning on my car. "So, should I come and meet you or would you like to stop by my office?"

"I'm not far from the radio station. I don't know if you've already left. I'm at my parents' place at Obalende."

"Oh, cool. I am still nearby. Send me the address. I'll come right away."

"Thank you so much." She sounds so grateful, and I can understand why.

"No worries at all. I'll see you soon."

When I enter my car, I raise my hands to the heavens and praise the Lord because *what?!* This can only be Him.

CHAPTER TWELVE - THE USUAL SUSPECTS

VICTOR

"Can you state your name for the record?"

"My name is Victor Okpara," I say.

"Thank you, Victor. Do you know why you have been brought in today?"

"No."

"Okay. We are conducting our investigation for the murder of your brother-in-law, Nnamdi Ukwueze, on the night of the 2nd of December 2025. We would like to ask you some questions to help us identify who might have had motive to kill him and his girlfriend that night."

I nod. "I understand."

"You should also know that this conversation is recorded and can be used in court as testimony against you or anyone else, and you have the right to have a lawyer present. Or you can waive it."

"It's fine. I don't have anything to hide."

The officer smiles. "Thank you. We appreciate your cooperation. So, can you tell us what you were doing on the night of the murder, specifically between the hours of 8 to 10 pm?"

"I was at home working on a project."

"Is there anyone who saw you, who can verify your statement?"

"Well, my wife, Amber, and our kids were around, but by 8:30, the children had gone to bed. My wife usually sleeps by 9 pm. I was with her before I went down to work on my project."

"Okay. How was your relationship with the victims, particularly your brother-in-law?"

I grind my teeth. "It wasn't good. We were cordial."

"And why was that?"

"He was cheating on my sister," I swallow. "Very openly, and she was in a lot of pain."

"So, you didn't like him very much…"

"I hated him! And I'm not the only one. He was a narcissistic bastard who thought he could do whatever he liked to whoever he wanted. I'm glad he's dead."

"Such strong feelings…" the officer says.

I shrug. "It's the truth."

"So, who else do you think wanted him dead? Your sister?"

I look the officer in his face, knowing his game plan. I am not a fool to out my sister. "Which one?"

The office smiles, raising a brow. "So, you think both of them might have had a motive?"

"No, I have two sisters. To which are you referring?"

"Let's start with Ada…"

I shake my head. "Ada couldn't hurt a fly. And I know she loved Nnamdi very much."

"Enough to kill him for leaving her for someone else?"

I grind my teeth. "All I know is she didn't do it. She couldn't have done it."

"Right…" he nods. "And…umm, Nneka? You think she could have."

"She doesn't even have a motive. Why don't you guys focus on his harem of mistresses and leave my family alone?"

"Well, sir, we are just doing our jobs. Two people were murdered in cold blood. We have to question everyone we suspect."

"That's fine. Can I go now?"

"If you know something, you have an obligation to tell us."

"It seems you are shooting in the dark here. Here's a tip. Start with Amarachi, his secretary. If there is someone with a motive and access to hurt him, she has both. I'm done talking."

AMARACHI

Honestly, I don't get paid enough for the shit I do around here, and then people want to come and be calling me 'Secretary'!

"Excuse me, I was Nnamdi Ukwueze's Executive Assistant not *Secretary*," I say to the police officers who have shown up to the office asking for "Amarachi, the Secretary."

"Sorry, ma'am. Please, we would like you to follow us to the station for questioning."

I stop stacking the files I have been sorting through and look at them. "Can you see that I'm busy? There's so much to do, especially with Nnamdi gone. Can't you just ask me what you want to ask me here?"

"Excuse me, ma'am," a police officer steps forward, distinguishing himself. "This is a high-profile, double-homicide investigation. I would suggest that you take it seriously and come with us right away. You can do it freely or under arrest."

I look at him amazed. "What? You think *I* killed him?"

"Ma'am, I'm not going to ask you again."

"Fine, I'm coming," I say, exasperated. "Just give me a moment."

My office line starts ringing, but the look on the officer's face prevents me from answering it. I call out to my own assistant as I leave my desk. "Janet, please look after things until I get back."

I follow the three officers to the elevator, and we wait for the lift. I can't believe they are causing this drama at my office. I know Nnamdi is dead, and they are just doing their jobs, but I also have a job to do, and it's piling up!

Nnamdi could not have picked a worse time to die! Just before Christmas?! If not for the salary I earn and my two kids, I would have quit.

Am I sad that he's dead? Truthfully, I don't think I care.

Oh, Nnamdi... Nnamdi was a bastard. A sweet bastard sometimes, but a cruel bastard most of the time.

When I first got the job, six years ago, I was so infatuated with him. No one had to tell me about his reputation. You could smell it on him. He just gave off that Casanova vibe. Despite the repulsiveness that comes with knowing that he is a 'free for all,' one look from him still managed to get me dripping.

Like a moth to the flame, I went the way of the others before me. I just couldn't resist his potent sex-appeal. And it sure didn't help that his performance matched his ego. He was better than I had even imagined...and his huge ego just wouldn't stop growing.

Yes, I will miss him. I miss him already. I've actually missed him for months...

Since he travelled to the States and returned with a new girlfriend. No one could have foreseen the change in Nnamdi. Instead of booking dates and rooms and sending flowers to this lady and that lady, Nnamdi had me diverting calls, cancelling dates, blocking off whole weeks. Everything was all about Rita.

Rita and his kids. He still went to visit his kids regularly. There was a rotation of baby mamas. One week it will be Ada's house, the next it was Adenike's place, then Cynthia's, then last but not least, my place.

If you're wondering how he was able to do all this and run a conglomerate, then look no further. *Secretary, my ass.* I run the place!

I wasn't like his previous secretaries, whom he shagged and sacked. Nnamdi needed me. Even when we found out I was pregnant, he just got me my own assistant, but I was still coming to run things until a

CHAPTER TWELVE - THE USUAL SUSPECTS

couple of weeks before I delivered my first child, Gloria.

But you see why I said Nnamdi is a bastard; he is too greedy for his own good. Even my assistant, he used to call her to give him blow jobs! He said at least they were not fucking... I have had to sack three assistants, and I know he screwed them all. To Nnamdi, if you didn't see him, it didn't happen.

But 'long throat' has killed him now. I know it must be one of his baby mamas. I doubt it will be his wife. She has put up with it for so long, it's like her life now.

These people are just wasting my time dragging me down to the police station. Well, we will get there, and I will send them the addresses of all his baby mamas. Who knows if it was even a baby mama. Maybe it was a jealous husband!

Nnamdi! Your cup don full.

*****

We are finally at the station, and I don't even know why they would prefer to chat with me here than my air-conditioned office. The place is so stuffy and poorly lit. And what's that smell? Like someone has been pissing on the walls.

"Can you tell us what you were doing on the night of the 2nd of December 2025?"

"What time exactly?"

"Between 8 to 10 pm."

"I was with my boyfriend..."

The officer raises a brow. "Boyfriend?"

"Yes, boyfriend! Am I not allowed to have a boyfriend?"

"Were you not also having an affair with Nnamdi?"

"It wasn't an affair. We screwed occasionally."

"And your boyfriend didn't mind?"

I shrug. "Are you going to tell him?"

The police officer smiles. "So, how do I know you and your boyfriend didn't plot to kill Nnamdi?"

"What would be the point of that?" I ask. "In case you haven't noticed, I like my paycheque. I had no reason to kill my boss."

"But your boyfriend did. Maybe he found out about you guys, decided to kill Nnamdi, and you agreed to cover for him."

I laugh. "Please. You're barking up the wrong tree. Temisan is too laidback to murder even a cockroach."

"Hmmm… So, do you know who else might have had a motive?"

"Why not visit his baby mamas? I have their names and addresses memorized."

"Oh, okay. Thank you."

I reel off the information of the two other baby mamas in Nigeria. "There's another one, Susan Harrison. She's 26!" I say, with emphasis on the six. "Nnamdi met her last year when he took Ada to Spain for their anniversary. Can you believe that mess? But she lives in the UK. I doubt she did it," I add cheekily.

"Okay. Thank you for your help."

"Of course, Rita's ex could have killed them too…" I chuckle. *Good luck finding out who killed Nnamdi.*

"Do you have his information?"

"Nah… Just a name. Jack Stevenson."

"Okay, thank you."

I inhale. "Can I go now?"

"Yes, ma'am. We'll contact you if we need more information."

ADENIKE

"Adenike Rogers?" one of the two police officers at my door says.

"Yes…?"

"You're wanted for questioning on the murder of Nnamdi Ukwueze and his fiancée, Rita Osineye. Can you come with us, ma'am?"

CHAPTER TWELVE - THE USUAL SUSPECTS

"Can I bring my two children? Because I don't have anyone to watch them."

The two officers look between themselves, then the other one asks, "May we come in, ma'am?"

I step aside with the door wide open for them to enter.

"I'm sorry. It's a mess. My nanny has abandoned me."

They remain standing until I point for them to take a seat on the sofa.

"Ma'am, we want to know where you were two nights ago."

"Oh, I went clubbing with my friends."

"Oh, really?"

"*Noooo!* I just told you that I don't have a nanny! She left since the end of November. I have been home with my twin boys, Taiwo and Kehinde. Do you want to see them?" I look in the direction of the stairs as I shout, "Taiwo! Kehinde!"

"Yes, Mummy!"

The officers exchange looks again. "It's alright, ma. Thank you for your time."

I watch as they let themselves out. My boys are already downstairs before the officers shut the front door behind themselves.

"Yes, Mummy?" Taiwo says.

"What is it, Mum?" Kehinde asks.

I exhale. "Nothing, baby."

The boys leave me again to go back to their room and play their video games. I shut my eyes against the pool of tears accumulating in my eyes. Despite the shield my eyelids present, the tears escape and run down my cheeks. Before long, I am heaving, sniffing, and shaking as I sob. And I don't even know why...

I met Nnamdi eight years ago during Fashion Week Lagos. I was one of the designers showcasing a new collection. He came up to me afterwards during the reception. He complimented my designs and my brand as a whole and said he was interested in becoming an investor. We exchanged cards.

I didn't really know who he was then. I called him to follow up on his interest, and he invited me to discuss over lunch. But at lunch, he seemed to have a different interest.

"Mr Ukwueze, let me stop you right there. I'm engaged."

I can't forget how his eyes lit up, and his smile grew wider, like he knew something I didn't.

"You're not married yet. There's hope."

"Let's just focus on our business, shall we?"

Thankfully, we were able to do that. I told him I needed a showroom and a few other things. He said he would see what he could do.

It didn't even take him a week to present me with my showroom in the heart of Victoria Island. I was amazed. But what was more amazing was how he filled the showroom with bouquets of flowers. It was clear to me that accepting that gift came with conditions. I had to turn him down. My wedding date had already been set.

By then, I knew he was married, and I'd also learnt he kept other women. Apparently, his wife was okay with that. But I wasn't. I didn't want to be his side piece.

"Look, don't worry about me. We can just keep this professional. You need the space, accept it as my investment. No strings attached."

"Are you sure?"

He gave me a small smile as he said, "I will always know that I tried. I respect you for your decision. So, yes, I'm sure."

I fell for the trick. I took the place, and I was giddy with excitement. He didn't make more advances at me. But as we spent time together decorating my new showroom and discussing my launch, I began to see him differently. I started wanting him to want me again.

On the day of my launch, he brought his wife, Ada, and I remember having this weird jealousy over the way he was with her. She didn't

CHAPTER TWELVE - THE USUAL SUSPECTS

look like a miserable wife, like I had imagined. He brought her over and introduced us, and she requested a few of my pieces to be customized for her. My fiancé, Patrick, also came, and I introduced him to Nnamdi and Ada. After that, Nnamdi left with Ada.

Nnamdi returned to the showroom the day after the launch, and he had never looked so good to me. As he shared his thoughts and asked me how I thought it went, I was just noticing things I hadn't noticed before, like how kissable his lips were, how thick, long, and smooth his fingers were, the scanty bush of hairs on his muscled chest, which could be seen through the opening on his shirt.

"You're okay?"

I blinked, realizing I hadn't responded to him but had been staring. "I'm sorry. I think I'm tired." My crush was full blown. I didn't know when it snuck up on me.

"Understandable… Want to take a break?"

I nodded, as my heart raced within me.

"I know a great place we can go for lunch. Interested?"

Again, all I could do was nod. I left my assistant, Funmi, to man the place as I followed Nnamdi to the elevator.

When we entered and the doors shut, Nnamdi turned his head to the side to look down at me just as I turned to look up at him with longing. I saw in his eyes that he knew what I wanted, and when he brought his lips to mine, I didn't try to pretend. He kissed me so gently, with a hand cupping my face, and I just leaned into him, pressing my hand on his chest, wanting to enter his arms, but knowing that when the doors opened, we would have to separate.

Instead of taking me to a restaurant, he took me to his Pearl Tower apartment, where he had his chef prepare us some lunch. In his bedroom, he gave me more than I bargained for… All I wanted was a taste of him. I had no plans to leave Patrick for a married man. But he turned me out!

My one taste became an all-consuming need. I wanted him every day. Sometimes, we even did it in my office, at the showroom. When Patrick walked in on us, one day, I was so far gone that I couldn't even stop. I literally couldn't, as Nnamdi had me pinned on my desk, and he didn't stop.

I will never forget the horrified look on Patrick's face before he ran out crying. I didn't follow him, or beg him, or even try to explain afterwards why I'd been so callous. My engagement scattered, but I was hooked on a married man.

Months passed, my business was thriving, and I was still getting my daily fix from Nnamdi. I knew I wasn't his one and only, but it was out of sight, out of mind, until it got too real.

I was pregnant with the twins when I caught him with my assistant. I had heard sounds coming from the storage room, and I went to check. He had her against the wall, humping like a dog in heat. I couldn't even get mad. I just shut the door and walked away. And he didn't come out until they were done.

I didn't know it could hurt that badly. I never expected that he would do that with someone who worked so closely with me and in my very own workplace. He stopped by my office afterwards and just watched me as I cried at my desk.

"Nike, I'm sorry…" he finally said after a while.

I looked up at him, my face wet with tears and mucus. "Don't ever come here again. Get out of my office!"

That changed everything. Nnamdi broke my heart, and I never let him touch me again. The sad thing was that he moved on so easily… He had gotten what he wanted, and it was on to the next.

If not for the fact that I was already pregnant, I would gladly never have laid eyes on Nnamdi again as long as I lived. I was a fool! I gave up so much for nothing.

I'm not surprised he was murdered. I'm surprised it took so long.

CHAPTER THIRTEEN - MATTERS ARISING

SEGUN

I arrive at the address Adaeze sent me. It is a two-story detached house with a comparatively large compound. The building is old and a little run down, but the garden is green with some spots of yellow, and there are three short trees gathered together to provide shade for the cars parked under them. I park beside Ada's Mercedes and walk the short distance to the entrance.

Ada is at the door just as I get to it. She smiles at me, and I can't help thinking what a pretty smile she has. I've always had a thing for ladies with gap teeth. But I shouldn't even be thinking about that.

She extends her hand to me. "Adaeze," she says. Clearly, she has a sense of humour.

I chuckle. "I thought I recognized you before. Nice to formally meet you. Olusegun Adetokunbo. But you can call me Segun."

"Thank you," she says, stepping aside so I can enter her home.

I bow slightly as I greet her parents, "Good morning, sir, good morning, madam."

When I see them rising, I say, "Please, do not stress yourselves standing."

Still, they stand until we shake hands, both with pleasant smiles on their faces, even though I'm sure they are going through the toughest time of their lives.

"Thank you," I say when they sit again, and I take a seat on the sofa across from their two-seater. Expectantly, I look at Ada when she returns to settle on the armchair, not sure if she wants to get me acquainted with the facts in front of her parents. "Are we meeting here?"

She nods and looks at her parents momentarily. "I have nothing to hide. I just want to know what I need to do and how I can prove my innocence."

"Okay," I nod. "Well, I'm going to need you to tell me everything you know about what you did that night, so that we can construct your alibi. I'd need trustworthy witnesses to corroborate your statement, and we can build our case on the fact that you could not possibly have been in two places at one time, regardless of if you had motive or opportunity."

"Oh, okay," she swallows. "You don't need me to tell you everything about my marriage."

"Oh, no, ma'am. There's no need for all of that, unless you want us to make a case for self-defence."

"No, I wasn't there. I didn't do it. I mean, I wanted to kill the man, but I didn't."

"So, only tell me what you think will help me prove your innocence. You can also provide information about your husband that will help me understand who else might have had motive and opportunity to kill him. What we want is to meet the criteria for reasonable doubt that you didn't kill Nnamdi and Rita."

ADAEZE

After about 30 minutes, Segun has gathered enough to construct a good alibi for me. Since we had a security guard at my house, my matron, and my two children at home with me at the time the crime was committed, they serve as my witnesses that I was nowhere near the scene of the crime. I also told him all I know about Nnamdi's lifestyle, which shows that a multitude of women, including husbands of women he slept with, are potential suspects in his murder.

Segun rises to take his leave.

"Please, won't you stay for lunch?" my mother asks.

"No, ma'am. Thank you so much, but I have a meeting to attend on the Mainland."

"Oh, okay. Thank you again," my mum beams at him. She seems to like him, going by how she is looking at him, as though she wishes she had children his age she could offer him.

I shake my head as I follow Segun to the door. We walk to his car, and I examine the damage I caused earlier.

"Feel free to add that to my bill, alright?" I say.

He smiles. "Sure."

"Thanks again for coming at such short notice."

"It was my pleasure, really. I will have my office send you our engagement letter right away, and I'll call to give you an update later today."

I nod. "Good, thanks."

He gets in his car and says, "Bye."

I smile and wave before walking back into my parents' house.

CYNTHIA

I thought the fact that I live in Abuja would rule me out of being a suspect in Nnamdi's murder, but apparently, my bitterness at being one of his used and discarded women is too much to discount.

I open the door to let the two officers into my house. It's a three-bed house in Maitama that my baby daddy got for me.

"Can I get you something to drink?"

"No, ma'am. We're here on official police business. We would like to ask you some questions about the murders of Mr Nnamdi Ukwueze and Miss Rita Osineye."

I indicate for them to take a seat, while I sit across from them, my hands between my legs, a nervous habit. "What do you want to know?"

"First of all, we want you to know that, though you are not under arrest, you are a suspect in the murders of Mr Ukwueze and Miss Osineye, and at any time during our interview, if we see sufficient reason, you may be arrested and taken to the police station for further questioning."

I swallow.

"So, you have the right to have a lawyer present at this time, or you can waive that right. But you should know that anything you say or do can be used against you in the court of law."

I nod.

"Are you waving the right to having legal representation?"

I shrug. "For now. I don't have anything to hide. I am just concerned about my children."

"If you have someone who can watch them, we can have the interview at the police station."

I think for a minute. "No, here is fine. I hope it won't take too long."

"No, ma'am," the police officer says. "Please state your name for the record."

"My name is Cynthia Adesola."

"Where were you the night Nnamdi Ukwueze and Rita Osineye were murdered?"

"I was here, in Abuja."

"In your home?"

"Yes. I had friends over. It was my birthday."

"Oh, okay." The officers look at each other, then the taller one asks. "How was your relationship with Nnamdi before he died?"

"He wasn't at my birthday party… He hadn't called or visited me or

CHAPTER THIRTEEN - MATTERS ARISING

his kids in months. I don't know if that answers your question."

"Do you know anyone who might want to hurt him?"

I chuckle at their question. "Really? Do you not know him by now? Nnamdi was a very selfish human being. Even a Priest would want to kill him after spending a day with him!"

The police officers exchange looks again. The tall one sighs and nudges the other to rise up. "Thank you for your time, ma'am"

"Are we done?" I rise up too.

They both nod, and I show them out. That was easy. I can't help but wonder who could have killed Nnamdi, though. Who had the balls to kill Nnamdi?

It has to be a husband he pissed off, I think. But then, why kill Rita? I guess she was collateral damage. *Oh, mehn. Nnamdi!* Someone that will be looking like a tall, handsome drink of water, but he's just poison.

I remember the day we first met like it was yesterday.

*****

I and a few friends were out clubbing in Victoria Island, Lagos to celebrate my 24th birthday. That was back in 2015.

I was in birthday-mode. I was happy, drinking, and ready to have a wild time. I saw him sitting at the bar watching me. He had a couple of friends with him. I turned my back to him, knowing he was still watching me, and continued dancing with my friends.

The DJ was playing all the songs I loved, and occasionally, my friends and I would jump up screaming when one of our favourite anthems came on. Guys had come to dance with us, and we would dance with them before returning to dance with ourselves. We didn't come to get tied down but to be free.

When Usher's "Yeah!" came on, it was on! I was getting ready to bust my moves as the intro played when the look on Gina's face and her finger pointing above my head alerted me that Nnamdi was behind me. I turned around, and he started dancing with me, a drink in his hand. He was fine!!! And the man had some moves!

I started winding up on him, and we were bumping and grinding on the dancefloor. Before the song was over, I already knew he was ready for me. I could feel him. And I was ready.

But he surprised me. He took me to the bar and bought me a drink. He said he wanted to get to know me first. I told him it was my birthday, and he said, "Happy Birthday, Beautiful."

Then he said, "I'm going to be honest with you. I got a girl. I really like her. But I'm so into you... Can I get your number?"

I should have walked away then. But I thought, 'Wow, he's so honest!' And he didn't say he was engaged. I'm not saying it would have made a difference, 'cos engaged isn't married, but anyway. I gave him my number.

We chatted and danced together the rest of the night, but we didn't go home together. I thought it was because he was a gentleman or because of his girlfriend, even though I wondered why she hadn't gone out with him.

I have since learnt that Nnamdi's actions are very calculated. He knows how to wait and when to strike. You don't know you have been seduced until it is too late to reason.

Do you know Nnamdi didn't sleep with me until after he got back from his honeymoon? I mean, we did a lot of the sexy stuff, but he never crossed that line. The night we eventually had sex, I was the one begging for it. I didn't care that he was married. He told me he had to get married for his inheritance, but that his wife was cool with them having an open marriage.

When he found out I was pregnant with our first child and that it was a boy, he got me a house in Abuja. That was as close to marrying me as he could get, he said. But he hardly came to stay. It was a lonely paradise, but he set me up *so nice*; I didn't want for anything.

CHAPTER THIRTEEN - MATTERS ARISING

Nnamdi was always busy, resolving one issue at work, or with his wife, or kids, or away on holiday. Even though I bore him three children, as the years went on, I saw him less and less. It was a hard pill to swallow when I eventually realised that I was just a number among a fleet of women at his disposal.

When he sent me a WhatsApp message to say that we couldn't be together anymore because he wanted to commit to Rita, I knew I had been cheated. I had been sold a lie.

He hadn't even regarded me enough to tell me to my face!

Instead of a manhunt, there should be an award for whoever can prove that they killed Nnamdi Ukwueze!

SEGUN

Ada told me that Nnamdi used to sleep with his secretaries, and it makes sense to me that, even if they didn't commit the murders themselves, they will have important information to point the investigation in the right direction. So, after my meeting on the Mainland, I head over to LionsGate Inc. in Victoria Island. The 12-storey building is as grand on the inside as it is imposing on the outside.

I take the elevations to the top floor for the CEO's office, arriving just after 4 pm. I walk over to a large C-shaped desk in front of the double-doors that I think leads to the CEO's office. The lady behind the desk looks at me as I approach.

"Excuse me, miss. My name is Olusegun Adetokunbo. I would like to see the person in charge of this floor, please."

"You're looking at her," the lady says, rising from her seat. "I am Amarachi Chukwudi. What is this about?"

"Thank you so much, madam. I am representing Mrs Adaeze Ukwueze, and I need your help, so that I can clear her name. I understand that it is a very busy time for you, so I plead your grace in assisting me with this."

Amarachi bites her lips as she looks at me, and I give her my most innocent smile. "Okay... What do you want from me?"

"I understand that you are privy to a lot of confidential information that could be pivotal in this investigation. For example, bank statements of the deceased, his journal, or appointment book. I am looking for unusual activity."

Amarachi sits down and says, "Okay, take a seat over there."

"Thank you. You are so gracious," I say, and she smiles.

"I am looking at his schedule. Honestly, that has been unusual for the past six months... You know, because of Rita." She looks at me and smiles. I can tell she likes to gossip. "No, no. Nothing here. Let me check his statements. But that will take a while. Do you want to come back?"

"Please, if it's no trouble, I would like to wait. If you don't mind, I can help you look through them..."

She narrows her eyes as she looks at me. "Can I see some ID?"

"Well, of course." I dip my hand in my pocket and pull out my driving license. I also pull out my business card, and she compares them.

"You are a SAN?"

I smile. "Yes, proudly so."

"Hmmm... Aren't you a little young?"

I chuckle. "I get that all the time. But if you can believe it, I'm not the youngest in the country."

"Okay. I'm only doing this because he is dead. And I like Ada."

"Oh, wonderful. Thank you."

I watch her for a few more minutes, then she rises from her desk to go to the printer. She collects the documents she just printed and hands them to me. "These are his personal financial statements with FCMB for the last 12 months. I'm looking through the corporate statements, *'cos, y'know,* it's corporate."

"Thank you, Amarachi. I appreciate this."

CHAPTER THIRTEEN - MATTERS ARISING

I look through the statements, not knowing what exactly I am looking for. There are lots of outflows and a few regular inflows of large amounts. I study the outflows, and I think I see something.

"Who is Nneka Aregbesola?" I ask.

"Nneka? She's Ada's sister. Why?"

"Well, it looks like, up until October 2025, she was receiving a significant monthly allowance from Nnamdi…"

Amarachi rises up to have a look. "Oh, wow. Is that something?"

"It is worth investigating. Let me keep looking."

"Okay," Amarachi says, as she returns to her desk.

CHAPTER FOURTEEN - SUSPECT #2

NNEKA

I knew they would come for me. I had actually expected them to come sooner. A part of me is still hoping that they will ask me about my sister's marriage to Nnamdi and not uncover the secrets I have kept for nearly twelve years.

I shut my eyes as I recall the day Nnamdi returned to my life eleven and a half years ago. I had known when he got back to Nigeria some years earlier, from studying in the States, because people used to say that they saw him at different events, but our paths never crossed, and I didn't have his contact. I hadn't heard from him since he left for America in July 1998, after his A' Levels. I had just completed SS1 then.

We started dating when I was in JSS3, but we didn't go all the way until his prom night when he took me to a hotel. He had been my first time and my first love, and our break up, after two years of dating, tore me apart. I couldn't even beg him to stay in a local university when he had been accepted into the most prestigious university in the world, Harvard. He said he didn't believe in long distance relationships but promised me that he would look for me when he returned to Nigeria.

I don't think I really expected him to, but the possibility of us reuniting was something I visited every now and then. However, when he returned to Nigeria and didn't reach out to me, I allowed

CHAPTER FOURTEEN - SUSPECT #2

myself to move on and began dating Dotun Aregbesola, who worked in my bank. He had been on my case for a couple of years.

On Valentine's Day, 2012, Dotun proposed to me, and I remember thinking of Nnamdi then. I had heard through the grapevine that he was engaged to some celebrity, one Big Brother contestant, so I believed our time had passed. Dotun was a good man, and though he wasn't the stallion Nnamdi was in bed, he was a generous lover. I said "Yes," and we got married in October that year. But by then, Nnamdi's engagement had scattered.

I have often wondered if I had just held on to hope, if he would have come for me and married me. However, it wasn't until February 2014 that our paths crossed again. Seeing him in the flesh was so different from seeing him on social media or on gossip blogs. He looked so good and exuded such sex appeal that would make even a nun rethink her commitment to celibacy!

I was rethinking my marriage vows.

Dotun had been headhunted and now worked in a more demanding role in another bank, so we didn't spend as much time together as we used to do. He worked late a lot. I always had a nagging thought that he was being unfaithful, but maybe it was just because that was what happened to my mother.

Anyway, seeing Nnamdi again at my friend's wedding, I was taken back to my High School days, and the desire I felt for Nnamdi was overwhelming. He seemed to know, and he hung out with me the whole wedding, making me feel even more special. We exchanged phone numbers, and that's how we started talking again.

By March, after just a couple of weeks of chatting, I was ready to end my marriage if only Nnamdi would ask me. I told him one night that I still loved him, and I'll never forget how amazing it felt when he said he felt the same way. But he said he couldn't marry me because of his inheritance, as I was already married. He called me and cried, saying how he wished I had waited for him. I couldn't believe that he actually still loved me.

I cried for a whole week!

We kept on chatting and meeting at different events. Then in May, I attended another friend's wedding, but this time, knowing he was going to be there, I didn't drive. I was sure he would offer and was delighted when he *told* me he would take me home.

That night, as he drove me home, he asked me about my marriage, and I told him it was okay, but I suspected that my husband was cheating because he didn't seem to have time for me anymore. I remember he parked the car right there and then and affirmed me.

"Nneka, you deserve a man who appreciates all that you are. You are such an amazing, beautiful woman. If you're not happy, leave him."

I just looked at his mouth moving, and I lost myself. I dove into his arms and started kissing him. After making out for a few minutes, Nnamdi asked if I would prefer to go to his place, and I was thrilled. And so, our love affair was rekindled.

The day I conceived, I knew, and I knew I had to get my husband to sleep with me as soon as possible. So, I picked a fight, accusing him of never being around. It worked like a charm. He apologised and decided to make it up to me with a date night. And I gave him a good seeing to. Till today, he thinks that was the day I conceived our first son. But Demilade is Nnamdi's, and he knew it. All my children are Nnamdi's. I'm quite sure my husband is infertile.

I knew Nnamdi was dating my sister, Adaeze, from their first date. He actually asked for my permission to date her before he sent the flowers to her office. I thought it was so considerate of him because he didn't really need my permission. He didn't owe me anything, and I knew he needed a wife. It might as well be my clueless sister. I knew I was the one he loved and wanted, and it was my fault that we couldn't get married.

CHAPTER FOURTEEN - SUSPECT #2

When she came to tell me of their engagement and 'ask' my permission then, I just pitied her. I couldn't tell her the truth about him because, well, I would have had to out myself, and I had too much at stake, with a husband and a baby on the way. Maybe I would have advised her differently if she had had the decency to come to me first. She knew I was crazy about him. She knew he was my first love, yet she dared to believe that he would truly love her.

I knew Nnamdi and I were still in love. He was with me every chance he got. He used to tell me how inexperienced Adaeze was and how he needed me. After his marriage had lasted five years, and he had not only gotten his inheritance but also his blasted heir, Chinedu, who Adaeze bore to him, I told him we could finally come clean and be together. We had nothing else to lose.

But Nnamdi wouldn't even discuss it. He said we shouldn't spoil what was working out well for everyone. I had since learnt that my husband had gotten his breakthrough with some strings pulling by Nnamdi, which made him mostly absent and allowed Nnamdi and me more time together. Nnamdi had even convinced Adaeze, with a little help from me, that they could have an open marriage, which made him so much more available to me. It was perfect, except it wasn't.

I wasn't his wife, I didn't get my own house, and my babies were not even regarded as his! He wasn't even there for the birth of any of our kids, and that hurt like hell! I got the short end of the stick.

And what was worse, neither I nor my four children stood to gain anything from his inheritance. I used to ask him all the time about writing a will, so that I knew I had some security, especially if Dotun suddenly figured out what was going on. But all he ever did was send me a monthly allowance.

Of course, I knew he slept with other women. I wasn't as naive as my sister. But nothing prepared me for the day that I caught him shagging his sister! His fucking sister! *How the hell?!*

I shiver in disgust at the memory. He didn't know I had seen them. I'd stopped by her place one evening to return a purse I had borrowed but kept forgetting to return and saw them through the kitchen window, humping on the kitchen island. I felt so sick to my stomach, I threw up. I found out a week later that I was pregnant with our last born. I still haven't returned the purse.

I didn't know how to bring up what I'd seen with him, so I kept it to my chest. It was bargaining power to serve me later, but I didn't know when.

However, a year later, he met 'Rita the Whore' in Las Vegas, and nothing was the same again. It was as if Nnamdi died because I didn't hear from him at all. He didn't even call to check on my kids, and he was the only one in the world who knew they belonged to him!

Nnamdi broke my heart, but why would I kill him? The truth is, Nnamdi was already dead to me before he died.

*****

"Mrs Aregbesola, is it?" the interrogating officer starts, bringing out a pen to write on a jotter.

I swallow and nod.

"Do you know why we have invited you here today?"

"I guess to ask me what I know about Nnamdi and Ada?"

He smiled. "Yes... But really about your relationship with the victims. Care to tell us about it?"

"Well, Nnamdi was my brother-in-law. We weren't exactly close."

"How do you mean? You didn't used to meet him at his Pearl Tower Apartment to have sex, 'cos, we have witnesses who say that they saw you there, several times a week..."

I swallow.

"You don't want to talk anymore? Or would you like to change your statement of not being that close?"

CHAPTER FOURTEEN - SUSPECT #2

"So, we fucked, so what? I didn't kill him."

"Okay, so I'm putting it on record that you 'fucked.' We are only gathering evidence here. No one has accused you of anything yet."

"I'm not saying anymore without a lawyer present."

"Wow, you have practically confessed," he laughs. "We know he was sending you an allowance every month until October 2025... Is that why you killed him? Because he stopped paying you for sex?"

"He wasn't paying me for sex! How dare you?!"

"So, what was the money for?"

I fold my arms and say nothing.

"Do you know we can arrest you right now, with this information? Because money and sex are the two biggest motives for murder, and Nneka, you reek of guilt!"

"Money and sex?" I chuckle. "Why don't you ask his sister all about money and sex! He used to fuck her!"

I smile when I see the alarm on the officer's face. Let him go find his scapegoat elsewhere.

"Can I go now?"

"Excuse me for a moment."

DOTUN

It's early evening when I finally decide to do what I should have done yesterday morning. The truth is, I've been afraid. I'm still so afraid about the damage that will be done to those I love when the truth comes out. But, as much as I hated his guts, I still have to do what I know is right, and the sooner the better.

I walk into the police station near my home at Ikate, determined to do what I came to do. At the reception desk, I ask for the Investigating Police Officer (IPO) in the Nnamdi Ukwueze murder.

"He isn't here. He's at Police Headquarters, VI. Do you want to leave a statement?"

"Ummm, no. Can I drop my number, so he can call me?"

"That's fine. What is your name, sir?"

"Dotun Aregbesola."

"And your number?" I call out the number for him. "Okay, sir. Someone will call you in an hour or two. Thank you."

I nod and walk back to my car. I feel a little lighter. I've taken the first step.

CHAPTER FIFTEEN - REVELATIONS

A **DAEZE**

I am at home with my children, but I feel restless. I keep looking at my phone wondering when Segun will call. He said he would call with an update this evening, but it's only 5 pm now. I am considering calling him when my phone starts ringing, startling me. It's the Barrister.

"Good evening, Segun," I say when I pick up.

"Good evening, Adaeze. How are you doing?" He has a lovely phone voice, I think.

"I'm fine, thank you. Any news for me?"

"Actually, news and questions… But let me ask first. Do you know why your husband would send Nneka 2.5 million naira a month?"

"WHAT?!"

"Yeah, I feared you didn't. I just discovered this, and I'm sorry that I had to share it with the police right away. I believe it is a significant piece of information that shows that Nneka had a motive to kill your husband, especially as he stopped sending the payments in October."

I swallow. "Where's Nneka now?"

"She's being questioned at Police Headquarters. I have sent one of my lawyers to represent her. But there's something else…"

"What?"

"The police did their own digging around, and they learnt that Nneka used to go to Nnamdi's Pearl Tower apartment, several times a week. But none of this is proof of murder… It's just important facts for consideration."

I am speechless. What am I hearing? "Are you saying… My sister? And my husband?" My vision is blurred as my eyes pool with tears. "Oh, my God!"

"I'm so sorry, Ada. I really am. And I hate that I am the one to share this information with you."

"It's not your fault, Segun. I have to go now." I don't wait for his response before I hang up.

Immediately I do, I scream! "Noooo!!! Why??? Nnamdi… Nnamdi… Why???"

My heart is breaking all over again. The thought never entered my mind that my husband could be sleeping with my sister also. To think I cried to him about sleeping with my friend, and he had been screwing my sister! *My sister!!!*

The tears rush from my eyes unbidden. How long was that going on for? Were they together when we first got together? Was it a new thing? Did he decide to go for her after he beat me emotionally to submission over Rita? Was there no one out of bounds for him?!

Though it looks like I no longer need a lawyer, it feels like I need a new heart because this one has been pummelled to death. I didn't think Nnamdi could take more from me even in death.

Why did Nneka do that to me? What did I do to her to make her hate me so? Just like Rita, she knew my pain over Nnamdi's infidelity. Why did she stab me in the back?!

"Mummy, are you okay?"

I realise my screaming had startled and scared my children, and now Osinachi is crying as she looks at me. "Why are you crying, Mummy? Please don't cry!"

I just take her in my arms and hug her. As she cries, I cry too, and

CHAPTER FIFTEEN - REVELATIONS

I know I might not get a better opportunity to let her know what is happening.

When I've sobered down, I release her to sit in front of me, and I use my right hand to wipe her tears from her face.

"Mummy?" Chinedu is on the stairs. "Why are you and Osinachi crying?"

"Come, baby. Come here," I say to him, and he does. I place him on my left thigh and sit more comfortably on the sofa. "Mummy just got some really bad news, so I was upset. But I want to tell you the good news first." I swallow. "You have me, and I love you, and we are going to get through this together. Do you believe that?"

Chinedu nods vigorously, and Osinachi nods too.

"Your daddy has gone away. Someone hurt him, and he got sick, and he can no longer be with us…"

Osinachi's eyes water. "Who hurt Daddy?!"

"We don't know yet, baby. The police are going to find out who took your daddy from us. But the thing is, he can't come and visit you anymore…"

Osinachi cries. "Did he die?"

I just nod my head slowly as I cry. "I'm sorry, baby. I'm so sorry."

Osinachi leans into me and sobs. "I'm going to miss Daddy. I'm going to miss him so much."

"We all will, baby. But remember the good news… We still have each other. I'm so glad that I still have you," I say, stroking Osinachi's face. "And you," I kiss Chinedu on his cheek. "We will get through this together. Okay?"

"Okay, Mum."

"Okay," Chinedu says, turning to give me a big hug.

SEGUN

After Ada hangs up abruptly, I know it's because she is in pain. I too feel pain over the news, even though I am supposed to keep my emotions separate to be professional and better able to help my clients. But Ada's situation is so painful to me.

When she told me about how she found out that her husband liked sleeping with other women and, at times, multiple partners at once, and even invited her to join in his orgies, my heart broke for her. I cannot think of anything more horrific than watching someone you love have sex with someone else.

God made sex not only for procreation but also to bond a man and his wife together. I see Nnamdi in the spirit as a beast who tore apart something sacred. Obviously, he was under a Satanic power, and it is a shame that he was never delivered of it before he died. May God have mercy on his soul.

I decide to call Barrister Gbenga to see if he has gotten a chance to speak with Nneka.

"Yes, I'm here. They are keeping her a little longer while they interview Nnamdi's sister, Adaora."

"What for?"

"Apparently, Nnamdi was sleeping with his sister as well… So, she's now a suspect."

"No way! What?! This is terrible!" I bow my head in my hand as the tears I fought to stay away return. How am I supposed to tell Ada this? Can she even take any news like this?

I'm afraid she will hurt herself, so I decide not to call her about it. She's too fragile. She has been through too much. And besides, if Adaora is innocent of the murder, it's something Ada can live without ever knowing. At least Nnamdi is already dead.

Chai! So, these things actually happen. I wonder how long it has been happening.

"Learned Silk, I'm going to give them another hour and then insist that they let Nneka go if they have nothing to charge her with."

CHAPTER FIFTEEN - REVELATIONS

"Yes, yes. That sounds good. Well done, and thank you."

"Thank you, sir. Have a good night."

After he hangs up, I just want to get on my knees to pray, but I'm still in the lobby at LionsGate Inc. I head to my car in the parking lot and drive home. I want to get home so I can pour out my heart to God because this is a lot! Ada needs prayers tonight. She needs someone to hold her and comfort her, but I know it can't be me. Not tonight.

God, please send someone to comfort her with Your love tonight.

I want to be the one to hold her, I realise, and the thought that it will never be makes my heart sick. I don't even know her.

As soon as I get into my house, I get down on my knees while leaning over the sofa, shut my eyes, and pray, "Father, Lord, thank You for causing Your daughter, Adaeze, to find me today. God, I thank You that she is not alone because You are always with her. Through all that she has suffered, You have been with her, even when she didn't know You as her God. I ask for Your healing, oh God, that You will mend her broken heart and restore to her faith and love.

"Breathe life into her bones, so that she will not be consumed with sorrow. Lord, I trust You because You alone are God and You love and care for us more than we can begin to comprehend. I cast my cares before You tonight and ask You to take control. Fill Adaeze with Your peace and direct her with Your Wisdom. In Jesus' name, I pray."

After that, I feel a burden to wait in prayer, and the Lord ministers to me. As He reveals to me His plan for His daughter, I agree with Him in faith and pray that it will be as He has ordained.

"Thank You, merciful God. I trust in You. Thank You for using me to reveal Your love to Your daughter, Adaeze.

"Lord, I also pray for Adaora. I don't know what happened that caused her and her brother to dishonour themselves and defile Ada's marriage, but I pray You will deliver her from this stronghold in the mighty name of Jesus! Let her be free and fill her with Your peace.

May she also come to know You as her Lord and personal Saviour and be used mightily in Your Kingdom to deliver others.

"Thank You for hearing my prayers tonight, Lord. Thank You for Your Holy Spirit that You have sent to be with us and lead us into all Truth. Amen."

ADAEZE

I tuck my children in bed and kiss them good night. It's 8 pm, and they have school tomorrow. I go downstairs and put on the kettle because I feel like a cup of tea to lift my spirits.

I hear movement from the doorway and turn, feeling a little wary. I'm pleased to see it's just Mrs Abike.

"God, you startled me!" I say.

"I'm sorry, ma. I didn't mean to."

She's looking at me weirdly, like she has a favour to ask. "Are you okay?"

"It is you, ma. I heard you with your children earlier. I'm so sad about what happened to you in your marriage, and now that your husband was murdered. Ma, I'm so sad!"

Oh, wow. "I'm sorry..."

"No, ma. I am sorry for you! I want to give you a hug. Please, say it's okay."

I'm so surprised. I smile and nod, and my weepy matron comes to hug me. It's a big, tight, long one. And I feel comforted. "Thank you, Mrs Abike. I didn't know I needed one."

She wipes her tears when she releases me. I feel like I need another one, so this time, I hug her. And she laughs weepily. She's a little shorter than I, but she's round like a bear, and I enjoy the squeeze. I exhale. "Thank you," I say again.

She nods and smiles at me. "No problem, ma. Thank you for being a good person. I know my God will bless you for how you have blessed me over the years."

Oh, wow. She's not done. I swallow as I listen.

"You have such a big heart. Huge! You are so thoughtful and kind. Please, don't let this thing make you angry… God has something good for you, I know it. You will see it soon."

I smile as I look at her speaking so passionately and let my tears fall. "Thank you for telling me and reminding me that I have goodness in me. I appreciate you, Mrs Abike."

She smiles and exhales. "Good night, ma."

"Good night to you too." I heave a sigh as she leaves me alone again. Except, I don't feel alone. There seems to be a Presence she has left. Today has been so mysterious.

The sound of my kettle boiling makes me jump. *God!* I bring out my mug and make my tea. I think about Mrs Abike's words again, and I feel healing in my body. *Hmmm...*

I take the stairs up to my room, after switching off all the lights downstairs, and settle on my bed with my mug. The sensation of a Presence remains.

Then my phone rings. It's the Barrister. I smile, even though a call from him would likely be about my sister, I just feel good whenever I hear his voice. I marvel at that realisation.

"Hello," I greet.

"Hello, Adaeze. How are you doing?"

"I'm fine, thank you."

"I hope you are not too upset about what you found out today…"

"I was… I cried. I even screamed. Then my children came to me, and I told them that they wouldn't see their father anymore…"

"Oh, really? How did that go?"

"Osinachi was really upset, but I don't think Chinedu really understood. But they're both fine now. They are sleeping."

"That's good. You're doing really well. I'm proud of you."

I chuckle. "What's with all the praises today?"

"How do you mean?"

"Well, just before you called, I went downstairs to make myself a cup of tea, and my matron came into the kitchen crying and asking me to hug her…"

"What? Wow!"

"And then, she starts telling me what a wonderful person I am and how I've been a good boss to her. She said something good is coming… It was so strange. But it felt good."

"Oh, my God! You are amazing!"

"Okay, stop it. It's not funny anymore."

Segun laughs. "I was talking to God! I was telling Him that He's amazing…"

"Oh, okay…"

"Because I prayed for you. At least, I think I did. I told Him you needed a hug, and since I couldn't be there, He should send someone. And He did!"

"Oh, okay. Now, you're spooking me!"

"Don't be spooked, Ada. You are loved. Much more than you know."

"Okay. Thank you."

There's a brief silence, and it's not uncomfortable, which is strange.

"Was there something you wanted to tell me?" I ask.

"No, I'll tell you tomorrow, okay?"

I feel a yawn coming on. I let it pass and stretch. "Okay. I'm so tired."

"I bet you are. Sleep tight, Ada. I'll see you tomorrow at 9 am."

"At my parents' place?" I ask sleepily.

"Yes. Good night."

"Good night, Segun."

I lay my head on the pillow and sleep without ending the call.

CHAPTER SIXTEEN - SUSPECT #3

DAORA

I was a little surprised when the police showed up at my door this evening and said I was wanted for questioning in connection to my brother's murder. I didn't think anybody knew about us. We had been very discreet about our liaisons, but I guess not enough.

As I sit and wait to be taken into the interrogation room, my life seems to flash before my eyes.

My life with Nnamdi had been like a game of Russian Roulette. I knew that one day it might kill me, but I could not leave him. I could not stop loving him. Even as the stakes got higher and higher.

It all began on a Summer Holiday we took to New York to stay with my mum's brother, Uncle Onyeka and his wife, Aunty Beatrice, when Nnamdi was eight years old, and I was ten. Uzo, who was four years old at the time, stayed back in Lagos with our parents.

My uncle and aunty lived in a small two-bedroom apartment, and they had no kids, so Nnamdi and I shared a room and a bed. I used to wonder about the muffled sounds coming from my uncle's room each night. At times, it was so bad that we were both kept awake. I eventually figured out what they were doing and started to get aroused by it.

One night, when we had both been awakened by the sounds, I

decided to put on the small television in our room to watch a cartoon. As I switched channels, we stumbled upon one where two people were making sounds similar to what my uncle and aunty had been making in their room. Nnamdi and I turned to look at each other and back at the screen, where two completely naked people were rubbing their bodies together. I quickly turned the volume completely down, and we watched the pornographic movie together in silence.

When it ended, another one came on. And we just kept on watching, even after the sounds from my uncle's room stopped. Eventually, the films stopped, and with wide eyes, Nnamdi and I looked at each other. We knew we were not supposed to have watched it, so I changed the channel to Cartoon Network and switched off the television. It was hard for us to go back to sleep that night, but somehow, we eventually did.

The next night, after lights out and the whole house was quiet, we turned to the porn channel again. When the usual sounds began in the other room, Nnamdi turned to me.

"Ada," he whispered. "It hurts…"

I was shocked to see what he was talking about. He showed me his erection with tears in his eyes. Immediately, I switched off the television.

"Sorry, Nnamdi," I muttered with my head on the pillow facing him. "Let's try and sleep," I said soothingly.

About thirty minutes later, Nnamdi tapped me. "It still hurts. How can I make it stop?"

"Maybe we can try to…you know?" I swallowed.

Nnamdi nodded. "Yes, please."

And that was how I lost my virginity to my brother.

After that first time, we developed an itch for sex every night. At first, we relied on the films for ideas, but soon, we began to experiment on our own. We continued our sexual relations, which had become

CHAPTER SIXTEEN - SUSPECT #3

very enjoyable for both of us, even when we returned home two weeks later.

I had my first pregnancy when I was 14. My mum found out when I started complaining of abdominal pain and a visit to the doctor confirmed that it was pregnancy. When they asked me what happened, I blamed it on our driver because I didn't know what they would do to me or Nnamdi if the truth was discovered. Mr Abdullai was a nice man, and I knew he had a wife and kid, but I didn't know who else to blame. He was fired and arrested, and my mother took me to a special clinic to have an abortion.

Still, we didn't stop our dangerous game.

The pregnancy was a shock to both of us, and I did some research on what I could do to stop it happening again. I was too young to go on contraceptives, but we were able to get condoms from attending Sexual Health Clinics and workshops. But with or without protection, we continued to take more risks with our sexual exploration, until the night my mother caught us in Nnamdi's bedroom.

She had grown suspicious when I started showing signs of pregnancy again, just six months after the first, and had installed cameras in parts of the house to identify my abuser, even wondering if it could have been my father. It was discovered that, not only was I pregnant, but I had also contracted an infection following the first abortion, which had resulted in a more serious disease, pelvic inflammatory disease. Not only did I need an abortion, but I also needed to have a hysterectomy. At the time, I didn't really understand the significance of this diagnosis. All I knew was that I couldn't get pregnant again.

When we were found out, I had just turned 15, and Nnamdi was still 12 years old, and so I was blamed. My parents sent me away to an all-girls boarding school for my last year in Secondary School, so Nnamdi and I couldn't get up to any more mischief. But the damage had been done. Nnamdi was left with a sexual addiction, while I was made infertile.

When I came home for the Christmas holiday, Nnamdi had replaced me with the house help. Miss Bisola, as we called our 23-year-old maid, was my first rival. I hated her, but I didn't want to get my brother into trouble, so I kept their secret. However, I used to make her jump through hoops for me, the only way I knew to punish her for screwing my brother.

Because of how closely we were watched, Nnamdi and I could not continue sleeping together. I had to find other means to satisfy my cravings and urges, but there was no therapy to resolve the emotional bond and sexual attraction I had developed for my brother. At 13, he was still much too immature to understand what I was going through or give me the emotional support I needed.

I turned 16 in July 1994, after I completed my Secondary Schooling. To keep us apart, my parents arranged for me to attend College in the US, and I returned to stay with my Uncle Onyeka and Aunty Beatrice. By then, they had had their first baby, and I came in time to lend my support.

One day, when my aunty went to the hospital with their baby, my uncle walked in on me masturbating to porn. He decided that he would relieve me of my urges thereafter. It was a sweet deal for the one year I stayed with them to do my Advanced Placement Courses because I never got pregnant. But my aunty eventually caught us and threw me out.

My parents were devastated when they learnt of it, but rather than bring me back home to be a temptation to Nnamdi, they supported me to remain in the US and attend Boston University. My uncle's marriage didn't survive his infidelity, and it also destroyed his relationship with my mum and our family.

Nnamdi was in his second year of Senior Secondary School when I started university. I used to call him from the US, and he told me

CHAPTER SIXTEEN - SUSPECT #3

about his adventures in Lagos, attending parties and meeting girls. In his final year, he began his first serious relationship with Nneka, a girl from his school who was in JSS3. He seemed to really like her and said she was 'an innocent girl.' Though I was pleased when he told me they weren't having sex, I knew it was only a matter of time before they would. Even with the passing of time, I still craved for my brother and was jealous whenever he spoke of the liaisons and relationships he had with other women.

After a year of A' Levels in Nigeria, Nnamdi got accepted into Harvard University, and we were reunited in Boston. For me, it was love, for Nnamdi, it was sex, but I didn't care. Even though I had to share him, I got to enjoy him again, and it was better than ever. By then, Nnamdi had learnt of my inability to conceive, and we both knew that I would never get married. He promised to do right by me and give me a portion of his inheritance.

We both returned to Nigeria after we were done with our studies to take executive positions in our family businesses. Nnamdi casually dated for years, getting into a couple of serious relationships, both of which eventually scattered because he just couldn't stay faithful. But when he turned 34, he intensified his search for a wife, even vowing that he would not sleep with another woman unless she was his wife. Of course, that didn't include me.

He told me of his interesting encounter with Adaeze, the sister of his High School girlfriend, Nneka, the day it happened. We were together that night, and he said he thought she would make a good wife. I told him to go for it. They seemed to hit it off, but I never believed it was love for two reasons. One, I was sure Nnamdi was incapable of that emotion. Two, the night before he proposed, he was in my bed.

I think he thought he loved her, though. He just couldn't be faithful. I remember how he told me off because she had complained that I didn't like her. He was so upset; he refused to have sex with me until I promised to apologise to her. It was such a trip.

Anyway, everything worked out in the end. He got his adoring wife, he got his inheritance, and he fulfilled his promise to me. But everything changed when Rita came into the picture. Nnamdi changed.

*****

"Adaora Ukwueze?" I look up at the officer. "Follow me."

I rise and follow him to a room lit only by rays of sun sipping in through a window with broken glass. A single bulb hangs from the ceiling, where a fan spins. There's a computer on the desk that looks like it belongs in the 1970s, and stacks of dusty files line the wall. *Nigeria, my country*, I think, holding back a hiss.

"Take a seat," he indicates for me to sit across from him in a white plastic chair that looks like it can't support my weight. I swallow as I perch slightly on it.

"First of all, I'm sorry about your loss," the officer says, surprising me. "Did you kill him?"

I'm mortified that he would even ask me that. It appears his first comment was insincere after all.

"No, I didn't."

"Do you know who did?"

"No, I don't."

"What was your relationship with your brother like?"

"He was my best friend," I say without a second thought. The truth of my words stirs up emotions and causes my eyes to moisten. *He was my everything.*

"Can you say more about that?"

"No. Our relationship was private and personal."

"Hmmm," the officer smiles and licks his lips. "I heard about the private and personal nature of your relationship… I bet it sucked when

CHAPTER SIXTEEN - SUSPECT #3

your sex buddy decided he didn't want to fuck you anymore."

I look at the officer alarmed, wondering what exactly he is getting at. Did they really believe I would kill my brother?

"Why would I kill my brother? I loved him!" I say.

"You know what they say, *'there's a thin line between love and hate,'*" the interrogating officer says with a smirk. "It happens all the time in relationships. I bet that's what happened here. I bet you were so jealous when he fell in love with Rita, it drove you mad." He leans forward as he adds, "That's motive for murder."

"He was my brother!" I cry. "I could never have killed him! I am devastated! How dare you?! *How dare you?!*"

As I break down in sobs, he rises from his desk and steps out of the room.

I miss my brother so much! I still can't believe he is gone. I know his actions seemed cruel to many, but he was just trying to find his way like the rest of us.

I remember the last time I saw Nnamdi alive, when he returned from the US after spending three whole months living with Rita. He came to see me, and I was so angry that he had left me alone for so long.

"Hey, sis," he said when he walked into my house.

He looked different. His eyes shone, but not in the usual way that said he wanted to have sex. He kept his distance from me as he went to sit on a sofa.

"What happened to you?" I asked him, choosing to remain standing.

He looked up at me, a bright smile on his face. "I'm cured, Ada. I found sexual healing."

His words weakened me and forced me to sit on the couch opposite him. "I don't understand."

"Rita, she fixed me," he said with a chuckle. "She's like my dick's happy place. I don't understand it either, but I don't get aroused by just anyone anymore. It's like, she's the only one it wants…"

"So, you're saying, for the last three months in the US, you have only been with Rita?"

He nodded excitedly. "Can you believe it? And I'm satisfied. I'm so happy, I finally know what it feels like to be sexually and emotionally fulfilled. I'm going to ask her to marry me."

"You're already married."

He swallowed. "I know. I know, but Rita's the one. I want to commit to her. I just came here to let you know and to say I'm sorry."

I swallowed. "What for?"

"For denying you the chance to find this kind of love and fulfilment. But it's not too late, Ada. I'm sure you will find someone who will satisfy you…someday."

I just looked at him, speechless. I didn't know what to feel. Yes, I was angry, hurt, jealous, but also, I was happy he had found peace from his constant craving. I told him and hugged him.

It was our first hug since we started having sex as children that was purely emotional. I hoped I would see him again, but somebody took him from me forever.

CHAPTER SEVENTEEN - AN ARREST

NNEKA
- Sometime Last Night -
"Excuse me a moment" seems to go on forever, as I stay in the stuffy interrogation room. Something doesn't feel right.

The door opens, and a suited man walks in. I look up at him with one wish: *Please be my lawyer...*

"Good evening, Nneka Aregbesola," he says, taking the seat in front of me. "My name is Gbenga Balogun. I'm from the office of Barrister Olusegun Adetokunbo (SAN). I'm here to represent you."

I stick my hand out to receive the one he has extended and let out a sigh of relief. "Did my parents hire you?"

"Actually, Barrister Segun Adetokunbo, who is representing your sister, sent me as a courtesy. To make sure you receive fair treatment and do not say anything to implicate yourself."

I nod. *Fair enough.* "Okay, what now? Can I go?"

"No, not now. They've requested that you wait while they interview another suspect. She just arrived at the police station and is being interviewed somewhere else."

"Do they have the right to keep me here?"

"Yes, they can arrest you, but they haven't done so yet. After they speak with the suspect, they can decide to arrest you both, if there is sufficient evidence, or release you both, or arrest one of you. It all depends on what their investigation produces."

"But I didn't do anything!" I say.

"Well, you are going to help me prove that. I just need you to be patient a little longer, and hopefully, they will let you go. But if we push them, they might just make an arrest on the information they have."

I swallow. "Okay. Thank you."

He rises from his seat. "I'm going to be right outside. If you need me, just call."

I nod, and he leaves the room. *What the hell?!*

*****

It feels like it's been another 30 minutes before the door opens again. My lawyer walks in followed by two police officers.

Barrister Gbenga stands by my side, and one of the officers takes the seat across from me while the other stands by the door.

"Well, have you thought more about your story?" the officer says.

"Nneka, you don't have to answer anything," Barr. Gbenga says, and I'm glad he is here.

The officer smiles. "Fair enough. But let me tell you what I know. Nnamdi was the father of your four children… He met Rita and decided he didn't want anything more to do with you or your children. You got angry, and you decided he didn't deserve to live."

I'm shocked that they have found out about the kids. *How?* If they know my kids belong to Nnamdi, it means my husband does or will very soon. But it's not only him that will be destroyed by this revelation.

I think of Ada finally knowing the truth about me and Nnamdi, my parents, my brother… I don't know how I will ever be able to face them if I ever get out of here.

"You're not going to confess?"

I say nothing. They can't prove anything.

CHAPTER SEVENTEEN - AN ARREST

"Stone cold," he says as he rises from his seat again. "I'm afraid I'm going to have to place you under arrest," the officer says, then looks at his colleague at the door, who walks towards me bearing handcuffs.

"Wait, what?!" I freak out. "Barrister Gbenga, please do something."

The officer behind me pulls me from my seat. "Nneka Aregbesola, you are under arrest for the first degree murders of Mr Nnamdi Ukwueze and Miss Rita Osineye," the officer continues, while his colleague puts my hands behind my back and slaps cuffs on them. *Ouch!*

I can't believe it. What are they basing this on?! "Look, you have the wrong person! I didn't do it! I loved Nnamdi!"

"Please be advised that anything you say can and will be used against you in the court of law!"

"Listen… What if I tell you of someone else who had a motive?" I ask when we are at the door.

"Nneka, I'd ask that you remain silent and let me defend you," Barr. Gbenga says.

"Please, I didn't do it," I cry as I am taken out of the room in handcuffs. "I need to call my family!"

ADAEZE

I head over to my parents' place again, immediately after dropping the children at school. Segun is supposed to meet with my family at 9 am, and Victor is expected to join us too.

Victor is already there when I arrive at 8:30 am. As soon as I enter the house, he draws me into his arms and holds me tight.

"I'm so sorry. I'm so sorry for everything," he cries. "I should have known. I should have checked him out first."

"You're my younger brother, Victor. What could you have done?"

He wipes his tears. "I could have paid more attention. I mean… The bastard was sleeping with both my sisters, and I didn't know… What kind of brother is that?"

"The kind that supports his sisters' rights to make their own decisions and mistakes. Please don't blame yourself. It wasn't your fault."

Still, Victor heaves. "Thank you, sis."

I leave him to go and greet my parents. I kiss them both on the cheeks and hug them one by one, before I find my seat. I choose the armchair because I need the space.

The doorbell goes off, and it can only be Segun. Victor opens the door to him, and he steps into the house. I watch as they make each other's acquaintance. He looks so good, dressed in a black native suit.

I adjust my gaze and wait for him to enter the living room properly. He greets my parents first before he finally looks at me and gives me a soft smile.

"Good morning, Adaeze. How are you today?" he asks.

I nod and return his smile, trying not to get lost in his eyes. They are so warm and inviting, calling out the vulnerability in me. I look away at last, and he takes a seat beside my brother on the three-seater sofa.

"So, I have news. I was informed of this last night, but I didn't want to alarm any of you. I thought it would be best for me to tell you all at the same time."

I swallow, looking at him, but he isn't looking at me. He keeps his eyes on my mum, who looks like she's about to have a heart attack.

"Nneka has been arrested."

"Nooo," my mum cries, and my dad holds her hand.

"Why?" he asks.

"New evidence was delivered last night that the defence is not yet privy to. But we should have that information by the close of work today."

"Are you saying she is now the primary suspect in my husband's murder?" I ask, and at last, he looks at me.

CHAPTER SEVENTEEN - AN ARREST

"Yes, Ada."

"Why? Why would she want to kill Nnamdi?" I ask, rising from my seat. This isn't making sense.

"There's something else. I'd suggest you take a seat."

"I can hear you from over here," I snap.

Segun inhales and exhales. He rises and comes to me. "Just take a seat."

"Tell me what you know!"

Everyone looks at Segun expectantly as he bows his head. When he lifts it, he says, "Nnamdi was the father of her children. All of them."

I hear my mum wailing, but it gets distant quickly. It feels like my heart stopped or the ground shifted, but something gives way, and I collapse.

SEGUN

Just as I feared, she doesn't take my news well and faints. Thankfully, I am close enough to catch her before she hits the ground. She feels heavier than she looks, but I manage to lift her in my arms and carry her to lie down on the three-seater, which Victor has vacated.

While her father comforts his wife, Victor rushes to get water to rouse Ada back to consciousness. I stay by her side until Victor returns with a small bowl of water and a face towel, which he dips into the bowl. I collect the damp towel from him and use it on Ada's face. Eventually, she opens her eyes, and everyone breathes easier. *Thank God!*

Ada looks up at me, and the pain in her eyes cuts me deeply. I swallow. "I told you to sit down." She looks away and tries to sit up. "Please, rest a while."

Ignoring me, Ada pulls herself up and sits, staring into nothingness and looking like she has lost another part of herself. Her mother is still crying like she just lost a child, and her father is stoic. Victor has returned to his position, sitting at the other end of the big sofa, and he is cradling his head in his hands.

I get off the floor, where I sat to attend to Ada, and rise to my feet. I know I cannot leave now, but I don't know what I'm supposed to do.

I sit to the left of Ada on the sofa, so I am between her and Victor, and wait. She doesn't look at me. Then the words come to me.

"Can I pray with you?"

She turns and looks at me, searching my face for what I don't know. I swallow. I can't help thinking how beautiful she looks, despite the pain I see and the lines of sorrow caused by neglect. I don't wait for her response any longer. I intertwine my right hand with her left, and it feels like home. Our hands fit so well together. *Focus.*

Shutting my eyes, I pray, "Father, Lord, thank You for bringing us all together again today. I ask for Your Holy Presence to fill this place. Bring Your peace as we trust in You to take control of this situation. Lord, we know that there is no weapon of the enemy fashioned against us that will prosper because You have set us apart for blessing. Even now, Lord, let Your blessing fill this place; heal our broken hearts, bring clarity to our minds, and renew our strength, we pray."

"Amen," Ada mutters to herself.

"Father, Your daughter is hurting so much. Please comfort her, the way only You can. I pray in the name of Jesus."

"Amen," we all say.

Ada turns to me. "Thank you."

I give her a small smile. "No problem."

"What do I owe you?"

"Absolutely nothing." I swallow. "I have appointed a lawyer to defend your sister. They will do their best for her. Please, do not worry. God is in control here."

Ada nods, still sullen. I squeeze her hand before I let go and rise to take my leave.

CHAPTER SEVENTEEN - AN ARREST

"Please, before you go… What's going to happen with our daughter, Nneka?" her father asks, rising to his feet too.

"They are going to keep her in remand until her arraignment. Hopefully, on Monday."

"Will we be able to bail her out then?"

"Unfortunately, murder is a felony and not a bailable offence. She will have to stay in jail until she is either acquitted in court or sentenced to…death. Unfortunately, the penalty for murder in Nigeria is death."

Her father sits with a thump, and her mother starts crying again. I look at Ada and Victor, then back at their parents.

"She might actually be taken to prison before conviction because the jail will not be secure enough to hold her while the trial is ongoing. This is a very serious charge against your daughter, and since I don't know the strength of evidence against her, I can't say more now. I will get back to you when we know more."

"Thank you, Barrister Segun. You have been a godsend to our family." Victor says. "Please do what you can for my sister."

I look at him and nod. "I will try my best. Mr and Mrs Okpara, thank you for inviting me into your home," I say. "Anytime you need me, please don't hesitate to call." I look at Ada now. *This isn't goodbye.* "I'll call you," I mutter.

She swallows as our eyes meet. They seem to lock each time we gaze upon each other, and now, I don't want to leave her. I exhale and look away.

Victor escorts me to the door, and I say, "Goodbye," as I walk out.

Adaeze is a widow, a broken woman. It will be hard for her to receive love, I know, but it doesn't stop me from wanting to love her, I realise as I get to my car. I remember what the Lord ministered to me yesterday, and I'm comforted.

ADAEZE

After Segun leaves, my mum comes to me and holds me in her arms as we cry. Our mourning today is different. In our house, we do not mourn Nnamdi, but the loss of myself to him, and the loss of my sister too.

I want to go home. Honestly, I don't care what happens to Nneka anymore. Whether or not she murdered my husband and his girlfriend, she can rot in prison for all I care.

"What's going to happen to the children?" my mum asks no one in particular.

"I'm calling Dotun," Victor says.

We all watch him as he greets Dotun when the line connects. The call ends after less than a minute. "The children are at home with Dotun. He knows that they are not his."

"Oh, my God," my mum laments. "Please forgive us!"

"All four of them?" I say, unbelieving. I know Segun said so, but it can't be true. *All of them???*

If they are not Dotun's, then it means that before I got engaged to Nnamdi, before I even met him at the bank, he had been having an affair with my sister!

And the bastard pretended like he had not even thought of her in years. I recall the conversation we had ten years ago as if it was yesterday. I was played for a fool! I feel murderous!

I recall Nneka's all too easy acceptance of my engagement, and how she even advised me to stay on as some sort of trophy wife, while my husband screwed everything that moved. I can't help but wonder now if she had set me up... Maybe they had been laughing at me the whole time. I feel pain, physical pain in my heart, and I reach to hold my chest.

God, I wish I could kill him again! God, why did You let me marry such a monster?! And Nneka... Oh, Nneka... Why are you so evil?!

I cannot forgive her. I will never forgive her for this!

CHAPTER SEVENTEEN - AN ARREST

I rise and hasten to my car, ignoring my parents and Victor as they ask me where I'm going, telling me to calm down first. No, calm was Nnamdi's forte. I'm MAD as hell!

CHAPTER EIGHTEEN - MYSTERIOUS WAYS

DAEZE

It is a miracle that I arrive at my sister's place in one piece because the way I drove through the streets of Lagos wasn't just murderous, it was suicidal!

I didn't know where I was going when I started driving. I thought of going home, but it would be too quiet. I thought of going to a bar, but that seemed too rowdy. I just kept on driving until I remembered that there was someone at my sister's place as betrayed as I, someone with whom I could find some solace.

I drive into the compound and park my car. I take some deep breaths before I get out and walk to the front door. The nanny opens up after I press the bell a couple of times.

"Good morning, ma," she greets, stepping aside for me to enter.

"Good morning, Funke. How are you?" I walk into the living room, but I don't see Dotun. Demilade, Dapo, and Seun are in the living room. The younger ones are on the rug, watching a cartoon, while Demilade is playing a game on his phone.

I guess they didn't go to school today.

"Fine, ma. How are Osinachi and Chinedu?"

Demilade looks up from his phone briefly and greets, "Good morning, Aunty."

CHAPTER EIGHTEEN - MYSTERIOUS WAYS

"They are fine, thanks. Hi, Demilade," I respond to him, but his focus is back on his phone. Dapo and Seun are so engrossed in their show, they haven't noticed me. "Where's Oga?"

"He's in his room, ma."

"Okay, I'll go up," I say as I take the stairs.

"Ma, please, let me go and inform him."

"It's okay…" I say, ignoring her and continuing up the stairs. I pass the nursery, where Sade is napping in her crib. Curiously, I step in.

She's sound asleep, and for the first time, I see the resemblance to her real father. I don't know how I didn't notice it before. I leave the nursery and walk a little further to the master bedroom. I knock and wait.

There's no response. I knock again.

"I told you I don't want to be disturbed!" Dotun shouts.

I open the door and look in. The room is dark, and he is lying in bed. He lifts his head when he sees me.

"Ada?" he says, visibly surprised. "What are you doing here?"

"I came to check on you," I say, feeling like it's a lie because I'm not really sure why I'm here. I walk towards him, and he sits up in bed. "I heard about Nneka and the kids."

Dotun bows his head and gives a little nod. I sit close to him and put my right arm around him. "I'm so sorry," I say.

With my left hand, I lift his head up so he can look at me. When our eyes meet, we both know what I want, why I came. I lean into him and kiss him, but he doesn't kiss me back.

He turns away. "What are you doing, Ada?"

I swallow. "Making us feel better?"

He shakes his head. "This fixes nothing. If you want to hurt Nnamdi, you are wasting your time because he is dead. And well, Nneka doesn't care about me, so you're not hurting her either. The only one you're punishing is yourself."

I move away from him, stung by his words. But he grabs my hand and draws me back to sit on the bed.

"I'm only telling you this because I learned the hard way…" He swallows. "When I found out about them, I wanted to die. I wanted to hurt them, to hurt Nneka. I went to a prostitute, thinking it would also make me feel good to have sex with someone else. It didn't. It didn't fix anything. It made it worse."

I look at him, amazed but confused. "How?"

"I got genital herpes from the one-time I had sex outside my marriage!"

"No! Oh, Dotun, I'm so sorry."

He sits back and rests his head on the headboard. "We can't punish them by doing what they do. I realise that now. We punish them by thriving and making the right decisions and living the good life they denied us."

"It took you getting herpes to realise this?"

Dotun gives a small chuckle. "God works in mysterious ways…"

"Wait, you believe in God now? After all that has happened to you?"

"Ada, get up… Let's go elsewhere and talk. It's not good that you're in my room."

I nod and rise from the bed. "Okay. I'll wait for you downstairs."

*****

When I get downstairs, I sneak up on Dapo and Seun and tickle them, causing them to scream and laugh hysterically.

"Aunty Ada!" they cry, finally acknowledging my presence.

"How are you guys?! I've missed you."

Dapo, who's seven years old, hugs me. "I've missed you too, Aunty. Why didn't you bring Osinachi and Chinedu?"

"They are at school. I came to see your father. But I'll bring them around tomorrow, so you guys can play, okay?"

CHAPTER EIGHTEEN - MYSTERIOUS WAYS

"Yeah!!!" Dapo jumps up excitedly, and Seun joins him.

"Why didn't you go to school, though?"

"Daddy is not feeling fine. He overslept and said we could stay home today," Dapo answers.

I turn to Demilade, who's head hasn't lifted from his phone since. "Hi, D'Lads," I call him by my nickname for him.

"Hi, Aunty. I'm sorry… Can't talk…trying to beat my best score."

"Roblox?"

"Yeah. You want me to teach you?"

"No, I'm good." I turn back to the TV screen.

After a while, Dotun's footsteps can be heard on the stairs. He's wearing shorts and a Polo. He steps into the kitchen first, then comes to meet me where I'm sitting.

"Wanna drive, or should I?"

"You drive," I say, even though I don't feel quite as murderous as I did earlier today.

*****

Dotun drives us to a local eatery in his car. We find a secluded place upstairs to have our private conversation.

"Want to order something?" he asks me. I shake my head. Food is the last thing on my mind. "Me neither."

"So, you said God works in mysterious ways…" I say as a recap.

Dotun gives another half chuckle. "Well, He does." He swallows and I watch him. "Do you know I have always wanted kids?"

I don't know what he expects me to say, so I shake my head. I don't really know him like that.

"Well, I found out recently that I couldn't possibly be the father of my kids. Well, it would have been a miracle in itself, 'cos I have low sperm count *and* my swimmers are slow…" he swallows.

"Okay…"

"Well, I now have four kids, when I wouldn't have had one otherwise..."

"Well, you would have if you guys realised on your own. You could have adopted, got a surrogate, or treatment."

"I know. I know all that. But that's me seeing the silver lining." He swallows. "When I first found out, I was mad, Ada. I was furious. My first thought was to locate Nnamdi and kill him."

Our eyes meet at this. I understand that feeling too well.

"I thought about it a lot... I also thought I'd kill Nneka too. Then what would happen to the children? Because I would no doubt end up in prison."

"Was that what stopped you?"

"No, I still wanted to, damn the consequences. One day, Nneka had gone out...to be with Nnamdi or whatever she does with her time, and I planned to follow her. But when I was heading out, Demilade cried for me. He was like, 'Daddy! Daddy!' I was like, 'Not now. Call your nanny!' Then he said, 'Please, Daddy, I want you! Please don't go...' Ada, it was like God Himself was holding me back."

"Hmmm..."

"I had already secretly installed a tracking device on Nneka's car, so I knew I could locate her even if I didn't follow her immediately. I shut the door and went to attend to Demilade. Can you believe it was just a stomachache? But when he said he felt better, Dapo developed a headache. One by one, they all had complaints. Even Sade did her own. That's how I decided I'd do it another night and settled down to watch TV with my kids.

"Do you know the TV was set to God TV? The moment it came on, a preacher started talking about 'When God gives you a second chance, take it!'"

"Wow..."

"I know! I didn't even know how to switch it off. I just watched the

CHAPTER EIGHTEEN - MYSTERIOUS WAYS

whole programme with the kids. Everything he said, it was as if it was me he was speaking to. That was where I got the lesson I shared with you about the way to pay back those who hurt us… It isn't by trying to hurt them back but about continuing to stand and choosing to be good even when it seems easier to be bad like them."

"Oh, my God. You know, I had a similar experience yesterday morning…"

"Really?"

"Yeah. I was driving to my parents' place, and I hit someone else when I was about to turn into Keffi Street. It turns out the person I hit is a Barrister, and he was going on the radio to talk about Nnamdi's murder…"

Dotun guffaws. "Whoa!"

"Yeah… I haven't even got to the mysterious part. So, he gives me his card, and I see his name and what he does. I get back in my car, I start the car, and the radio comes on, tuned in to the exact channel that he would be speaking on. They were like, 'Stay tuned… Don't touch that dial!' I was like, what? That's not even a channel I'm normally tuned into, and the radio wasn't even on before I hit his car."

Dotun bobs his head and smiles. "You see, God works in mysterious ways."

"I know… I just wanted to know why you said so," I say. "I actually prayed after my police interview, probably the second time in my life, for God to help me find a good lawyer to represent me. And this happened. I'm just marvelling like… Where was He before?!"

"You mean God?"

"Yes!" Tears arise unbidden, and I wipe them. "How did I end up with someone like Nnamdi?! I mean, before him, I hadn't even kissed anyone in my life. He was my first. If we count the stranger I kissed in the club to get back at him, that's three people I have kissed in my life. All I wanted was love, and I got screwed."

Dotun reaches out to hold my hand on the table. "I'm sorry, Ada. I'm sorry he did that to you. I'm sorry about Nneka too."

"It wasn't your fault…"

He shrugs. "I'm still sorry. But I know God will make it up to us in the end, if we do not decide to repay evil with evil."

"I wish I could believe that. I'm still so angry, honestly. Nnamdi… Nnamdi!"

"Don't waste your breath, dear. He can't hear you."

At that, I laugh! And Dotun laughs. Then we sigh.

"Want to order something?" Dotun asks again.

Suddenly, I don't feel so full. I guess the anger was taking up room in my stomach. I nod.

"Me too."

We decide to go down and get in line to order some food.

*****

"So, how did you find out about Nnamdi and Nneka?" I ask when we are back in our secluded spot eating our rice and chicken meals.

"Nneka became careless. When she got pregnant with Sade, I knew something was wrong because we hadn't even had sex in months. So, I did paternity tests on the others and found out that none of them were mine." He swallows. "I then decided to check myself because that was concerning in itself. So, that's how I discovered her infidelity."

"That must have been hard… Why didn't you confront her?"

"After ten years?! She had to be very cold and heartless to have done that to me for ten years… If I had confronted her, who knows if I wouldn't have been the one being investigated for murder." He shrugs. "I realised that her secret made her feel like she had power over me. I didn't want to take away the false security just yet. I wanted to know what I wanted first and what my options were, so I bid my time. Yes, I considered just walking out, but I had invested nearly ten years raising

CHAPTER EIGHTEEN - MYSTERIOUS WAYS

Demilade... Seven raising Dapo, Five raising Seun. You get? If I had adopted them, their biological father or mother wouldn't matter."

I nod. "And Nnamdi? How did you know he was the one?"

"I started paying attention," he swallowed. "I have been doing my own investigations for a while, thinking I would use it to fight her in court for the kids. Well, now, she has screwed up."

"How do you mean?"

"Because she killed Nnamdi, and I can prove it."

I just look at Dotun, shocked to my bones! Why didn't he say that sooner? My heart's racing in my chest as he tells me what he knows about the night Nnamdi and Rita were murdered.

"Oh, my God, Dotun. Have you told the police?"

"Yes, I have."

CHAPTER NINETEEN - A WOMAN SCORNED

NNEKA

As I lay on the bench in my cell, my mind replays memories of better times with Nnamdi. I shut my eyes as I recall the unforgettable night we conceived Demilade in March 2015. It was the one and only time Nnamdi came to my house and stayed through the night. But we did not sleep until dawn.

Dotun had gone on a business trip to Enugu for a couple of days, and I had the house all to myself. Nnamdi came over with Chinese food he had ordered from Oriental Hotel and a pack of my favourite chocolates for dessert, which he fed to me in bed later that night. He was really a man with a plan because I wasn't prepared for the ordeal he would put my body through that night.

In my pre-maternal body, I looked mad sexy when I opened the door to him in a cream, cotton mini-dress that hugged my body in all the right places, showing off my full bosom and wide hips. Apart from the thin dress, I wore only black stilettos and a smile. He was so turned on that we didn't even get around to opening the packs of food before he grabbed me by my waist, placed me on the kitchen counter, and ravished me.

I always thought men were exaggerating when they boasted about making love to a woman all night long, but Nnamdi literally did that,

CHAPTER NINETEEN - A WOMAN SCORNED

moving us from the kitchen to the living room, where we christened all the sofas, before taking me to my bedroom. It was like he wanted to brand the place with his essence.

It was after the second time in the living room that we finally took a break to eat the food he brought. I ate just for energy, and even then, I could only eat a little, as I looked at him lustfully across the glass coffee table, where he sat shirtless on my sofa. When he met my gaze, he just winked at me, a teasing smile on his face as he ate.

I wasn't bothered that he didn't say a lot. He was a man of action more than words. And he was a great listener. I never had to tell him what I wanted twice, and he was *sooo* eager to please. When we finally made it upstairs, he spent the next few hours doing just that, giving me orgasm after orgasm after orgasm. I cried for him to let me rest, but with just one touch from him, I was ready to go again.

I knew I was pregnant in the morning when I woke up in his arms, having slept barely a couple hours the whole night. Sometimes, I wonder if that was truly his intention, to plant a seed in me. We never had another night like that again, even when I visited him and stayed over at his apartment.

"I'm pregnant," I muttered when I felt him stir in the morning. I turned in his arms and looked into his face, and he beamed at me, making me feel absolutely wonderful. I was well and truly fucked in every sense of the word.

"Now you have something that is mine," he said.

I placed my head on his chest and wondered what that really meant. Was that his way of saying 'I love you,' an expression he rarely uttered? Or was it because I was married, he needed something to stake a claim on me? I didn't mind, though, because I wanted to be his baby mama, even if it had to be a secret.

I heave a sigh as I open my eyes. Demilade should have been his heir. I have always resented that he wasn't considered Nnamdi's first child.

Because of his proposal and marriage to my sister months later, he didn't actually get to see his child until six months after he was born, when he visited us at home. And it was the same way with my other children. Though I would sneak off to see him, he never visited us until they were several months old, when Dotun was out of town.

I know I went along with it, but I never expected him to stay with my sister as long as he did. I kept dreaming that we would one day divorce our spouses and get married. But it wasn't till he met Rita that I realised that I had been living a fantasy, and he never intended for us to be a family.

Tears slip from my eyes, and I wipe them with the back of my hand. Why did Nnamdi keep me hooked on him when he didn't really want me forever? I still can't believe how he discarded me like an old rag when Rita came along. I mean, I had just birthed our fourth child!

He left for Las Vegas without even seeing Sade and then stayed away a whole three months in the States. Even when he got back, I did not hear one word from him. It was through my sister that I knew he was around because he visited her to check on his kids. But I didn't even get a text.

I had to go looking for him. I cornered him in his office one day in October because I didn't care about hiding our relationship anymore.

He looked up at me that morning when I barged into his office. He was meeting with someone, but I couldn't have cared less. I approached his desk angrily.

"What did I ever do to you, Nnamdi?" I yelled.

He had to tell the man sitting across from him to excuse us, and I just folded my arms, waiting for his response.

"Nneka, you know you're not supposed–"

"Forget that! You left me no choice!"

"I'm sorry. I've been meaning to come, it's just been super demanding since I got back."

CHAPTER NINETEEN - A WOMAN SCORNED

"Since you got back from where?"

"I've been in the States."

"Doing what exactly?"

"I met someone. It's serious."

I extended my hands back and forth as I said, "WE were serious?! I'm the *mother* of your children!"

"Please, Nneka, go, and I promise I'll visit and explain to you later."

"You're gonna explain to me now. Because I have waited eight months for you to see your daughter." I swallowed, and he looked down. "Didn't you even miss me at all?"

He took a deep breath then said, "I'm in love with Rita. I'm sorry that I didn't tell you sooner, but what we had is over. I'm going to marry her."

"Who the hell is Rita, and why do you want to marry her?! Aren't you still going to be coming to me when you get bored of her?"

"Rita is my girlfriend. We met in Vegas. I don't know what else to say to you."

For a moment, we just stared each other down, me, not quite able to believe that he actually had nothing more to say for all the years of my life he had wasted. Then I remembered my wild card, my bargaining chip.

"Does she know you fuck your sister?" I asked with a sardonic smile.

For a split second, his eyes flared before he regained control. *Oh, I hate how he is so bloody calm all the time,* I thought!

"She already knows. I told her everything, and she loves me anyway."

And just like that, the power I thought I had dispersed into nothingness like a whiff of smoke. I walked towards him, desperate now.

"Why are you doing this to me? Nnamdi, I love you! You said you loved me. Please don't leave me like this…" I got down on my knees before him, crouching in front of his seat, behind his desk. "Tell me what you want me to do, and I'll do it."

He swallowed. "Please, get up, Nneka. Get up!"

I began to unbutton his shirt. "Let's fuck, please. Just one more time."

The next thing I knew, my butt was on the floor, and Nnamdi was standing over me. "NO!" he barked. "Get out of my office, Nneka!"

That was when I started crying. I never knew I could stoop so low to beg a man to have sex with me. Looking in his eyes, I saw only anger. He didn't care about me at all.

"Nnamdi," I cried as I moved away and stood to my feet. "Why are you doing this?"

He returned to take his seat and straightened his clothes. He took some deep breaths before he said, "Rita and I are committed to each other. She is everything I've ever wanted. I'm finally satisfied sexually with one person. Please forget about us. I'm sorry I hurt you."

Sorry, my ass! He didn't know what sorry was! I was livid!

"You're going to be sorry, alright! I'm going to tell Adaeze everything. She's going to divorce your ass and take *everything* you own."

"No, she won't. She's not like you," he threw back, and I flinched.

I left his office disgraced, sure that those waiting outside had heard our small commotion. Somehow, he had to pay for dissing me and my children. I needed to punish him, but I didn't know how. As I drove home that day, it was like my mind was in 'Disturbia' like Rihanna sang. I was losing it, and my every thought was on how I would make Nnamdi suffer for what he did to me.

However, Nnamdi played his hand first and got my husband fired in early November! I knew then that he really meant to end things with me. With no income coming from Dotun's work and no more allowances coming from Nnamdi, I was *crazy* MAD! How could he have so much control over my life?!

Weeks later, I heard the news about his engagement to Rita and how he was even building them a home at Eko Atlantic, where I had been begging him for years to get me my own apartment, and he couldn't

CHAPTER NINETEEN - A WOMAN SCORNED

even do that!

I turn to my side on the bench as I lie in the foetal position and weep for the love I lost, the time I lost, and the life I lost. Nnamdi took everything from me, even my beautiful figure, birthing his four kids. He took my essence, and he wanted to move on and give what was mine to someone else.

He really left me no choice.

*****

I hardly slept a wink last night. In the morning, an officer comes to release me from my cell and take me for more questioning.

However, the officer leaves me alone, and Barrister Gbenga, who visited me yesterday, walks into the interrogation room.

"Good morning, Nneka," he says as he takes a seat across from me.

But it's not a good morning. I just nod to acknowledge his greeting.

He gives me a small smile. "I know you're afraid. But if I'm going to defend you, I need you to be honest with me. You can tell me the truth; it's just us."

I look him in his eyes and say, "I didn't do it."

"I can't help you if you lie to me…"

"Look, I'm innocent, okay? They can't prove any of their accusations. Just do your job!"

Barr. Gbenga heaves a sigh. "Nneka, you're not being truthful. There's substantial evidence that has come to light."

"What evidence?"

He looks at me with pity and swallows. "Look, I know *why* you did it, the police know *how* you did it, and the prosecution can prove it in court. If you confess, we can appeal for a lesser sentence with a plea of systematic abuse and temporary insanity. But only if you confess," Barr. Gbenga says.

A tear escapes my right eye. I'm determined to go down fighting.

"Have you interviewed my husband? Maybe he found out about us... He probably got jealous and decided to kill Nnamdi."

Barr. Gbenga holds my gaze. "Hmmm... Actually, we have spoken to him. Dotun is a key witness for the prosecution. He is going to testify against you, Nneka. Like I said, they have evidence, and it's not looking good for you. I'd suggest you take a plea of insanity."

More tears fall from my eyes. *Is this really happening?* "And if I don't?"

"I don't think you will win. I'll be lying if I told you otherwise. You'll be looking at a death penalty verdict, which is the lawful punishment for murder in Nigeria."

I gulp, sniff, and blink as tears run down my cheeks. "What evidence do they have?"

"That night, when you returned home and thought your husband was asleep, Dotun saw you and what you did with your clothes. The police were able to find the gun you stashed with his help. There's also DNA evidence that puts you at the crime scene. That, and a tracking device on your vehicle."

My shoulders fall as I look at my lawyer and begin to sob. "He ruined me. Nnamdi ruined my life."

"We know."

"Do what you can for me, please."

"I will."

CHAPTER TWENTY - ONE NIGHT IN DECEMBER

NNEKA

Nnamdi hadn't been staying at his Pearl Tower apartment since he returned from the States. I figured it was because he had been gone too long and had rented it out, or it was his way of making sure I didn't sneak up on him. Either way, Nnamdi was too predictable.

Whenever he stayed at a hotel, he always booked the same room. He liked a corner room with a skyline view and always with a large balcony. For my plan to succeed, I had to make reservations a week in advance at three of his favourite hotels for the same night. I was lucky, really, because I hadn't expected him to travel to Paris, and I was nervous that he would return too late.

However, he got back just in time for me to execute my plan. I knew the hotel he would be staying at that night, and I arrived early to check into my room beside his. There, I waited for them.

I heard them when they entered their hotel room and smiled when I heard Nnamdi open the door to his balcony for fresh air. I knew him too well. That was key to my plan. Nnamdi loved to have sex on the balcony, where he could be seen.

I waited patiently for them to get vulnerable. It took a while. I heard water running in their bathroom and their muffled voices as they talked about God knows what. Then, the smooching began.

I got into position and slipped on my gloves. It was a hard feat because of the floor-to-ceiling dividers in the balcony that were decorated with climbing plants and other potted plants, so one could not easily snoop on their neighbour. I had to go over the balustrade and monkey bar to his balcony. But I had developed my upper body strength from gyming over the years and managed it.

By the time I got to his balcony, he was already inside of her, and she was moaning as he grunted. They did not hear me when I pulled myself from the balustrade into their balcony.

All the rooms on the floor were the same, so I knew there was a cushion on the sofa by the balcony facing the bed. Their sex sounds were even louder now, and the stupid whore was thrashing around like a fish out of water, her eyes closed.

I brought out the gun I had carried along, which I had kept in my back pocket, picked up the cushion, and made the first shot through it, right into the bastard's back. He fell on top of her wordlessly with a thud. I instantly silenced the bitch with another shot, straight through her breast, and she fell back on the pillow. Not wanting to draw more suspicion and not wanting a situation where they could be resuscitated, I brought out my army knife set and used a blade to slit their throats.

Pocketing it and my gun, I went back the way I came, ensuring the balcony door was shut behind me.

I had called in before arriving to cancel my reservation, so I knew the room beside theirs was available when I checked into the hotel. I paid cash for the room and wore a disguise on entry. I left the room soon after, wearing a different wig and outfit.

I was pleased to see Nnamdi hadn't employed security guards to man his room. He underestimated me.

I left the hotel and made it to my car. It was only after I had driven off that I heard the police sirens. I guess room service must have found

CHAPTER TWENTY - ONE NIGHT IN DECEMBER

them.

DOTUN

I kept a vigil for Nneka. Because of the tracker on her car, I knew when she was on our street, which hotel she had been at, and exactly how long she had stayed. This was proof that she was cheating, and I was ready to confront her about it.

I peeped through the window from our bedroom and saw that instead of coming into the house, she was changing her clothes outside, in the dark, hiding behind our big oak tree. That seemed a bit too suss for me. She even took off a short, black wig cut into a bob and stashed it in a bag. Something was fishy.

Then, she brought out a gun. That threw me off completely. What was my wife doing with a gun?!

She dug a hole by the tree and buried it, then carried the bag of clothes and wig as she walked towards the house.

Deciding that it probably wasn't the right time to confront her about her infidelity, I quickly got out of my clothes and went under the covers. I switched off the light and turned my head away from the door.

She took a while coming up, and I figured she was washing the clothes or something. About 30 minutes later - the bedside clock read 11:05 PM - she opened the door to our bedroom. Immediately, I began breathing deeply. I don't snore, so I didn't try to fake it, but I hoped my deep breathing would assure her that I was sound asleep.

She went into the bathroom and washed off, coming out about 15 minutes later. She went to her side of the bed and looked at me. I could feel her stare.

"Honey, you're awake?" she asked.

I knew it was a test, so I just kept deep breathing. After what felt like a minute, she lay beside me and put her head on the pillow.

I didn't move for a whole hour because I didn't want to risk that she was watching me to see if I was faking. But eventually, I heard her snoring lightly.

I knew she had done something awful, but I was shocked to my bones when I learnt that there had been a double homicide at the hotel she had spent two hours in that night.

My wife was dangerous, and I was afraid for my life.

UZO

Nnamdi and I were supposed to meet at 9 for celebratory drinks at his hotel that night. Just like the rest of the world, I heard of his engagement in the news, and I was shocked. When I chatted with him on WhatsApp, he said he was still in France and promised we would catch up when he returned to Lagos.

So, I was already at the hotel bar at 8:45 that night. I sent him a message and ordered a drink. The message was delivered, but he didn't text me back. I figured he was probably getting ready or doing the nasty with Rita. At 9, I sent him another message, but it was the same thing, no response.

At five past nine, I decided to call, but his phone just kept ringing. I gave it another 10 minutes before I visited the help desk to ask them to call his room. They said there was no answer, but that was odd. Nnamdi had messaged me at 8:15 pm to say he was in his hotel room with Rita and would see me at 9 pm as planned.

"Can we check it out?" I asked the receptionist. She said she would ask the manager.

He initially refused to "encroach" on the privacy of his guests but, after calling a second time, decided we could go up and knock. I followed him to their room, and we knocked on the door and waited for someone to open up. Nothing happened.

I dialled Nnamdi's phone, and we could hear it ringing from the

CHAPTER TWENTY - ONE NIGHT IN DECEMBER

hallway.

"Open the door!" I shouted.

The manager used his master key and unlocked the door. The scene I saw crumbled my knees.

Blood streamed down my brother's back where a bullet had entered his chest. His neck hung off weirdly to the side, revealing that his throat had been cut, and blood gushed out. Beneath him, Rita's chest, face, and neck were covered almost completely with blood, and her eyes remained open.

I screamed and shouted, "Call the police!" But the manager had already left to do just that.

I knew I wasn't supposed to touch anything if I wanted my brother's killer caught, so I leaned on the desk opposite the bed, my hand covering my mouth as I looked at my brother's naked body on top of his girlfriend and cried. As long as I live, I will never forget that horrific visual.

I didn't have to check if they were dead; they had bled out on the bed and were perfectly still. A cream-coloured pillow with a couple of bullet holes lay on the ground in front of the bed.

Who did this?! Who would do this?!

I don't know exactly when the police came, but they immediately ushered me out of the room, asking if I had touched anything. I shook my head as I was led outside. I sank to the floor outside my brother's hotel room and wept.

Why? Why would someone do this to my brother?!

ADAORA

I was in bed when I got the call from Uzo at 10:30 that night. Nnamdi was dead!

"Where? Where is he?" I cried.

"The Chandelier Hotel."

"I'm on my way." I hung up before he could say anything else.

My whole body shook as I dressed. *This has to be a joke! This has to be a mistake! Nnamdi, dead?! No...*

I slipped into my slippers, rushed down the stairs, grabbed my house keys and purse with my car keys from where I hung them by the door, and ran out of the house. After locking up, I hurried to my car and got behind the wheel. Instantly, I was on the road, going as fast as possible to get to Lekki Phase One.

When I arrived, I called Uzo, and he told me the floor and room number. I went straight to the elevator and pressed it impatiently. On getting to the floor, I followed the signs and ran to his room, but a police officer prevented me.

"Ma'am, this is a crime scene. You cannot be here."

"He is my brother! He is my brother!" I cried as I tried to fight my way past.

Uzo came to me and hugged me, moving me away from the door to the room. "You don't want to see it, sis. You shouldn't see Nnamdi like this."

"Please tell me it's not true," I cried, looking into his face, but he just sobbed. "What happened?"

"I don't know. That's what the police want to find out. We have to let them do their jobs, sis."

"Noooo, noooo, noooo, noooo..." I couldn't stop saying no as I cried into my brother's chest.

VICTOR

I was in my drawing room that night, working on a new design for an apartment complex, when the news broke first on Channels TV, where my television was tuned to.

"Breaking News at Ten," the presenter said. "We have just received word that there was a shooting tonight at the Chandelier Hotel. The

CHAPTER TWENTY - ONE NIGHT IN DECEMBER

number of victims and their identities are yet to be confirmed..."

What?

I opened my phone and checked social media. There wasn't more information about it. I continued to work on my drawing until 11:30 pm when I got a message from a friend.

"Do you know your brother-in-law, Nnamdi, is dead?"

"What?" I texted back.

He sent me a link to an Instagram post by an influencer who happened to have been at the hotel that night. According to her, the two people killed that night were Nnamdi Ukwueze and Rita Osineye.

Oh, my God!

I immediately called Uzo to confirm it. He said it had happened around 9 pm and crime scene investigators were still at the scene.

"I'm so sorry," I said.

I had grown to despise the man for how he treated my sister, especially when she told me the horrible thing he did in Las Vegas. Though I had thought of killing him myself, I knew it was something I could never do. Despite everything, Ada loved him.

I thought of calling her, but I figured it was too late. There was no point waking her up to cry. It's not like Nnamdi was in the hospital. He was dead. She would have to find out in the morning, just like the rest of the world. *Damn!*

III

THE AFTERMATH

"Blessed be the God and Father of our Lord Jesus Christ, the Father of mercies and God of all comfort, who comforts us in all our tribulation, that we may be able to comfort those who are in any trouble, with the comfort with which we ourselves are comforted by God."
(2 Corinthians 1:3-4)

CHAPTER TWENTY-ONE - THE MIND OF A KILLER

NEKA

Barrister Gbenga opens the door, and I'm taken back to my cell. The truth is out. Everybody knows what I've done, and though they may think they know why I did it, I doubt anyone truly understands my reasons.

The truth is, I loved Nnamdi. I would have died for him. There was nothing I wasn't prepared to do for him, for us to be together. Realizing that he didn't feel that way for me, even a little bit, hurt more than I could stand. It was as though he had said my entire existence was worthless...

Back in my cell and on my bench, I bend with my elbows on my knees, my hands behind my head, and my face buried in my bosom. I want to scream. I want to scream! The thought keeps coming until I do.

"Aaaarrghh!" I scream in agony. When I think about everything I've lost, I just scream. Even when the guard comes to bang on the bars and shout at me to shut up or else, I just keep screaming. It's the only freedom I have left.

*****

I wake up in a different room with no bench and no window. I seem to recall my hysterics getting out of hand, and officers charging into my cell to prevent me from breaking my head against the wall. My bench had been thrown and was upside down when I was pinned to the floor and cuffed, with my hands and legs folded behind my back. Then I was knocked out.

Wow, it came to this, I marvel, feeling sedated. I raise my hand to my head, where a throbbing headache prevails. I guess the next thing for me to lose is my mind. I feel like I am losing control of it. But before I do, it takes a trip down memory lane to the very first time I met Nnamdi Ukwueze…

Naturally, I had noticed him in school, like every other red-blooded female, but he didn't notice me until I was in JSS3. That was the year that I became very popular in school because my boobs began to grow exponentially every week! By the end of my first term, I had the wide hips to match, and all the guys were bidding for my attention, but he was the only one I wanted.

The day we met, he came up behind me on the cafeteria line and just started talking to me.

"Can you believe we pay ₦50k a term for this rubbish?" That was back when ₦50,000 was something.

I turned and looked at him, not sure if he was talking to me. I just gave him a small smile.

"What is this? I'm starving!" he complained to the server when she handed him a plate of rice and stew, twice the size of mine. "God, can you believe it?"

I turned to him again, figuring he was actually asking me this time. "Yeah, it sucks…"

"I mean, I'm supposed to study, and play football, and with the exams coming… I need my strength, *mehn!*"

At this point, I was just giggling. He was funny.

"It's not funny," he said, giggling too. "You're Adaeze's sister, right?"

CHAPTER TWENTY-ONE - THE MIND OF A KILLER

I swallowed. "Yes. Nneka."

"Nice. I'm Nnamdi," he introduced himself.

I felt like saying, "I know," but I swallowed the words. He didn't need to know that.

He carried his tray and said, "I hope to see you around some time," as he went to sit with his friends.

My friends surrounded me later to ask me how it was talking to Nnamdi, saying how lucky I was because, fine as he was, Nnamdi was a quiet guy. He hadn't developed a reputation of being a ladies' man at that point. He was studious and often pensive at school, even though he was friendly and outgoing at parties.

I can't really say when we started going out, but I kept seeing more of him, and he was always chatty and friendly with me. One day, he met me as I was walking to class with my girls and asked if I was going to be at Kunle's birthday party that Saturday. I told him I hadn't heard of it. So, he gave me an invitation and said I could come with my friends. It wasn't like a date, but after that party, everyone knew I was off the bench. Nnamdi had claimed me, and no one tried to hit on me again.

The first time we kissed was at another party, the following Friday. Nnamdi and I spent the whole time together as we danced to different Hip hop and RnB anthems. When a slow jam came on, he put his arm around my waist, as I put mine around his neck, then he brought his face down to meet mine. It was amazing. Even when the party jams started again, we just kept kissing. We eventually decided to find a seat, and we made out for the rest of the evening.

We were inseparable after that.

I fell headfirst in love with him because he was so sweet, sensitive, gentle, affectionate, attentive, gorgeous, and a great kisser. He wasn't just my boyfriend. He was my best friend.

I remember the first time he told me he loved me. It was Valentine's Day, and he got me the biggest teddy bear, with a big, red heart cushion on its chest. He also got me a massive box of Ferrero Rocher chocolates and a heart locket, inscribed with "Nnamdi loves Nneka."

Opening the locket with the red ruby stone and seeing the inscription brought tears to my eyes.

"I love you, Nneka. Forever and always," he said earnestly, before sealing his promise with a kiss.

As I lie on the bare ground in my cell, I can still see his young earnest face as he says, "Forever and always…"

Tears run down my cheeks and wet the cold ground. "I love you…" I say to Nnamdi. I reach out to stroke his face, but like smoke, the vision of my love vanishes.

SEGUN

I'm sad when Gbenga calls me back around noon with an update on Nneka. I don't know how I'll begin to share the news with her family. Ada especially. I decide to call her father, Mr Okpara, first.

"Good afternoon, Mr Okpara," I greet when he picks up.

"Barrister Segun, good afternoon," he says. "Any update?"

"That's why I'm calling, sir. Are you at home?"

"Yes, but Ada and Victor have gone. Please, what's the news?"

"I need you to take a seat, sir."

"Oh, God."

"Are you sitting down?"

"Yes."

"Nneka confessed to the murders." I pause briefly before continuing. "She's going to plead insanity. We will need to get medical evidence to substantiate this claim, however."

I can hear him sobbing over the phone. I should have waited to visit before I told him.

"I'm sorry, sir."

"Can we see her?"

CHAPTER TWENTY-ONE - THE MIND OF A KILLER

"Yes, you can. Do you want me to be there?"

"Yes, please. Where's the place? And can we bring food?"

"Yes, you can bring food. I'll send you the address. Let me know when you plan to get there, so I can be there before you."

"In the next hour."

"Okay, sir. See you then."

*****

I've been at the police station for 15 minutes before I see Mr Okpara's car. I have already spoken to the officers, and they agreed to take us to her cell to speak with her, but we only have ten minutes. Apparently, she caused a huge commotion in her first cell earlier, screaming, throwing furniture, crying, and even banging her head on the wall. They almost didn't allow us access.

"You brought two coolers?" I say as I see Mrs Okpara carrying the coolers, one in each hand.

"Yes. Rice and stew," she says, lifting one hand after the other to show what each cooler contained. "Too much?"

I shrug. I thought she would have brought one small cooler, which would have been enough for Nneka. "I guess they'll get eaten. This way."

I lead the way to the reception, where the warden is waiting to take us to Nneka's cell.

"You'll have to leave the coolers at the reception, madam," the warden says. "We'll make sure she gets the food when she's ready to eat."

Mrs Okpara looks at me, and I nod for her to obey. Hesitantly, she leaves them with the officer at the reception.

"She hit her head a few times against the wall before we could get to her, so she may seem a little bit confused," the warden says as he leads us to a separate building. "She's on suicide watch and may need to be transported to a more secure facility before her arraignment."

Mrs Okpara gasps, covering her mouth with her hand to hold back a sob.

Finally, we arrive in front of Nneka's cell, and she's lying on the floor, dressed in a pair of blue jeans and a black t-shirt, muttering to herself.

"Nneka, Nneka," Mr Okpara calls to his daughter.

NNEKA

It's like my mind's stuck in a loop as I keep replaying the night of the Senior Prom, where I accompanied Nnamdi, as his date. The same song - our song - plays over and over in my mind, as I gaze up into Nnamdi's face.

It feels like I'm right back there with him.

"You're so close but still a world away" takes on a new meaning as Madonna sings "Crazy For You."

"I never wanted anyone like this, Nnamdi…" I say. "I'm so crazy for you."

But my fantasy becomes a nightmare as I see her. "No! No! No, Nnamdi! Please don't leave me!"

"Nneka, Nneka…"

I hear my name in the distance. The visions fade away, and light is replaced with darkness. My eyes soon adjust, and I see a wall. I reach out with my left hand and touch it, then turn my head up in the direction of the call. I see the bars that remind me of my incarceration. I sit up with effort. My right arm feels numb, and my head hurts, but there's a hole where my heart used to be.

"Nneka, baby," I see my father at the other side of the bars, and for a moment, I wonder if I'm imagining it.

"Nneka," Mum cries. "Oh, Nneka, why did you do it?"

I blink back the tears. I don't know what to say to them. Why did they come? I don't want them to see me like this, like an animal in a cage. What will their words do for me?

CHAPTER TWENTY-ONE - THE MIND OF A KILLER

I shut my eyes and wish them gone.

"Nneka," my mum says again, stretching her hand into the cell to hold mine.

I ignore her. They are just making this harder. Nothing they do will change what has happened. When I think of the agony I was in the day I decided Nnamdi had to die, I remember why I did what I did.

I couldn't breathe. It felt like I was suffocating knowing he was alive and was in love with another woman when I had given up everything for him. However I think about it, like the endless loop of his prom night, the outcome is the same. Nnamdi is dead, and I die slowly in agony over losing him.

"Go away..." I mutter.

"Nneka, your mum and I—"

"Go away!" I shout. "Please, just leave me alone."

"Nneka, we don't know why you did what you did or why you are pushing us away now. But your mum and I want you to know that we love you, and we will be praying for a miracle."

I don't even look at him. If I look at him, I too will wish for the impossible, and that's just a different kind of hell. Let me die and meet Nnamdi in hell. Being alive, incarcerated in this world without him, is the hell from which I wish to be delivered.

"Honey, we brought you some food. The warden will bring the food for you soon," my mum adds.

I'm hungry. Starving even. I haven't eaten since they brought me in for questioning last night.

My babies! I suddenly remember my children, whom I left with the nanny when the police came for me. I am curious to know how they are doing, wondering if Dotun has abandoned them.

I turn to look at my parents through the bars.

"How are the kids?"

"They are fine. Dotun is with them. He knows..."

I swallow. He is choosing to stay? Tears run down my cheeks. He is a good man. I didn't deserve him.

I sit with my back against the wall, arms around my knees, and head on my knees. I shut my eyes again.

I want to dream of Nnamdi once more.

CHAPTER TWENTY-TWO - BETRAYED

DAEZE

A Dotun and I have finished our meals, and it's almost time for me to pick my children up from school. I can't believe what he has just told me. How did I not even have a clue?!

Yes, Nnamdi was the master of secrets, but Nneka?

Up to the time I left home to stay on campus and study Economics at the University of Lagos (UNILAG), we had been so close. When she was dating Nnamdi, in my final year of Senior Secondary School, we used to talk all the time. Yes, I, too, fancied him then, but it wasn't an all-consuming crush. It was like the way you crush on a celebrity you know will never love you back.

I never dreamed Nnamdi would look my way, and when he fell for my drop-dead gorgeous younger sister, all fantasies I had about one day being his girlfriend flew out of my head. It just didn't seem at all possible. I was quite sure he would end up marrying Nneka, the way they were carrying on, so my crush went into hibernation, only to awaken when I saw him again at the bank that cursed day.

I remember when they broke up because Nnamdi was going to study at Harvard. She was still in SS1 then, and I was busy with my studies at UNILAG. She visited me at university to cry and told me how much she loved him and would miss him. She even asked me to help her talk to our parents so that they would send her to Boston University, since she didn't have the grades for Harvard University.

I tried not to encourage her dreams because I knew nothing was certain and our parents were not so well off to send us abroad to study. However, I assured her that everything would be okay. I told her not to worry, using the cliché line, *"if it's yours, it will come back to you..."* I believed that for her; that Nnamdi would keep his promise and search her out when he returned, but I also hoped she would move on.

As it turned out, funds didn't permit my parents to send Nneka to study abroad. She was gutted! She was accepted into Enugu State University to study Banking and Finance and spent the next five years there. I know she thought I didn't try enough, but I thought she wasn't being reasonable. I actually thought the distance would do them good, so that time would prove their love, instead of her forcing herself to be with him at the expense of her education.

I remember asking her, "What if you get pregnant? Are you willing to give up your studies just to be with a man?"

"Not a man, Ada. *Nnamdi!*" she cried. "If I get pregnant for him, I know he will marry me. And I won't need to worry about money because his family is rich. But now, I'm stuck here, and some other girl is going to have his babies!"

That was just so confusing for me because, at that point, I wasn't sure what she wanted more; Nnamdi or the security he brought. But I knew that she was presuming on a lot. No man wanted to be trapped in marriage. As much as Nnamdi thought he loved her, he needed time to figure out who he was and what he wanted. I told her as much.

"You'll never understand..."

We didn't talk as often after that. The years passed, and Nneka moved on, just as I had hoped. There were always guys on her case, and she seemed happy. And when she got engaged to Dotun in 2012 and married him later that year, I was thrilled for her. I believed she had finally found love. I had no idea that she had clung to the dream of

CHAPTER TWENTY-TWO - BETRAYED

birthing Nnamdi's babies to the point of ruining not just her marriage but mine as well.

I guess Nneka was right. I'll never understand her motivation to do the cruel things she has done to people who loved her. I'll never understand how she could lie to our faces and carry out such deceit for over a decade! I'll never understand the value or satisfaction she got from being one of Nnamdi's whores because she certainly was not his wife!

"What are you going to do now?" I ask Dotun, my hands folded on the table between us.

He draws in a deep sigh. "Right now, I'm just trying to find a new job."

"Yeah… I'm sorry you lost your job. What reason did they give again?"

"They said they are still conducting an investigation, but a substantial amount of money got missing. Given my position in the company, they had to let me go."

"Wow!"

"I know I didn't do anything wrong…but I don't even know where to begin to fight it. I don't even know if I should now. That job was my entire life! I think I was so engrossed in working that I didn't see what was happening with my family. I didn't look into Nneka's eyes and see deceit. If I knew her, if I knew her at all, then I would have known she wasn't happy…"

Dotun's shoulders heave as he breaks down and sobs, and I just place my hand on his left shoulder as he cries.

"Dotun, please don't blame yourself. If she was unhappy, it was her responsibility to tell you. She didn't have to cheat on you and make you think you were in a marriage that you weren't. She could have divorced you when she found out Demilade wasn't yours, and then both of you could have moved on…"

"I loved her… I really loved her. I thought she was such a supportive wife. When it was just us at the beginning, and I had just been promoted, she used to complain, and I tried to make it up to her, with date nights and stuff… But when Demilade was born, she wasn't so demanding of my time, and I guess I just didn't realise that my priorities were square. I thought I was doing what I had to do, providing for her and the children."

I think of the N2.5mil monthly allowance Nneka had been receiving. That was even more than Nnamdi sent me! I guess she had four kids, and I had my own house, business, vacations, and so much more that he gave me, but still!

I don't know if I should tell Dotun about the allowance. It seems unnecessarily cruel at this time, when the one thing he thought he was providing, he might as well not have been.

"I'm so sorry about Nneka…"

"Are you going to apologise for Nnamdi too?" Dotun asks, meeting my gaze. "I just want to move on…"

I swallow and nod.

"I want to move out of that house so desperately. I even hate that I still sleep in the same bed. So, I really need a good job; one that will allow me to spend as much time as I can with my kids."

Hmmm… "Actually, this might not be for you, and you can totally say no, but I am looking to employ a new Executive Director at AdVi Grand…"

"What about Tamara? Hasn't she been with you since you started?"

"She just had a baby, and she and her husband are planning to relocate to Abuja. She's on leave now and was supposed to resume in January, but she gave me notice at the end of November. So… It's something to think about…"

"Wow, Ada. That would be so amazing! It would literally be an answer to my prayer."

CHAPTER TWENTY-TWO - BETRAYED

"Really?"

"It's not that demanding, is it? Not like you'll be sending me to remote places every month?"

"Oh, it would be nothing like that. It's not exactly nine to five, but there'll be a lot of flexibility and allowance for holidays."

"I'll take it!"

I throw my head back and laugh. "Okay, well... I'll have to talk to Victor, and if he says you need to apply like everyone else, then you will need to submit an application."

"That's fine." Dotun sighs. "Thank you."

I shrug. "I'm happy I can help."

My phone alarm goes off, reminding me that I have to pick my kids from school.

"You're ready to go?" I ask Dotun.

"Yes, yes. I'm ready," he says, standing up. "I'm so glad you came."

"Me too," I beam and follow him back to his car.

*****

I arrive a little late to pick up my kids from school. On Fridays, they close an hour earlier than the usual three o'clock closing time, but today, I arrive by quarter to three.

"Mummy, you're late," Osinachi grumbles when she gets to the car, where I am sitting with the engine running.

"I'm sorry, honey. How was school today?"

"It was fine. We did rehearsals for our Christmas party."

"Oh, nice. Are you doing anything special?"

"I'm in the drama group and the choir. Mummy, they said I need to wear all white on Friday for the drama presentation. I am one of the angels."

"Cool."

Chinedu arrives at the car, escorted by his class teacher. "Hi,

Mummy," he greets.

"Hey, baby," I say, as I get out to relieve his escort. I help him get settled in his car seat as Osinachi continues talking.

"And I need to wear a green shirt and Christmas hat for the choir presentation."

"No problem, dear," I say as I return to the driver's seat and strap myself in. "Chinedu, are you doing anything for the Christmas party?"

He nods excitedly. "My class is singing a song. '*Oh, little town of Bethlehem...*'" he begins singing.

"Oh, wow!" I speak over him as he continues to sing. "My children are stars! I can't miss it for the world. What time is it?"

"We have to be at school by 8 am for rehearsals, but the party starts from 1 pm," Osinachi says as I pull out onto the road to drive home.

"Got it!"

*****

When we get home, the children go up to their rooms to change, while I go to mine to rest. I lie in my bed, feeling intense mental fatigue, but sleep evades me.

Sorrow, like a blanket, wraps itself around me, squeezing the tears from my eyes. When will I run out of tears? *Ten years of crying, and I'm still crying for you, Nnamdi.*

I shut my eyes and pull up a memory that I have scanned many times before. I keep looking for the tell-tale sign I missed, the wayward look or smirk that would have shown that he did not truly mean it when he held my hands in the presence of a Minister and promised to love and cherish me till death do us part.

For ten years, I have searched but haven't found it. I only remember the look of pure love and adoration on his face, as he spoke his vows to me. Did something change? Did I become so unlovable that he could not keep his promise? Or was he as deceived as I was about his true

CHAPTER TWENTY-TWO - BETRAYED

emotions?

How do you stand in Church, in the presence of your family and friends, in the presence of your bride's family and friends, knowing full well that you are sleeping with her sister and God knows who else, and yet pledge to love her so convincingly? How do you promise to forsake all others, all the while knowing you will never keep that promise?

Nnamdi, how did you lie in my bed and say you love me, then leave me to go and lie with my sister?

When my phone rings, I do not pick it. I cannot pick it, even though I see it is Segun calling. Instead, I put my phone on silent.

I just want to wallow in the pain of his betrayal. Nnamdi has buried me in shame and sorrow. He has caused me grievous bodily harm.

If I had killed you, Nnamdi, it would only have been self-defence.

I hope it hurts, it burns, where you are.

For depriving me of love, joy, and respect in our marriage, I pray you never find rest.

I know I profess not to believe in God, Heaven, and Hell, but at such a time as this, I wish it were true, if only for Nnamdi to suffer in death for what he did to me while he lived.

CHAPTER TWENTY-THREE - BEREAVED

DAEZE

A I wake up in the middle of the night, having been carried away by sleep, my flighty visitor. I look at the time on my phone, and it's 1:05 in the morning. I can also see that I have ten missed calls.

Feeling curious, I check and see that three were from Segun, two were from my mum, another two from Victor, and three from my friend, Omi. *Hmmm...* I'll call them back in the morning.

Across from my bed, on the coffee table, I can see that Mrs Abike has been in my room and left a tray of food. Grateful, because I'm hungry, I rise to collect the tray and carry it to my bed.

As I eat my delicious but now cold meal of special fried rice with turkey and dodo, I turn on the TV and look for a world to escape to. I can't think of anything else I can do or even want to do at this time.

I have no interest in browsing social media. In fact, I'll probably never go back on it again. It's too late for me to call Omi back, or even my mum, so I just keep scrolling for something to watch.

None of the romcoms recommended by Netflix appeal to me, so I settle for something with action. I still haven't watched their new series, 'Supacell.' I've heard so many good things about it. I hit play without watching the previews.

CHAPTER TWENTY-THREE - BEREAVED

I'm still wide awake watching the show about Black people in London with superpowers when my alarm goes off at 5 am. It's telling me to do my morning exercises, but I don't give a damn right now. I silence it, and keep on watching, even though I'm finally feeling sleepy again. The series is so interesting!

*****

I stir hours later to find my television switched off and someone lying in bed beside me. I stretch my hand to touch my friend, and she stirs and turns to me.

"At last, you're awake," Omi says. I give her a small smile. "How are you, darling?"

I just nod, then inhale deeply. I'm so happy to see her, but still I ask, "What are you doing here?"

Omi sits up in bed. "I had to come and check on you when you were not picking up your phone. I spoke to Victor, and he told me about Nneka."

It seems my eyes have finally dried because the mention of her name doesn't provoke tears to fall.

"I'm so sorry, Ada," she says.

I just look at my best friend and breathe. A part of me is afraid that she too betrayed me with my husband. The lack of evidence over the years does not prove anything anymore, since I had no clue that Nneka was doing what she had been doing to me.

Nnamdi's betrayal didn't just destroy my relationship with him but fractured all my intimate relationships, poisoning them with distrust and fear.

I left Las Vegas without saying goodbye to any of my friends, so traumatized was I. They had all seen firsthand what my husband was capable of, and I wondered which of them he would go after next, if he hadn't already. But the day after I returned home, Omi was at my place. She didn't need to say anything, she just held me and let me cry. She and Titi, who I'd also met at UNILAG and had invited on the trip, were the only ones who stood by me and who I've kept in touch with since I returned from Las Vegas.

I, Rita, and Titi were besties back in university, and Titi was also mortified when she learnt what had happened during my birthday holiday. She also came around later to debrief the 'incident.'

"*I dey fear oh!* Ah, Rita!" she marvelled.

"You have to leave him, Ada. You cannot continue in this kind of marriage," Omi said.

"Yes, you have to leave. Not for anything but your sanity. You have tried, *abeg*."

But still I stayed, waiting for the final nail on the coffin of our marriage, his publicized engagement to my former best friend.

At last, I blink and look away. I will never know. But at least he is dead now. He can't continue to hurt me with his lifestyle, but I wonder if I'll ever be able to trust another man - another soul - as long as I live. I have been shocked in this life.

"Ada, I can't imagine what you're going through," Omi says, reaching out to hold my hand. "But I want you to know that I'm here for you. You're going to get through this."

I look at her, nod, and mutter, "Thank you."

I want to know the time, so I reach for my phone as a yawn passes. I'm wide awake now, and I see it's 11:30 am. I now have 15 missed calls. Still, I'm not ready to hear my phone ring.

I rise from my bed and tread to the bathroom to ease myself. While there, I decide to have a shower. I hear the TV again, as Omi unpauses the series I was watching in the night.

"You finally decided to watch it. It's great, isn't it?" she says.

I can't remember where I stopped. The last thing I recall is how the fifth episode ended, so I figure I probably slept off during the sixth.

CHAPTER TWENTY-THREE - BEREAVED

"Please, watch something else! I haven't finished watching it," I shout before entering the shower.

I'm happy when I hear the theme song for Friends. Omi can watch Friends from now until Kingdom come!

*****

I'm finally able to leave my room at noon. Omi walks behind me as I climb the stairs, and I'm surprised to see that she isn't the only one who has decided to come and check on me today. My mum rises when she sees me and meets me at the bottom of the stairs.

I can't imagine the pain she's going through, being the praying woman I've known her to be. It must be devastating to see that despite all her prayers, Nneka turned out to be a murderer, and my marriage suffered a shipwreck worse than the Titanic.

She pulls me into her arms, and for a moment, we say nothing. I wonder if she knows that Nneka is guilty. I wonder if I should tell her. At last, she says with tears, "She did it, she did it... I'm so sorry."

She has succeeded in squeezing more tears from my eyes. "It's not your fault, Mum. You did your best for us."

I hold her hand as I walk over to my dad. I'm even more surprised he came. I bend to greet and kiss his cheek. "Good afternoon, Dad," I say, sitting beside him. "Why are you guys here?"

"We came to pray with you. We have lost one daughter already... We cannot lose you too."

"You didn't have to come to my house."

"This one that you're not answering your phone," Mum says. "You had us worried, dear."

I sigh. "I just wanted some peace."

"We will leave. Just let us pray with you."

It's a little late for that, isn't it? I want to say it, but I don't, though it feels like administering medicine after death.

I nod and move on to greet my other uninvited guests. Victor and Amber are sitting on the two-seater sofa. From the noise I hear coming from the basement, where my children have their games' room, I know they brought their children with them.

Victor rises to hug me. Then Amber hugs me too. There is no need for words.

Lastly, I see Dotun sitting on my armchair, my favourite seat. He too rises to hug me, and I wonder who decided to organize this small get together. I'm comforted by their show of support at this time. Each of us has been hurt so deeply by the actions of my husband and my sister.

"Thank you for coming," I say to all at last, and they just smile at me.

I smell something delicious, so I follow the fragrance into the kitchen. There, I see Titi, whipping up her signature ugwu leaf and goat meat stew on my stove, assisted by Mrs Abike. She drops her spoon and comes to give me a big hug.

I wanted to be alone, but I didn't realise I wanted this more.

*****

When the food is ready, Amber calls her nanny to bring all the children up for lunch. Including Dotun's boys, there are eight children seated at the dining table. While Dotun's nanny feeds Sade, Amber's nanny eats with and supervises the older children, and my matron caters to the adults, serving my parents first.

When we have all been served and are holding hands, my father leads us in prayer, saying, "Dear Heavenly Father, have mercy on us. We are bereaved and are in desperate need of Your comfort. As we gather and eat together, may Your Presence fill this place and restore joy in our hearts. I know that You, who knows the beginning from the end, have seen all and knew what would happen even before it did, and I trust that You are making a way, and You will bring good out of this mess.

"I pray especially for my daughter, Adaeze, that You will reveal

CHAPTER TWENTY-THREE - BEREAVED

Yourself to her as the God who is near to the brokenhearted, who saves those crushed in spirit. Help her to stand through this storm and see Your wonders in her life.

"Lord, I lift up my son, Dotun, to You. I pray that You will bestow to him greater grace to be able to love and raise his children, despite the betrayal he has suffered. Draw near to him, o Lord, as he draws near to You. I pray that as he waits on You, trusting in You, he will truly rise up on new wings like an eagle and prosper in everything he does.

"And for his wife, my daughter, Nneka, we plead Your mercy. I know there's no depth You won't go to save the lost. We pray that You will forgive her and grant her favour in this court case. Please bring her home to her family and heal the wounds of betrayal.

"Finally, Lord, for the food we are about to eat, we ask Your blessing on it, upon the cooks, and upon our generous hostess. We pray all this in Jesus' name, amen!"

"Amen!" everyone says soberly.

I am sitting beside my father on the three seater sofa, while my friends are beside me, on two visitor chairs they carried from my home office. My father looks at me and smiles, and I return a small smile.

Everyone tucks into their food - Basmati rice and Titi's signature stew, with moin moin, dodo, and coleslaw - and we eat in silence.

"Dotun, have you told the children about their mum?" my mother asks after a while.

He looks up and shakes his head. "I haven't. I don't know how I can begin to have that conversation."

"You have to try, before they hear it from their friends. I know it's hard, but you're the only one who can tell them. Demilade, especially, because he's much more aware than you might think," my dad says.

"I know. I'll try," Dotun says, and I feel his pain anew. It's one thing for your wife to be a cheater, it's quite another for her to be a murderer as well.

I can see him tearing up, and I want to go to him, but my dad holds me back with his elbow. Victor rises to comfort him. Dotun gets up and goes out to the verandah, and Victor follows him.

I look at the three boys sitting in a row at the dining table, beside Chinedu, and they seem so unaware as they talk about the latest video games and Roblox. Osinachi turns and meets my gaze for a moment before returning to chat with her cousins, Amber's twin girls, Emma and Eva. Their younger brother, Ethan, sits beside Eva.

I wonder how Dotun's family feels about the kids now that they know their mother is in jail for murder and they are not related by blood. Or has Dotun not told them yet? I can imagine that will also be a difficult conversation.

After a while, Dotun and Victor return from their break outside, and Dotun looks more composed. Victor returns to sit beside his wife. I find myself looking at Amber now, wondering if she was spared from the Nnamdi tornado that swept through my family. I wonder if I should suggest a paternity test to Victor because I wouldn't even put it past Nnamdi, *the devil!*

Rubbish! Wicked snake! I seethe.

I take deep breaths to remain calm. I have to stop thinking everyone screwed my husband, but if I can't rule out my sister, who can I rule out?!

My parents take their leave when they are done eating, and I escort them to their car. My mum holds my hand as we walk out.

"Your daddy and I went to see your sister at the police station yesterday," she informs me.

What can I say? She's their daughter. My late husband's whore and murderer is their daughter. I can't blame them.

"We want to go again tonight," she says when we have arrived at their car, and I've said nothing. "Do you want to join us?"

CHAPTER TWENTY-THREE - BEREAVED

"No, mum. I'm not ready to see her."

My mum swallows and looks up at my dad before returning her gaze to me. "I understand, dear. But please, find it in your heart to forgive her too. She's family, and she's already being punished. You cannot punish her more…"

"Leave her alone," my dad says. "She will go when she's ready."

I think hell might freeze over before I visit that wicked witch in jail!

I give him an appreciative smile and exhale. "Bye," I say as I kiss them both.

When they drive off, my phone starts vibrating in my hand. I smile when I see my caller.

"Hi, Segun," I say, jovially.

"Good," he exclaims. "You're alive!"

I laugh. Funny guy. "Why wouldn't I be?"

"I should not have worried. I know you're stronger than you look."

I exhale at the compliment. Instead of returning into the house, I settle on the patio sofa on the verandah. I don't really know what to say in response, so I ask, "How are you? Enjoying your Saturday?"

I smile as he tells me what he has been up to so far, and his plans for tomorrow. He asks if I would like to attend his church, and it's an easy "No, thanks." When he asks me about my day, I remember that I still have friends and family visiting.

"It's a full house, but my parents just left."

"Do you have any plans for later?"

"Yeah… I'm going back to my bedroom to finish watching Supacell! And after that, I might start on Prison Break!"

Segun laughs. "Have fun! I'm glad you're okay."

"Thanks for calling. Bye."

I hang up and smile. *That was nice.*

CHAPTER TWENTY-FOUR - THE ARRAIGNMENT

ADAEZE
I attend Nneka's arraignment on Monday with my parents, Victor, and Amber. Dotun said he would go to the court only when required to testify. Across the room, I see Nnamdi's family for the first time since the news of his death broke out. Actually, I think it's the first time I'm seeing any of them all year. I swallow as I face forward.

Nneka is brought in chains, her hands and feet bound as she is led to the witness stand. Her lawyer rises to address the court and make their plea. When asked by the judge, Nneka pleads guilty but asks to be pardoned due to temporary insanity.

The Prosecutor from the Attorney General's office rises and presents pictures of the murder scene. They are rejecting her plea and, instead, insist on the maximum penalty for "two counts of premeditated murder in the first degree."

The judge looks at the pictures and then at my sister. She agrees to set a date for the commencement of a trial, and the case is adjourned. Nneka breaks down in sobs as she is led out of the courtroom in chains. My mum whimpers beside me, and my dad wipes tears from his eyes. Victor is stoic as he holds my hand.

I don't feel sorry for her. I don't know why she did what she did to

CHAPTER TWENTY-FOUR - THE ARRAIGNMENT

me, why she hurt Dotun in such an unforgivable way, and why she felt justified to kill the father of my children. Yes, she did the world a favour because that man - Nnamdi - deserved to die a rotten death! The more I have learnt about him, the more I believe he was a spawn of the devil because how can someone be so blessed, so loved, and yet be so wicked?!

Because love him, I did, even as much as I hate him now. I shut my eyes to quell my rising fury. It wasn't just me he treated as worthless; it was his children too. But we have to move on.

I rise and leave the courtroom, and my brother and his wife follow, then my parents. Nnamdi destroyed my family; he can burn in hell!

ADAORA

I'm relieved to know that Nneka won't get away with murdering my brother. I don't care what he did to her. She wasn't innocent! She agreed to play a deadly game with him, and she got burnt. She should deal with it!

In contrast, I sympathise with Adaeze because I know she was innocent. She loved my brother and was good to him. Even though he cheated on her and treated her so badly, she never once stepped out on him. At least, I didn't hear anything...

Yes, she was probably naive, but if I knew my brother at all, she didn't stand a chance against his charms. Nnamdi did not play fair, that much I know. He knew how to use everything and everyone to his advantage.

I occasionally glance in her direction as her sister is arraigned in court. I can't imagine how hurt and broken she feels to discover the truth about Nnamdi and Nneka this way. It was bad enough what he did in Las Vegas, leaving her on her birthday to shag Rita, her best friend. I swallow. *He was awful!*

Nnamdi didn't tell me about everything he did, and I wasn't really aware that he continued a sexual relationship with Nneka after marrying Adaeze, but I occasionally wondered about them. I'm as surprised as everyone else to learn that he fathered all her children. My brother had balls; I'll give him that.

My family and I leave the courtroom when Nnamdi's case is adjourned. I see Adaeze up ahead, and I feel like I should say something to her. I'm not sure what, and I'm not really sure she's ready to be consoled, but I feel terrible about all she has suffered loving my broken brother.

ADAEZE
"Ada!"

I turn at the sound of my name, and I'm surprised to see Adaora. I stand and wait for her to catch up with me. She does and looks at me. I can't even bring myself to smile at her.

"I'm sorry for your loss," she says, sounding a bit nervous.

"Which one? My husband, my sister, or my wasted years?"

I didn't mean to sound so bitter, but I can't help it.

"All of it. I'm really sorry for what he did to you," she swallows. "He didn't mean to hurt you…"

"Can you not apologise for him? How do you know what he meant to do?" I ask, irritated.

"Because I knew him well. He loved you, he just had…problems."

I look away, as unbidden tears wet my eyes. I don't want to stand here and listen to this. I heave a sigh and hold back a sob as my lips tremble.

"Look, now isn't the place. But I'll come to you later. We need to talk."

I nod, and she hugs me. I stand limp in her arms. She lets me go and walks back to catch up with her family.

I slowly begin to walk to join mine again. *'He loved you…'* He had a

CHAPTER TWENTY-FOUR - THE ARRAIGNMENT

terrible way of showing it!

SEGUN

I'm at the court when I see Adaeze standing by her car. Her brother, Victor, hugs her as I approach them.

"Hello, Adaeze," I say when I'm close enough not to shout.

"Hi, Barrister Segun," she greets.

"Please, Ada. I said you can just call me Segun. How are you today?"

She nods, "Fine, thanks."

"Hello, Victor," I say, as I extend my hand for a shake.

"Hi, Segun. Can I also call you that?" he jokes.

I chuckle. "You're free…when I'm not in court."

Victor chuckles and introduces me to the woman beside him. "This is my wife, Amber. Amber, meet the learned silk."

"Hello, Amber," I say, and she smiles.

Victor gives Ada a kiss on her cheek and takes hold of his wife. They wave and head to their car, leaving me alone with Ada.

"How have you been?" I ask, looking into her face. It is clear that she has been crying, and I just want to wrap her in my arms, but I restrain myself.

She nods and looks up at me slightly. "I'm okay. Thank you. How about you?"

I'm glad she cares enough to ask. I can imagine she doesn't really feel like making small talk with anyone. I smile at her, hoping I am conveying how much I enjoy being in her presence.

"I've been good. I'm happy that you're no longer a suspect."

She exhales with a smile. "Yeah, that's a relief."

"But I'm not happy that you don't need me anymore…"

She looks up and meets my gaze. She looks puzzled.

"Can we see? Later?" I ask nervously because I fear it is much too soon for her, but I'm convinced our meeting was fated. *No, ordained.*

She swallows and looks down. "I'm sure you're a good man, Segun, but I'm not in a good place."

I inhale deeply. "How are you going to get there? I just want to be there for you."

She looks into my eyes as she asks, "Why?"

I shrug. "God hasn't told me why yet."

She beams. "You're funny."

"Laughter is a good medicine for sorrow. We should go for a laugh," I persist, not knowing where the boldness is coming from. She just keeps looking at me, and now I can't help looking at her soft lips. "Maybe we can catch a movie or go to a comedy club…"

"You really want to go out with me?"

I nod because my words feel trapped in my throat.

"Can I think about it?"

"Sure," I say with a small smile. "Don't be too long."

She shakes her head and gets in her car. She looks like she wants to ask me something but thinks better of it.

"Drive safe," I say as I wave her off. I heave a sigh as I watch her drive away.

What am I doing?

ADAEZE

How flattering that the good Barrister wants to date me. I have sensed that the question was coming since the first night he called me. He called again yesterday evening to ask how I was doing. We had an even longer chat than on Saturday, and we didn't even discuss the case.

His interest makes me feel good, even though a part of me is wondering about his motives. Being the widow of a billionaire, I know I am due a substantial inheritance. But I've seen his car. He is doing quite well for himself. Still, you can't underestimate the greediness of men.

CHAPTER TWENTY-FOUR - THE ARRAIGNMENT

I also wonder if it was really God who caused us to meet. As it turned out, I didn't need a lawyer, so why should our accident be any reason to believe that God exists and answers prayers?

Hmmm... I don't know what to think, and I don't know if I should pray. I don't know how to hear from God, so what's the point?

I decide I will just leave it alone and see what happens next. I drive home, feeling like I have done what I said I would do. I thought about it, and it's too soon.

Yes, I would like to be with another man. I would like to be happy. I have been emotionally abused and neglected for practically my entire marriage to Nnamdi. I don't owe him any time of mourning nor abstinence. But I know I owe myself some quiet, to listen to my own heart and to choose me at last. I don't want to do anything just to please another man. *No, thank you!*

When I get home, the house is quiet because my children are still at school. They will be breaking for the Christmas holiday this Friday. I go up to my room and lie in my bed because I don't know what else to do with myself. I just want to sleep. And that's what I do.

*****

A knock on the door stirs me awake. I look at my phone, and it's already past the time I should have picked up the kids from school.

I can afford to get a driver, but I'm usually not too busy to pick them up myself, and I'm wary of trusting any driver with the responsibility of chaperoning my little children unaccompanied. I have heard too many stories that touch.

"Thank you, Mrs Abike," I say, sure it is my matron at my door reminding me to pick up the kids.

The door opens, and my brother sticks his head in.

"Victor... Why are you here?"

He walks towards me, where I'm lying on the bed, and I sit up.

"I picked up the kids from school."

"Oh, wow, thanks. I'm sorry I overslept," I swallow.

"They said they tried calling you, but you weren't answering."

I pick up my phone and realise that it's still on silent since Friday night. *My bad!* I finally remove it from silent mode. "Sorry, my phone was on silent. Thank you for picking them."

He comes closer and sits on the bed, looking at me. "Are you okay? Really? Do you need Amber to come and stay with you for a while?"

"I'm fine, honestly. I just needed to rest."

"Okay. But any time you need me or Amber, please just call us. You need to recover from all you've been through, sis. And we're here for you."

"I appreciate that, Victor. Thank you," I say as I hug him.

I get out of bed and follow him downstairs to see my kids and to see him off.

Mrs Abike is supervising the children as they are doing their homework on the dining table. Everything is tidy and clean, and I marvel at how she is able to do so much. Employing her was definitely one of the best decisions I ever made.

At the door, Victor gives me a big hug and says, "Take it easy, okay?"

"I will," I say with a smile.

"Bye, kids!"

"Bye, Uncle!" Chinedu and Osinachi shout back.

"Thank you, Mrs Abike," I say after shutting the door. But I wonder, "Why didn't you wake me up?"

"I know you need your rest, ma. The children will be fine."

Hmmm... "What's for dinner?"

"I cooked stew this morning, and I will boil rice later. There's also soup in the freezer if you want to take swallow today, ma."

I yawn and stretch. I can't believe I'm still so tired. "No, rice will be fine. I'll be in my room. Wake me for dinner, will you?"

CHAPTER TWENTY-FOUR - THE ARRAIGNMENT

"Okay, ma."

CHAPTER TWENTY-FIVE - THE WIDOW

ADAEZE

The days pass uneventfully. Because of the Christmas holiday, Nneka couldn't get a hearing this year, and she will be held in remand until January 15th, 2026, the date of her Preliminary Trial. I feel gutted for her, but not enough to want to visit her in jail.

Now that the investigation is over, the bodies have been released for burial, and funeral arrangements have begun. With my name cleared, I'm given due recognition as the widow of the deceased, and his family suddenly feel a need to acknowledge my existence and pain. One by one, they call to check on me and offer to bring me food, as if I lack anything. Nnamdi gave me everything but himself.

We are still waiting for the contents of his will to be divulged and his estate to be divided. I know that whatever the outcome, I and the kids will be fine. We have my house, cars, my flourishing business, and lots of money in my bank account. I don't need anything else from Nnamdi.

Well, except maybe an apology from the grave, then he can drop dead again and rest in peace!

I remember Adaora said we need to talk, and I wonder what it is she has to say. It's not until Thursday, three days after the arraignment, that Adaora calls to ask if she can come over for our chat.

CHAPTER TWENTY-FIVE - THE WIDOW

"Sure. I'm at home."

*****

Adaora arrives around noon, and Mrs Abike lets her in. She's in the living room, looking at the pictures of me and my children that I've hung on the walls. There's not a single picture of Nnamdi, since the day I had the house cleaned after he defiled it by screwing our housekeeper. *The shit I put up with*, I think as I walk to meet her.

"Thanks for agreeing to see me," she says, taking a seat.

I don't know what to say to that, so I say nothing. I settle on the armchair, which has a nice view of my garden.

"I don't really know how to tell you this…or even if I should," she swallows nervously. "It's just, when I saw you in court, I felt like you deserved to know, and since you might eventually find out anyway, I thought you should hear it from me."

Can I really take any more revelations about my late husband? Will anything she says matter? But I'm too curious to pass it up. I know now that ignorance isn't bliss.

"Please, go on," I say.

"Nnamdi was a sex addict," she says, and I just look at her like, "*Is that it?!*"

She picks up the glass water on the counter, which my matron brought for her, and takes a sip, then another. *Wow, she's really nervous.* It's so out of character, though. She has always been aloof around me.

"I… I am a sex addict too."

She holds my gaze, as if she expects me to get it. "What are you saying?"

"When we were kids, we were exposed to porn. I was 10, but Nnamdi was only 8. We started experimenting…together."

I swallow and hold her gaze.

"Nnamdi didn't cheat on you because he didn't love or respect you.

It was something that was out of his control."

"Did he ever get help for it?"

She shakes her head. "I don't think so. We just lived with it, I guess."

"But he knew when he married me that he had this problem."

Adaora nods.

"So, if he really loved me and wanted my unconditional love, he should have told me then and given me liberty to choose to love him through it… But he didn't."

She swallows.

"He deceived me, with your help. You knew, he knew, and I didn't. You took the choice from me. So, I can never believe he loved me."

Her head is bowed now.

"So, why did you think I needed to know that?"

Adaora sighed. "Because you are hurting, and because I don't want you to feel like—"

"I married a monster and a liar?"

She remains quiet.

"So, if I'm reading between the lines correctly, you too were *fucking* my husband…" I say, leaning forward and pointing my finger at her. "For the almost ten years that we were married and all the years before… And I'm supposed to accept that because *'he couldn't help it,'* when he never really tried to get help?!"

"I'm sorry. I shouldn't have said anything." She rises to leave.

"Please stay. I think it would be more cruel to dump this on me and walk away."

Adaora sits down again.

"I think you are looking for someone you can be honest with, someone who can understand how much you loved your brother and offer you comfort in a way no one else can."

Adaora wipes tears from her eyes.

"That can't be me. Your experience of your brother and mine are

CHAPTER TWENTY-FIVE - THE WIDOW

worlds apart. The love I had for him was pure and wholesome, but he gave me filth! He threw it away for *filth*. You think what he went through as a child was an excuse, I think what he did as an adult was inexcusable!" I heave as tears pool in my eyes. I wipe them. "If you want my forgiveness, you can have it. But I will not excuse you."

Adaora weeps on the sofa, and I don't know whether to feel disgust or pity.

She fucked my husband! Everybody fucked my husband! They robbed me of the right to choose and forced me to love the unthinkable!

I can't watch her crying over him. It hurts too much. So, I leave her there and go up to my room. And there, I cry.

*****

Adaora is gone by the time I return downstairs about an hour later.

How dare she come to me for pity? Just the thought of her having sex with Nnamdi makes me want to vomit. All the time I thought we were in love, they were both playing me for a fool.

I realise now that it was why we were never close. She kept her distance from me, and she could never look me in the eye. How cruel and disgusting they were! I wish I had nothing more to do with their incestuous family! I wish I had no more memories of any of this. It hurts so bad!

But Nnamdi has gone and stuck me with two kids! I love my babies, but I hate that I see Nnamdi every time I look at their faces, or every time Osinachi gives me attitude or Chinedu comes to play and cuddle with me. They have so many traits from him, even though he was hardly ever around, it seems so unfair!

I'm supposed to go and pick them up, but I don't feel up to it again today. I call Amber to help me, and she's more than happy to. Before she brings them home, I change to go out. I just need to get out of the house.

SEGUN

I haven't been able to stop thinking about Ada since Monday. I have wanted to call her so many times, but the last thing I want is for her to feel pressured. I hoped she would call eventually, but up till now, she hasn't, and it's twisting my insides. I might just have to give her a call tonight. I think enough time has passed.

I look at my colleague, Barrister Oliver, seated across from me and try to remember the last thing he said. I decide to just listen and respond to what I hear.

"So, that's why I think this would be the best defence strategy… You agree?"

He's looking at me, and for the life of me, I don't know what defence strategy he is advocating for. I run my hand down my face to force myself to focus.

"I'm sorry… Can you repeat that?" I ask instead.

"Okay, sir. Is everything alright?"

"Yes, I'm fine. Just another case that's been on my mind—" the words stop mid-speech as I see the object of my distraction walk past to be seated in a secluded area of the restaurant.

"Who's that?" my colleague asks, having followed my gaze.

"Someone I met last week." I rise and put a finger up as I say, "Excuse me, one second."

ADAEZE

As if on autopilot, I drive to my favourite place to chill and have a nice meal. The ambience at the Wheatbaker Hotel, Ikoyi is always so relaxing. A waiter escorts me to my preferred corner of the restaurant, which I'm glad to see is unoccupied.

"Thank you. Yes, bring both," I say when he asks if I need both the drinks and food menu.

I actually didn't feel hungry until I started driving. To be honest, I

CHAPTER TWENTY-FIVE - THE WIDOW

haven't had much of an appetite of late. Right now, I just want to order some sandwiches and sip some tea.

"May I join you?"

I look up, and I'm shocked to see Segun. I raise a brow. "Are you stalking me now?"

"Actually, I was just about to ask you the same thing. You see that gentleman over there..." He points to a table near the bar at the entrance where a young man is seated. "I'm having a meeting with him. Actually, I was *trying* to have a meeting with him when you walked in here..."

"Coincidence then."

Segun beams. "It's nice to see you again. Hopefully, you will still be here when I'm done with my meeting..."

"We'll see," I say with a small smile, my heart thumping against my chest.

I feel light as I watch him leave. He doesn't command the room like my late husband, but he is confident and kind. At least, he seems kind. He's also very good looking. But he looks young.

I noticed that before, which is why I was surprised that he was even taking an interest in me. I hope he isn't too young...not that I'm seriously thinking of dating him.

SEGUN

I'm able to focus a bit easier on my meeting, now I know Ada is just a stone's throw away. I still find myself looking at her every now and then, but for the most part, I am able to carry on an intelligent conversation.

"So, I'll head back to the office and draw up the briefs..." Oliver says.

"Great, thanks."

I wait for Oliver to pack up and leave before I go where my heart has been longing to.

"Excuse me, ma'am. Is this seat taken?"

She shakes her head, a smile on her face.

"I like your smile," I say sincerely.

She laughs aloud. I love that sound too. "You're full of lines, Segun… Is this your normal?"

I let out a breathy chuckle. "Actually, no. I don't know how to talk to women. I just want to talk to you."

"Wow! The lines!"

I laugh this time. I can see why she will think it's a line. I take a deep breath as I look at her. "You're looking relaxed today."

"Actually, it's this place. I come here to relax. Like my home away from home."

I bob my head. "That's cool. So, have you ordered food?" She nods. "Okay, let me place my order."

I indicate for a waiter to come with a menu. I already know what I like, so I show him on the menu.

"That's exactly what I ordered," Ada says, her eyes lit.

"Wow, really? I always get that. I love the avocado texture mixed with the prawn."

"Yeah, me too."

I just look at her beaming at me, and it seems unreal. I swallow.

"What drink will you have, sir?" the waiter asks.

"Hmmm… Do you have mango?"

"I'm sorry, we are out of that for now."

"Okay. Just bring orange juice and water. Thanks."

"You see, I ordered tea," she says cheekily.

"Nobody's perfect."

She gives me that hearty laughter again, and I feel something twist in my insides.

"I really like you," I blurt out. "Have you thought more about our date?"

CHAPTER TWENTY-FIVE - THE WIDOW

She shuts her eyes for a moment. "You don't want me," she says when she opens them to look at me.

"Why would you think so?"

"I'm much older than you, for one…"

"Wait. How old do you think I am?"

She gives me an appraisal. "34?"

"I'm 38. Is that too young?"

She chuckles. "Boy, I'm 44, with two kids and a shattered heart…"

She doesn't look 44. I even thought she was in her mid-30s. "I don't mind."

She exhales. "Just leave me, will you? I don't have any love to give you."

Her food order arrives, and the waiter places it between us. We remain silent until he has placed the last condiment on the table and leaves.

"I know Someone who restores broken hearts…" I say, seeing an occasion to evangelise.

"Don't tell me… Jesus?"

I smile. "So, you've heard of Him."

"Who hasn't?"

"You'll be quite surprised. So, can I introduce you?"

"To religion?" she asks, a brow raised.

"No. To Jesus."

"No, I'm good." Ada takes a bite of her sandwich, and I try not to look disappointed.

She's not ready yet, I hear in my spirit. I have to deal with this longing I have for her a little longer.

"Do you want me to give you some space?" I ask.

She looks at me and then back at her food. "I don't mind the company. Tell me about yourself, Segun."

"What do you want to know?"

"How come you're still single?"

Hmmm... "I'm waiting for the right woman."

She raises her brow at me. "At 38? You haven't found someone worthy?"

"Well, timing hasn't always worked out. I know that the race is not to the swift, so I'm not pressured. I was engaged before, but she died."

"Oh, I'm sorry." I nod in acceptance, giving her a small smile. "Ummm... Why did you decide to be a lawyer?"

I beam. "That's a sermon!"

She beams. "I'm not going anywhere."

CHAPTER TWENTY-SIX - THE REDEEMER

A **DAEZE**

I wait expectantly for Segun's answer.

"Well, the short answer is that my dad was one, and so was his father. I was trained to love law and justice," Segun says. "The long answer is my personal faith in God, the Father to the fatherless. The Bible says in Psalm 82:3-4 that we should *'defend the weak and the fatherless; uphold the cause of the poor and the oppressed. Rescue the weak and the needy; deliver them from the hand of the wicked.'* I find that I am able to obey this scripture through advocacy and legal reform, hence my passion for my profession."

"Hmmm... Wow. You really believe in this stuff," I say, putting a potato chip into my mouth.

"This stuff...?"

"The Bible, God etc."

"Why don't you?"

I shrug. "It's not that I don't... I just haven't been convinced of its practicality in my life."

"What exactly do you find impractical?"

I pick up another chip and dip it in Ketchup before inserting it in my mouth. "Like this whole 'Jesus died for you so you won't go to hell...' Like *really*? How does that work? How does that help me live in a world where I have bills to settle, children to raise…? I don't know if I'm making sense."

"You are… But could it be that you just don't understand it? Maybe someone hasn't explained it to you."

"That's the other thing… Something that is considered so important, so dire that if I miss it, I will end up in hell, *shouldn't* be that hard to understand. It just sort of seems like a clique thing or made up or something."

"The Gospel is actually very simple. Jesus likened it to a seed that is sown in different types of fields or terrain. So, depending on where it falls, it will spring up and bear fruit or it will wither and die. So, I think it's really about the condition of our hearts and our readiness or willingness to receive it."

I take a sip of my tea and look at Segun. He seems so sincere. "So, you're saying it is my fault that I don't believe?"

"Not that exactly…" He seems a bit confused. "Jesus also said in John 6:44 that *'no one can come to Me unless the Father who sent Me draws them.'*"

"Clique thing!" I say proudly, sticking my index finger up to emphasize my point. "So, it's the Father who has not called me?"

His eyes meet mine. "The Father is always calling you… He loves you. He is the One who sent me to you…"

I lean back, taken aback by the intensity of his speech just now. It's almost as if he wasn't the one speaking.

"Are you okay?" Segun asks.

"You said you were sent to me… How do you know this?"

"Because God speaks with me."

I swallow. "Audibly?"

"Actually, yes. Sometimes, I hear Him audibly through other prophets and messengers He sends. A lot of the time, it's an inner but distinguishable voice. Other times, it's from my Bible reading."

CHAPTER TWENTY-SIX - THE REDEEMER

"Hmmm..."

He reaches out to hold my hand on the table. "Ada, God sees you, He hears you, and He wishes that you will be comforted in knowing that He is always with you. He loves you so much."

"Even when I don't believe?"

"Yes. You didn't have to believe before He sent Jesus. The Bible says in Romans 5:8 that, *'While we were yet sinners, Christ died for us...'*" he says. "But the truth is, His death only saves us *when* we believe. It's like a lifeline that is thrown to someone drowning. If you don't grab it and hold on to it, you will die. But if you believe it can save you and take hold of it, you will be lifted from the water into safety. So, it's not just you...and it's not just God. He's extending His hand to you right now, Ada. Are you going to take it?"

My heart is thumping in my chest as I look at Segun. I can hardly believe what he is saying. It does seem so simple. *Too simple.* "Where was He? Where was He when I was about to marry that monster? Why didn't He send you to stop me then?"

Segun brings his other hand to clasp my hand between his hands, and he looks like he is on the verge of tears. "Please don't harden your heart now. Please, Ada. Don't close your heart to God. I love... *He* loves you!"

"You *love* me?! You don't know me!"

I rise from the table. I've had enough of this. I'm tired of men pretending to love me so they can use me.

When I look at Segun, his tears have fallen, but his eyes beg me to stay. I can't. I walk away.

SEGUN

I love you?!

I am as shocked as she is that I almost said that. The need to profess my love was like my need to breathe in that moment. But even though

I stopped myself, it was too late.

I watch as her eyes widen in alarm, wishing I could gather the two words I had uttered back into my mouth. How could I have been so careless?

I want to run after her, but the Lord impresses on me to wait. It was too soon. She's too hurt and angry. She doesn't know who to trust or what to believe. But my prayers will save her. So, I start praying for her with an urgency that feels like life or death.

When my food comes, I ask them to pack it up to take away. I leave my glass of orange juice on the table because I don't think I can or should put anything in my mouth right now. I feel a burden to fast as I pray for Ada.

"Soften her heart, oh, Lord. Help her to see You! Open her eyes so she can see," I pray out loud.

The waiter returns with my doggie bag, and I carry it as I walk out of the hotel.

ADAEZE

Again, as if on autopilot, I find myself in Obalende, on my parents' street, turning into their compound. It's just after five o'clock in the evening, but I know my dad, being a retired civil servant, will be home. At this time, Mum will likely be at the clothing shop she owns at Falomo. I park my car and march to the front door.

My dad opens up almost as soon as I start pounding. "Hey! Ada, what's wrong with you?"

"Daddy, why did you do it?" I ask him outrightly as I enter the house overcome with fury.

"Do what, dear?" He looks at me as if he is absolutely clueless what I'm talking about.

"Cheat on Mum!"

"Oh... Ada," he says, as his expression changes to one of understand-

CHAPTER TWENTY-SIX - THE REDEEMER

ing. "Please, come and sit."

"I don't want to sit. Just tell me why you did it. Why did you hurt her like that and put our family through all that pain?"

"What can I say, sweetheart? I was a selfish man. I didn't have the love of God in me."

"Are you saying you had no control over what you were doing?"

"Please sit down, Ada. Let's talk."

I take a calming breath and follow him to the lounge, taking a seat beside him on the two-seater sofa he chooses to settle on.

"In a way, you could say I had no control because I had not trained myself to have control. I didn't have any discipline, and I didn't know I needed it or that I could actually be disciplined and self-controlled sexually. I had trained myself through practice to always satisfy my urges, and as quickly as I had them, I wanted them met. That's why I said I was selfish."

"So, what changed?"

"I don't know how to explain it, dear. But it felt like, one day, the scales just fell from my eyes, and I could actually see the wickedness I was doing for what it was. I think it was just grace, Ada. The mercy of God."

I shiver at his mention of God again. "So, just like that," I click my fingers, "you stopped?"

"No, just like that I began to see. God caused me to see your mother's pain, her love, and her sacrifices, and I began to despise my weakness and unfaithfulness. I prayed and asked for His help to stop, and He began to help me and strengthen me, and soon, I no longer desired the things I once thought I couldn't live without. It was gradual, but it was also sudden."

I exhale, trying to process all he has said.

"You know what I later found out?"

"What?"

"Your mum had been praying for me. Before I suddenly began to see, she was praying for God to restore me to wholeness and sound mind. God heard her prayers, and He had mercy on me, giving me the grace to overcome what I thought was impossible."

"Are you saying if I had been praying for Nnamdi, he would have changed like you did?"

"I'm not saying that… I don't know about Nnamdi, but I also know it's not impossible. I've come to know that with God, all things are possible. But if we do not have the faith to believe for it, we cannot pray to Him for it…"

"But He knows we need it. Why doesn't He just help us?! Why do we have to pray?"

My dad swallows. "It is so much easier for God to work with us when we are willing and ready than when we are headstrong and unbelieving. When we pray, we take a step towards Him that shows that we really want His help, that we are ready to be blessed.

"It's like having two daughters. One of them goes about doing everything for herself without ever coming to you for help. And the other seeks you out continually, asking you to get involved and help them with the things she struggles with. I bet you would give more help to the one who requests it, who believes that you are able and willing to help them, than the one who never or rarely comes to you…"

"I guess. But I think I might get annoyed or tired with the one who doesn't seem to know how to do anything for herself," I say with a small smile.

My dad chuckles. "That's where the comparison ends, dear. God always wants us to come to Him. Even for the smallest things. He wants to be involved in our lives and guide us in the best path that will bring us peace and happiness. He can see it, but we can't. When we try to do life without Him, we show that we are proud because, though we can't see where we are going, we refuse to ask for help. The Bible

CHAPTER TWENTY-SIX - THE REDEEMER

says, '*God opposes the proud and gives grace to the humble.*'"

I look at my dad, and suddenly, I get it. It is as though the scales he spoke about have fallen from my eyes. I have been so proud living without God's help, not believing that He could really help me or even wanted to.

From nowhere, my eyes flood with tears, and I begin to sob. My father holds me close as I cry, leaning my head on his shoulder. I weep for like five whole minutes as I think of all the times I could have prayed to God but didn't. And I think of how when I prayed for a lawyer, He brought Segun into my life. *He heard me.*

I suddenly remember Mrs Abike's words last week when she said *"God has something good for you... You will see it soon."* I wonder now if she was talking about this new friendship I have with Segun.

Then I recall Segun's words to me, about God extending His hand for me to take it. But I refused.

I look up at my dad. "Is it too late?"

"For what, dear?"

"For me to accept God's help?"

"*Never!* As long as you have a breath and can call on Him, He will save you. Baby, do you want to call on Him?"

I nod and cry, "Yes! Please. I need His help."

"Then tell Him. You can speak to Him yourself."

I bow my head as I pray. "God, I need You. I need You so much! I'm so tired of trying to do everything by myself and thinking I know best. Please help me now. Please come into my life and make me whole. Please take away this pain and anger I've been holding on to for years. I'm ready to be blessed. I'm ready now."

My dad is wiping his tears when I look at him. "Thank you, Daddy."

He puts his arms around me, and it feels different. It feels like God is holding me, and all my pain begins to melt away.

CHAPTER TWENTY-SEVEN - THE AWAKENING

ADAEZE

I'm still at my parents' place an hour later when my mum gets back from work. Apparently, the good news of my conversion, my profession of faith in Jesus Christ, reached her office via a text from my dad, and she had to close up as soon as she could to get home and give me a hug!

"Ada, I've been praying for this day for years!" she says as she embraces me. "I'm so glad you finally made the decision to receive Jesus as your Lord and Saviour. You have truly crossed from death to life, and now I'm not worried about you anymore. Glory be to God!"

I just beam at her, feeling so much lighter than I did when I came. Years of anger and bitterness have been washed away in just an instant, as I have come to see God for the Father that He is. The One who sees me, and Whom I can go to whenever I have cause or need. The One who has been waiting for me to say, "Yes, I trust You with my life," so that I never need to walk in darkness again.

Practically, I know that I haven't touched the surface of all that I need to know and do as a Christian, but in the spirit, I do feel like I have crossed from a realm of despair and death to a realm of hope and life, like my mum said. I don't really know how to describe it, but I feel clean, I feel justified, I feel loved, I feel amazing!

CHAPTER TWENTY-SEVEN - THE AWAKENING

"You will stay for dinner, won't you?" I hesitate, and she pleads, "Please stay. The kids are with Mrs Abike, right? They'll be fine for a couple more hours."

I smile and exhale. "Sure. I'll let Mrs Abike know I'll be home after dinner."

"Great! I'll just warm up the egusi soup. You'll eat semo?"

"Yes, Mum." I love my mum's egusi soup. "Let me come and help."

"No, please, sit! It'll be ready in ten minutes."

"Okay, Mum."

I return to sit with my dad, as we continue reading the Bible he just gifted me. He took me to the Book of John, saying it's the best place to start to get to know Jesus. I'm already enjoying what I am reading and learning so much. I can't wait to get home and really get into it.

*****

I arrive home at 7:45 pm, just before my children have to go to bed so they can wake up early for their Christmas party and last day of term tomorrow.

"Mummy, where were you?" Chinedu asks. "You didn't pick us from school, and we didn't see you at dinner."

"Sorry, darling," I say as I sit on the edge of his bed, where he is already lying under the covers. "I had to go and see Grandma and Grandpa. And we had a good long talk. I really needed it," I end with a smile.

"Okay. Are you going to come for our party tomorrow?" he asks.

"I won't miss it for the world! Are you ready for your performance?" He nods eagerly. "Awesome! Well, close your eyes and get a good night's rest."

I rise to leave, but I feel a strong burden to stay longer and pray with my son. It's not something I've ever done, but I believe it is one of the promptings my dad told me the Holy Spirit would give, which, as I obey, will help me become better at hearing God.

So, I go back, kneel at my son's bed and begin to pray. "Father, thank You for Jesus Christ, whom You sent to be our Saviour. Thank You for never giving up on me and welcoming me into Your Kingdom today. I pray also for my children, Chinedu and Osinachi, that they will receive Your free gift of salvation, and they will be blessed because they put their trust in You. Please watch over us tonight as we sleep. I pray that we will have a wonderful time tomorrow at their party, and we will have the best Christmas we have ever had…"

I feel like I'm rambling, so I wrap up with, "In Jesus' name I pray," like I have heard my parents do many times. "Amen."

"Goodnight, Mummy," Chinedu says sleepily.

I give him a kiss on his forehead and leave his room. I go next door to his sister's bedroom, and she's still brushing her teeth.

"Were you praying just now?" she asks me, with a brow raised.

"Yes, I was," I say, as I sit on her bed.

She spits out foam. "Why? I thought you didn't believe in God?"

"Well, I didn't have an understanding of who He is in order to believe… I didn't know Him enough to believe in Him, but I've encountered Him recently, and now, I know He's real, and I believe He is good."

Osinachi rinses her mouth out, puts away her toothbrush, and comes to sit beside me on the bed. "What's He like?"

I smile at her question and the sincere curiosity in her eyes as she looks up to me. I swallow, "Well, we are just getting acquainted, but I know He's very mysterious… I know He is patient because He has been so patient with me. He is compassionate and merciful, just like a good father."

"Like Daddy?"

I'm taken aback by her question, but rather than deny her father was good, I say, "Better. He is the best father, and the most reliable and

CHAPTER TWENTY-SEVEN - THE AWAKENING

trustworthy. Do you want to get to know Him too?"

Osinachi nods.

"Then let's pray. Dear Lord, Osinachi wants to get to know You as her Father too. I've heard people say You are the Father to the fatherless, so please reveal Yourself to her, and to Chinedu, as the *best* Father. Let us all come to know You for ourselves and Jesus Christ, Your only begotten Son who died for our sins. Fill us with Your Holy Spirit now, so that, as Your beloved children, we too will do the things that please You. Amen."

"Amen," Osinachi says. She throws her arms around my waist and nestles in my bosom affectionately. "Thank you, Mum."

I kiss the top of her head. "Thank you, baby. Go to bed now."

"Goodnight, Mummy."

"Goodnight."

She gets under the covers, and I switch off the light as I leave her room.

*****

I am finally in my room and eager to continue reading my Bible. I feel like I still know so little about the Father, Jesus, and the Holy Spirit. Their relationship boggles my mind, how they are all the same God, but separate enough that the Father sent Jesus Christ to die, yet God never died... And then Jesus went to Heaven and sent the Holy Spirit to live in our hearts, so that those who believe are now God's temple!

Mind boggling!

But it's also very interesting and inspiring. I figure I probably won't understand it all until I finally see God face to face, but with the Bible, God's love letter to me, as my dad called it, I can learn as much as I can about Him. My dad said the Holy Spirit will also teach me and cause me to understand what I read if I pray as I read, so I am excited to continue reading and praying to God.

I'm still reading at 9 pm when my phone rings. I'm happy to see it's my brother.

"Hey, Victor," I answer cheerfully.

"Hey, sis! How are you?"

"I'm great," I say, and I'm thrilled that I'm not even exaggerating.

"Wow, so it's true! Mum told me you have given your life to Christ... Amazing!"

"Yes, I have, and yes, it is amazing! Although, it's still new..."

"Let it be new every day. That is what we need to keep our hunger for God."

"Hmmm," I mutter.

"You know, I made the decision ten years ago, about the time I met Amber... She was actually my motivation, if I'm being honest," he giggles. "But God took my confession and held on to me, even when I forgot how desperately I needed Him. It can happen like that sometimes. Life happens, and you revert back to doing what feels easiest rather than what is necessary and right... But God is so gracious. We just have to keep going back to Him, and He'll wash us white as snow and remind us of how much we are loved."

I swallow. "Thank you, Victor. I'll try to remember that."

"I'm really happy for you, sis. But I'm curious, what prompted this change?"

I draw in a breath and think for a minute. I keep thinking of my mysterious encounter with Segun last week. But would I have met him if I had not prayed for God to send me a lawyer? Then again, I wouldn't have needed a lawyer if my husband hadn't been murdered... I stop that train of thought because it is potentially endless.

I decide to start with my meeting with Segun today. "Well, I bumped into Segun at the Wheatbaker, and we started talking. He talked about how his faith in God was the main reason he became a lawyer..."

"Oh, wow... You guys have been bumping into yourselves a lot,"

CHAPTER TWENTY-SEVEN - THE AWAKENING

Victor says.

I shrug. "Well, just three times…and the court doesn't really count because that's like his office."

"I think he likes you… I saw something on Monday when he came over. Hmmm…"

"What are you hmmming for?"

"It's all so exciting! Do you like him?"

"Victor, I'm reading my Bible. I'm not trying to think about him…"

"Well, don't be afraid to ask God about him because I don't think he is random in your life," Victor says, confirming my own thoughts. "I know you probably don't feel ready to love again, but I can't wait for you to know what it means to be loved in a committed relationship and to experience true love. I too will pray about him. We don't want another time-waster in your life!"

"Thank you, Victor. He actually did ask me out, but I said no."

"Oh, okay. I like that he came correct, though. Anyway, let's pray that God will make His will clear for you, so you will have peace about your decision."

"Yeah, thanks. Please greet Amber for me."

"I will. Goodnight, sis."

"Goodnight."

*****

After Victor's call, I finish the tenth chapter of the Book of John and decide to call it a night. I have absorbed so much in one day. I'm particularly struck by Jesus' words in John 10:10, *"The thief comes only to steal and kill and destroy; I have come that they may have life, and have it to the full."* It speaks to me in so many ways.

I think of Nnamdi as a thief who came to devour me, while pretending to have good intentions. I know that there are also many other thieves that I've looked to for satisfaction, but now I see that only

Jesus can satisfy. He is the only one who can fulfil what He promises and do even more than I can imagine.

I get down on my knees and begin to pray for Him to satisfy my hunger and thirst to know Him more, to deliver me from every lying thief, to deliver my children and family from those who seek only to manipulate and devour us. I ask Him to help me see, to be able to distinguish the gifts that are truly from Him and not to fall for the lies and illusions of my enemy, Satan. I identify him as the original thief who sought to destroy me, but today, God has delivered me from his grip. Today, I am saved. As I pray, I thank God for His kindness and mercies towards me, and I ask Him about Segun.

"Lord, Segun said You sent him to me and that You talk with Him. Please talk with me too so that I'll know if he is really from You or just another thief looking to take advantage of me. I admit that I like him. Every time I see him, I feel happy, and I don't know why. I enjoy talking with him, and yes, he is very attractive. But my husband isn't even buried yet.

"I don't want to rush into anything, but if You have brought him for me to love, help me to love him and not push him away. But if he was only sent to help me with the case or to bring me to You, then keep him away from me before I fall for his charms. Thank You for listening to my prayer. And thank You for answering my prayer for a lawyer.

"Lord, thank You for being 'Father' to my children who are now fatherless. They have been fatherless for a long time, even before their father died, because he was hardly around to care for or mentor them. I don't know if I'll ever get married again, but I know they need a man in their lives. Father, I pray that the man who loves me, and whom I love, will love my children as his own too. Amen."

CHAPTER TWENTY-EIGHT - MAKING PEACE

DAEZE

A I have never slept as peacefully as I did last night. I know something has truly shifted in my world. I get down on my knees immediately I wake up to thank God for yesterday and for today. I pray that the day will be blessed and for God to reveal what He wants me to do. Aside from going to my children's school party, I don't have anything else planned.

Business-wise, I have a Chief Executive Officer that I employed five years ago, who has been doing a fantastic job at AdVi Grand. So good that I'm content to receive communication and reports about the business via email. On occasion, I visit the office and attend important meetings, but it really hasn't been demanding on my time.

I'm thinking I would like to go to the gym today, and maybe I can finally go to the spa and saloon as well, but I have this feeling, like the burden I had last night, that there's something else I'm supposed to do.

I bring out my Bible and the daily devotional my dad gave me yesterday to aid my spiritual growth. I open the devotional to today's date, Dec 12, 2025. The heading reads 'Make Peace,' and I'm immediately intrigued.

As I read, I feel like God is asking me to do something I would never have done…something I don't know how to do.

Citing Psalm 34:14, which says, *"Turn from evil and do good; seek peace and pursue it,"* the author makes a case for reconciliation, which he called "God's Supreme Will." He quotes 2 Peter 3:9 and 1 Timothy 2:1-4 to back up his teaching about God's desire to be reconciled to everyone.

He ends the devotional with a challenge. *"Who is it that you feel you cannot pray for? Make peace with them today."*

I am so convicted because I can think of a few people who are not dead, but who I have already buried in the archives of my mind.

Nneka. I know now that I need to see her. I'm not sure when or how, but I know it should be soon. I'll probably need to accompany my parents on their next visit.

Nnamdi's parents. I hate that they have never made an effort to reach out to me, but I now know I can't wait for them to make the first move. I must give up my pride and follow God's example. He sought and made peace with us; He came down to us and offered us pardon, even when we didn't regard Him nor seek peace with Him. And because He did so, I'm saved today.

I would like to visit with the kids, so I think tomorrow will be a better day for that. I decide to send Nnamdi's mother a message to let them know of my plans to visit with the children tomorrow. I'm not quite ready to call.

*****

I finish my time of devotion and prayer and go down to check on the children. They are at the table having their breakfast. Once they're done, I'll take them to school and go to the gym. While I wait, I decide to call my mum.

"Hi, Ada. How was your night?"

"It was good, Mum. Thank you. How are you and Dad?"

"We're good, dear. Still so happy about yesterday."

CHAPTER TWENTY-EIGHT - MAKING PEACE

I beam. "Me too. That's why I'm calling actually. I'm thinking I should go and see Nneka."

"Oh, my God!" my mum cries. "God, You are too good."

I just chuckle. "Can I follow you on your next visit?"

"Sure, but we don't really know when that will be. They moved her to Kirikiri. Wouldn't you like to go by yourself, or maybe ask Barrister Segun? He was the one who helped us with our first visit."

"Oh, okay," I swallow. "I'll call him."

Thinking it might be rude to call too early, I decide to call Segun after I return from dropping the kids at school. He picks up on the third ring.

"Hello, Adaeze. Nice of you to call."

"Hi, Segun," I say softly, feeling the usual pleasure from hearing his voice. "How are you doing?"

"I'm great. And you?"

"I'm good. I… I'm sorry about how I left things yesterday."

"Oh, please, don't be. I shouldn't have pressured you."

"Actually, I needed the push. I went to speak with my dad afterwards, and we had a good talk. He helped me to understand why I need God and why I need to pray."

"That's great."

"Yeah… So, I prayed and asked God to help me. I accepted His hand," I say, beaming.

"Thank You, Jesus!" Segun exclaims unashamedly, and I giggle.

"Yes! Thank You, Jesus."

"I'm so happy to hear that, Ada. I've been praying for you…"

"Really?"

"Yes. But You know, Jesus has been praying for you even longer."

"Hmmm… Well, I was actually calling because I want to go and see my sister. My mum said you can help me."

"Oh, that's great. I'd be happy to help. I'm actually heading there this morning to see another client. Want to go together?"

"Ummm... I don't know if I can. I'm supposed to be at my children's school at 1 pm today."

"Oh, okay. Then, let's do Monday. Cool?"

"Yes, please," I breathe with relief.

"Great, I'll make the arrangements. Should I pick you up? So we only need to take one car?"

"Yes, if you don't mind. I'm kind of nervous about going to that place."

"Don't be. You'll be fine."

"Okay, thanks."

There's a momentary silence as I wait for him to say bye, but he says, "So, ummm, now that you're saved..."

I beam and giggle.

"Any plans for Sunday?"

"Ummm... I actually haven't thought about it."

"It'll be good for you to meet and fellowship with other believers. If you're looking for somewhere to grow, I'd love for you to come to my church..."

"What? Are you like the pastor or something?" I tease.

Segun chuckles. "No, no. My legal work keeps me very busy. But you will soon know that we are all labourers in God's Vineyard, and because we want everyone saved, we have to keep inviting them to fellowship."

"I understand. I was just teasing..." I can hear the smile in his breathing. "Ummm, where's your church?"

"It's in Ikoyi."

"Oh, okay. Not far then..." He's beaming again. I giggle. "Okay. I don't mind."

"Yes!" he exclaims. "Praise God! I'll share the address with you... unless you want me to pick you up?"

CHAPTER TWENTY-EIGHT - MAKING PEACE

"Just share the address," I say, amused.

"Alright, then. I'll look out for you on Sunday."

"Cool. Bye," I mutter before I cut the call. Afterwards, I just exhale. *God, hold me, o!*

*****

Holy Light Fellowship in Parkview Estate, Ikoyi was easy to find. The building stands majestic surrounded by beautiful homes that share the same street. Cars of all brands line the street leading up to the church, and I struggle to find somewhere to park. Eventually, I find a spot a minute's walk away to park.

After dropping my children off at the Kid's Church, I head towards the main hall. An usher takes me to a single unoccupied seat, three rows from the front. As the choir leads the congregation in worship songs, I close my eyes and thank God that I made it to church today.

Yesterday, I took the children to see their paternal grandparents. Chief and Mrs Ukwueze were very happy to see us, and Nnamdi's mother cried as she embraced me. I hadn't even expected that emotional response. I almost cried. Almost.

The children told them all about their performances the day before, at their school's Christmas party.

"I sang a solo," Chinedu said proudly. "Mummy, do you have the video?"

I sure did. He sang like an angel! I also enjoyed Osinachi's performances. They both did so well.

I sent all the pictures and videos I took to Nnamdi's mum's phone, and she was thrilled as the children stood either side of her to look through and watch them with her. After that, the children were served plantain and egg for lunch, while Nnamdi's parents ate amala with ewedu soup. I didn't feel like eating.

"Have you spoken with Adaora and Uzo?" Mrs Ukwueze asked when we were about to leave. "They have fixed December 22nd for the burial. I hope you'll be there."

I swallowed. "I haven't. But I'll reach out and see what they need me to do."

Chief Ukwueze nodded his approval, and Mrs Ukwueze said, "Thank you, my daughter. God bless you."

They asked after my parents, and I told them they were okay. Though they didn't say the words, "We're sorry" or "Please forgive us," I knew that they regretted how things had turned out between me and Nnamdi. Nnamdi's dad thanked me for coming and blessed me and the children before we left.

The choir is singing a new song, and it's a little familiar. It's so beautiful, and I join the congregation as we sing, "Firm Foundation (He Won't)," by Maverick City Music.

"He won't fail… He won't fail," I sing as my eyes water.

When the pastor takes the podium to preach, I'm ready to be watered. I listen as he gives a sermon titled, "Beauty for Ashes," and I'm blessed. The word is for me.

"God doesn't owe anybody anything. He is a debtor to no one. If you feel you have been wronged in this life, just know that God is working on something! God is not done with you yet! If you feel discouraged, crushed, broken, let me speak to your dry bones…

"*'This is what the Sovereign Lord says to these bones: I will make breath enter you, and you will come to life. I will attach tendons to you and make flesh come upon you and cover you with skin; I will put breath in you, and you will come to life. Then you will know that I am the Lord.'*

"That's taken from Ezekiel 37, verses 5 to 6. If you're a child of God, you can hold Him to this word, knowing that there is nothing too hard for our Lord to do. Do I have a believer in the house?!"

I nod and then join the congregation in shouting. Yes, I'm going to hold God to His word. He will bring to a beautiful end what He has

CHAPTER TWENTY-EIGHT - MAKING PEACE

started in me. *He won't fail!*

When they asked earlier about those who were visiting the church for the first time, I raised my hand to collect a welcome card, which I filled and submitted to an usher. Before the service is over, an usher comes to stand by me, saying she would like to escort me to their welcome desk so I can learn more about their fellowship and consider becoming a member.

I'm not surprised when I see Segun at the welcome desk. The way he's looking at me as I approach, I feel like a bride on her wedding day, walking to her husband. I'm so happy to see him; I can't even stop smiling.

"Welcome to Holy Light Fellowship, Adaeze," he says when I'm finally at the desk, extending a hand to me.

"Hi, Segun," I say, taking it. "Thanks for inviting me."

"It was my honour to. I trust you were blessed by the ministration?"

I smile and nod. "Very charismatic!"

Segun chuckles. "We keep the boring sermons for the disciples." My jaw drops. "Just kidding!"

I chuckle too. "Okay, so, what do I do here?"

"Well, this is where I tell you more about the church and what we believe, and then we ask about you, what you believe, and your interest in drawing near to God through service and fellowship."

I nod and smile. "The floor is yours."

As Segun laughs, I marvel that he has never looked more handsome. *God, abeg!*

*****

Segun escorts me to pick up my children from the Kids' Church, then follows us to my car. After I have secured Chinedu in his seat, and Osinachi is strapped in the front seat, it's time for us to say "goodbye," but God knows I'm not ready.

"What are you doing later?" Segun asks. I guess the feeling is mutual.

"It's my nephew's tenth birthday today. Nneka's son, Demilade."

"Oh, wow! You're having a party?"

"Not really. Just going to visit." I swallow. "We can't really do anything big, you know, because of his mum being…you know?"

"Yeah, I get. Well, wish him a happy birthday for me."

"Will do," I say with a smile, taking that as my cue to leave. I open my car door and get in.

"I'm really glad you came," Segun says.

"Me too. See you tomorrow."

He beams and waves. "Bye, guys," he says to my kids.

I pull out of my parking spot and onto the street. As I drive away, I keep looking into my side mirror as he just stands in the same spot watching me drive away. *God, let him be genuine*, I pray.

CHAPTER TWENTY-NINE - FORGIVENESS

ADAEZE

Monday couldn't come soon enough, and it wasn't because I couldn't wait to see Nneka…

One barrister like that has been on my mind since I saw him at church yesterday.

Today, I will be in close quarters with him for at least 90 minutes, which is how long it will take for us to drive from Banana Island to Kirikiri Women's Prison and back to Banana Island, if the traffic isn't too bad.

Segun arrives right on time at 9 am to pick me up. As usual, he's dressed smartly, this time, in a navy blue native suit that makes him look taller than usual. He has a fresh haircut and is looking mighty fine. But I'm not even going to trip.

"I bought some provisions to take with us. That's okay, right?" I ask after we have exchanged pleasantries.

"Yes, sure. Need a hand?"

"Yes, please."

Segun helps me carry the two boxes of noodles I bought, as well as a bag of rice, a pack of 24 toilet rolls, and a few other things in shopping bags.

"Wow, you really went shopping!"

Hmmm... "I hope they will use them for the prisoners."

"They will."

Soon, we are on the road to our destination, and I'm cosy in my seat as Segun drives expertly through Lagos traffic. I love the playlist of Gospel music that plays through the speakers, though I haven't heard many of them before. When Cece Winans comes on with "Believe For It," I find myself humming along.

"How did it go yesterday?" Segun asks, breaking the silence when we exit for the Apapa-Oworonshoki expressway.

It takes me a while to figure out he's asking about my visit to Demilade's house for his tenth birthday.

"It was good, thanks for asking. I took a cake and bought some gifts for him as well. He was happy we visited, though I could tell he was disappointed that his celebration wasn't bigger or that his mother wasn't there. My brother also came with his wife and kids, and we just chilled till dinner time."

"That's nice. What about her husband? What's his name again?"

"Dotun. He was in good spirits, actually. He has been holding up, despite everything. He applied for the Executive Director position at AdVi Grand, the architectural company I run with my brother, and he was perfect for it. He will be resuming with us after Christmas."

"Wow, that's great."

"Yeah... I'm happy for him. His old boss actually called to offer him his job back, but even with more pay, he turned it down because he wants something that won't take him away from his family so much, especially now that it's just him and the kids."

I sigh. I'm really proud of him. I know he will give the children his best. To think Nneka had it so good and blew it.

"Has anyone spoken with the children about what happened?"

"Yes. Dotun said they were able to talk on Saturday. He sat the boys down and told them that their mother was in prison because she had

CHAPTER TWENTY-NINE - FORGIVENESS

done something very wrong. He said he had to be upfront because the truth would soon be everywhere. They were all crying, but eventually, when Dapo stood up to hug him, they all hugged it out. I feel so sad for the boys."

"I pray God comforts them all. This is so heartbreaking. Dotun is an incredible man to continue to love the children as his own."

"They have been his since they were born. That's the way he sees it. He really loves them."

Segun turns to me and gives a small smile, and I wonder if he is thinking what I'm thinking. *Will he ever see my kids as his?* But why should my mind go there?

He returns to look at the road, which is congested with trailers carrying massive containers, one of the reasons I'll never drive to Apapa!

Dotun's family hadn't visited yesterday, and I took him aside to ask him about it.

"They are heartbroken. They have a choice, not like me. I know they will come around later. But now, it's just too painful."

"It's understandable," I said. "Again, I'm sorry about all of this. I know you don't think I should apologise, but she was my family, and my family hurt you."

"Thank you, Ada."

"I'm going to see her tomorrow… I don't know if you want me to pass on a message."

He shook his head and wiped his eyes. "There's nothing to say."

"You're okay?" Segun asks, and I realise I have tears on my cheeks.

I just nod. I don't even know what I will say to Nneka. *God, please help me find the words.*

SEGUN

I feel so proud of Adaeze for the way she has been holding up through this very difficult time. As much as I'm sad for her, I'm so happy that I got a chance to meet her, and through our encounters and interactions, I've had the chance to get to know her.

Looking at her now, as she cries, I realise that I don't just love her; I'm in love with her. *God, I'm in love with Ada.*

Since the very first day we met, it's like I found the piece that was missing. And whenever we're not together, I miss her. But I have to take this slowly because she has been hurt so badly. I don't want to lose her again.

The next song that comes on as we climb down the bridge into Apapa seems so appropriate, I remain quiet and let Britt Nicole's "The Sun is Rising" minister hope to Ada.

Finally, we arrive at the prison, and I find somewhere safe to park on the road. I put a call across to the Deputy Controller of Prisons. I informed her ahead that we would be coming. Thankfully, she is around and sends someone to fetch us at the reception. They also help to carry the provisions Ada brought.

Ada remains silent as we walk into the prison, looking about curiously. We are led to a room that's like a classroom and told to wait.

"I wasn't expecting this," Ada says after a while.

"What do you mean?"

"It doesn't look as bad as I imagined," she whispers. "The inmates look so young, though..."

I sigh. "This is probably the best correctional centre in Nigeria. Our prisons are very overcrowded, but this one is not. However, many of these women are still awaiting trial, like your sister, and some are brought in quite young. There is so much reform that needs to happen with the prison system, but not enough time nor resources are being invested into correcting the deficiencies."

I stop talking as Nneka arrives, escorted by a guard, and is directed

CHAPTER TWENTY-NINE - FORGIVENESS

to take a seat. Her gaze lingers on me, straying occasionally to look at Ada, but she says nothing.

Ada speaks first. "How are you, Nneka?"

ADAEZE

I don't know what I was expecting from this visit, but it isn't the silent treatment my sister is giving me. Since I asked her how she was about a minute ago, she hasn't said a word. But I came too far to leave without expressing myself to her.

"Nneka, you hurt me..." My lips tremble with just those four words, and she gives me a passing look. "Is that what you wanted? To hurt me?"

Still, she remains quiet, looking out of the window as if I'm wasting her time.

"You hurt Dotun! Dotun is a good man; he was faithful to you. He is at home, taking care of your kids, after you deceived him for ten years! Where is your compassion?"

She sits forward, shuts her eyes, and exhales. For a moment, I think she might say something, but she just opens her eyes and looks at me then away again.

"You hurt Mum and Dad. And Victor too. Do you not have anything to say?" I cry, unable to believe that she can be so cold.

She swallows. A sole tear that escapes her left eye tells me she's listening. But we deserve more than that. I have cried buckets because of her!

I feel anger rising, but Segun holds my hand, and the negative emotions lose ground. I remember why I came.

"You did a terrible thing, Nneka. And I'm not just talking about murdering my husband. I don't know why, but I guess waiting for an answer from you before I let it go would be injuring myself further," I say. A moment passes before I finally let the words form in my mouth and utter them with difficulty, "I forgive you."

She looks at me, still with the same dead eyes, as she grinds her teeth. "I don't need your forgiveness," she says at last. "I don't want your *fucking* forgiveness!"

"Hey! Language!" the guard shouts.

Nneka rises from her seat. "I want to go to my room."

The guard moves aside so that Nneka can leave, and I just sit there more hurt than I was when I came. How could it be? How does she not even care about what she has done?!

I break down in sobs. And Segun cradles me in his arms as I cry.

SEGUN

When Nneka rises to leave, even I feel injured. If I had known the trip would be so fruitless, I would have discouraged Ada from coming. I can't imagine how hurt she feels right now.

She begins to weep, and I take her into my arms and let her cry into my chest. My tears fall too because that was painful to watch. *God of justice, make this right*, I pray. It's a prayer I say often in my line of work. Sometimes, I feel like I cannot stand to see another injustice committed against someone.

Ada eventually stops crying, and she looks up at me. With her face so close, I could kiss her right now. I know from looking in her eyes that it's the comfort she wants, but I can't be so weak. I have to be strong for her...for us. So, I hold her by her arms and create distance, a professional distance.

It feels like the hardest thing I have ever done because, *God*, I want to kiss her!

She looks down and sniffs, and I hope I haven't hurt her too. "I'm ready to go home," she murmurs.

"Okay," I say and rise to leave. I want to hold her hand, like I did while we were seated, but she folds her hands, one over her breasts and the other clutching her waist. I walk quietly behind her as she heads to the car.

The drive back is filled with silence. I want to ask her how she feels so many times, but I think I know. *Devastated.* I feel it too.

Even the music doesn't seem to help, and when she switches off the stereo, I don't object.

I choose instead to pray for her, that she won't let bitterness seep into her heart again, that she will let God comfort her through His Holy Spirit. That is the true comfort she needs now. Not me.

I don't know when she'll be ready for me to love her, but by God's grace, I'll be waiting when she calls.

When we arrive at her home, she says, "Thank you. I appreciate the time. Please remember to send me your bill."

I shut my eyes at her words. She's creating distance between us.

I step out of my car to escort her to her door, but she says, "Please don't. I'm fine. I just need some space right now."

I watch her leave with a sinking feeling that I won't hear from her again.

My fears are confirmed when Sunday comes around, and she doesn't come to fellowship. She said she wanted space, and I fear calling her would only make her feel like she needs to run away, so I don't.

Still, I pray for a miracle.

ADAEZE

I was not prepared for the damage seeing Nneka would cause to my heart and spirit. I was so naive, thinking everything would be fine because now I have God, but I might as well have walked into hell with a water gun!

When I'm back home, I go to my bedroom, get into bed, and just let the pain have its way. I cry until I sleep. When a phone call wakes me from sleep, even though I see it's Omi, I put my phone on 'Do not

Disturb.'

Mrs Abike comes in to check on me in the morning, and I stir when she places her hand on my forehead, perhaps thinking I've fallen sick. It does feel like a sickness, but my temperature is fine.

"Ma, come down and play with your children," Mrs Abike says. "They are worried about you."

"I'll come down at lunchtime," I say quietly.

"Okay, ma," she says before leaving.

"God, why didn't You warn me? How do I move on from this betrayal?" I pray aloud.

It is already past...

I hear that word in my spirit, and I am revived. *God spoke to me!*

I understand immediately that I have chosen to carry again what I already dropped. I don't need to wallow in the pain of what I have already overcome. Like the labour pains of a pregnant woman, it's just a memory.

"Thank You, Lord," I say, as I feel His peace returning.

Even though I feel better by the time Sunday comes around, I don't feel ready to see Segun. He didn't do anything wrong, and I'm glad he didn't take advantage of my weakness at the prison, even though it hurt like hell. In fact, that made me realise that he is truly trustworthy, a man of noble character.

I don't know when I'll be ready to see him again, but it's not today, so I stay home. Maybe next week I will find another fellowship to attend.

Tomorrow is Nnamdi's burial. I spoke with Uzo on Wednesday to let him know I'd be coming and would like to contribute. But now, as I think about what led to his death and the pains I suffered in our marriage, the temptation to be angry and bitter returns. However, I console myself with God's words to me - *It is already past.*

CHAPTER THIRTY - LIFE AFTER DEATH

ADAEZE

Today should have been our tenth wedding anniversary, but it's now the day of Nnamdi's funeral. I'm in church, dressed in black, in honour of the dead. I'm sober as the Minister preaches his message of 'Life After Death,' talking about the hope of everyone who dies believing in Jesus Christ for their salvation.

"If you are here today, and you are yet to give your life to Jesus Christ as your Lord and Personal Saviour, let me invite you now to do so. You do not need to come to the front. Simply bow your head with me and sincerely pray for the forgiveness of your sins. Pray that the Father will be merciful to you and baptize you with His Holy Spirit. Pray that your name will be written in the Lamb's Book of Life. For this death will surely come for us all, but only those who have called upon the name of the Lord shall rise up in glory to live with Him in eternity. May you and I be among them."

As the minister speaks, I think of Nnamdi, and I'm sad because I don't know if he ever had the chance to call on God before he died. I am no longer consumed with anger and resentment over what he did to me. I see him as a broken soul who needed the Saviour but didn't know it. I wipe my tears as I pray for his soul to find rest.

I have forgiven him, but I say it again in a whisper, "I forgive you."

Neither my parents nor Nnamdi's parents are able to attend the funeral because it is not right in our culture for parents to bury their children. Victor sits with me for support at the front of the church. Adaora, who has a black lace veil covering her face, sits with Uzo on the adjacent pew. When the sermon ends, we all rise to sing the hymn, "It is Well With My Soul." Then Uzo goes to the pulpit to give his eulogy.

"Nnamdi Gerald Ukwueze was my one and only brother, and I loved him. His death has been devastating to me and our entire family. I have always known Nnamdi to be very popular and well liked, even back in Secondary School. I was so proud to call him my big brother. He had a lot of friends, and he was always fun to have around. It is shocking to think that anyone would want to end his life.

"Nnamdi was very thoughtful and generous, not just with his money, but with his time. It's like he loved to make people happy. One of the first things he did when he got his inheritance was to buy a house for me and my family, and he even opened a trust fund for my children. I mean, he went over the call of duty, and this was just his nature.

"I know he died in a less than honourable circumstance, and it's no secret that my brother loved women, but I know he loved his wife and children very much. I remember the day he called me crying that Adaeze had packed out of their home because she thought he had only married her to get his inheritance. I will never forget what he said that night: *'Without her, the inheritance means nothing.'*

"So, Ada, please forgive my brother. I hope you will remember him for all his good qualities because he was truly an exceptional human being, and I for one, will miss him dearly."

The tears flow freely from my eyes as Uzo wraps up his eulogy by letting me and the world know that, in his own way, Nnamdi loved me. I don't understand it, but I accept the consolation. I don't want to think about all the times he kissed me and told me he loved me

CHAPTER THIRTY - LIFE AFTER DEATH

because I don't want to cry more than I already am. In truth, Nnamdi was easy to love when he was not cruel. I miss him.

At the end of the ceremony, I and Victor walk out first, behind the casket that contains my husband's body. Adaora and Uzo walk behind us until we get to the hearse that will carry the casket to the burial ground.

"Ada," Uzo says, and I turn around to look at him. "I'm so sorry."

He doesn't need to say more. I throw my arms around him, and we hug for a whole minute. "Thank you," I murmur in his ear.

I see Adaora walking away to enter her limousine, and I know we have unfinished business.

ADAORA

I'm standing by my brother's grave, looking into his final resting place, and my heart is breaking all over again. When I look at the white casket with trim, I can't believe his lifeless body is in there. I can't believe I'll never see him again…

"We therefore commit this body to the ground, earth to earth, ashes to ashes, dust to dust; in sure and certain hope of the Resurrection to eternal life…" the Minister says as my brother's body is lowered into the ground. And I weep.

When the ceremony ends, and as the mourners begin to disperse, I remain standing as I weep for my brother. No one understands my love for him. No one will ever understand my pain.

I feel a hand on my lower back and turn to see his widow. "I'm sorry for your loss, Ada," she says, surprising me.

I am overtaken with sobs by her show of compassion, and she draws me to her chest and comforts me. I should be comforting her, but I can't seem to stop crying.

"I'm so sorry, Ada," I weep. "I'm so sorry! Forgive me. Forgive me, please."

"I forgive you," she says, crying as well.

ADAEZE

I agreed to host the reception in my home as Nnamdi's widow. I think it is only right for his children to be a part of the remembrance ceremony for their father. Omi and Titi are around to help me with the preparations, allowing me to sit and receive mourners from afternoon to nighttime.

Many mourners attend my house, and many of them are beautiful women. But I do not look at their faces. This time, a black veil covers my face to hide my tears. After today, it will all be over.

Amber is also around to assist, and she helps me watch the children in attendance, including the three she birthed to my brother. Dotun came with Nneka's children also, and with Uzo's two little children included, Amber has her hands full. Uzo's older kids, Uche and Chioma, now in their teens, assist my friends to cater for the guests.

I'm glad to see Amarachi, Nnamdi's Executive Assistant, make an appearance. She comes to me and expresses her condolences. "Tomorrow will be better," she says, squeezing my hand gently. I accept the blessing.

Tamara, my former Executive Director, also attends the wake with her three-month-old baby girl, Ariana. "I'm sorry for your loss, ma," she says as she bends down to hug me.

"Thank you," I say in a whisper. "Thanks for coming."

It's the same thing I say to all my well-wishers, until 9 pm, when I choose to retire. I'm exhausted, emotionally and physically. But it's over now.

*****

The next day, when I wake, the house feels empty. I go downstairs and see that my friends and matron have tidied up, so there's no

CHAPTER THIRTY - LIFE AFTER DEATH

evidence of the reception we held, apart from the three extra coolers purchased to hold food that have no place in my kitchen. They have been washed and turned upside down on my kitchen island.

I walk out of the house, eager to breathe the free fresh air. I settle on the patio sofa and lean back to enjoy the breeze from the Atlantic Ocean, which is most amazing here. I have thought of moving out of this house several times over the years, but Nnamdi did good when he chose my brother to redesign my dream home. Even location-wise, it is perfect.

I let out a breath. I don't have anything planned for today, although it is two days until Christmas. I could take the children away on vacation. But I know it would be no vacation for me.

Frankly, I'm exhausted and in need of some serious pampering. I haven't been to the spa in weeks, and I haven't been consistent with gyming since the news of my husband's death broke out earlier this month.

Actually, I feel like getting out of the house. I don't mind spacing out in front of a big screen...or maybe I will enjoy the film if they have a good action movie. But I have never been one to go to the movies alone.

I remember Segun suggested we could catch a movie together. I wonder if the offer still stands... I have thought often about his profession of love, or near profession, and it still gives me pause. Was it romantic or the "Brotherly Love" Christians profess to one another? If I'm honest, I hope it's the former.

I heave a sigh.

I wonder what he is doing now. Is he even in town? Perhaps he travelled to his village for Christmas, like many Lagosians do. I want to call him and ask him to watch a movie with me, but I'm a little afraid he will say no. I mean, if he really wanted, he could have called me since. I'm sure he knows that I buried Nnamdi yesterday. Perhaps I offended him… Or maybe he is interested in someone else now.

I swallow.

Remembering that I can ask God, I shut my eyes, look into my heart, and pray. *Should I or should I not get in touch with Segun again, Lord?*

"Mummy!" I hear Osinachi call me, and I turn to the doorway. "Good morning, Mummy."

She hugs me, and I squeeze her tight and kiss her cheek. "Good morning, baby. How was your night?"

"It was good, thanks." She settles down beside me. "What are we having for breakfast?"

I inhale and exhale. "I'm thinking of going out. Want to join me to eat at the Wheatbaker?"

"Yes, please!"

"Okay. Go wake your brother and bathe so we can go."

"Okay, Mum," she says, rushing back into the house and taking the steps two by two.

*****

My children like the buffet at the restaurant, whereas I prefer to order à la carte. Chinedu returns first with a plate filled with scrambled eggs, bacon, and sausages. Not one vegetable or even starch in sight.

He beams at me as he sits down to devour his meal. Osinachi returns with a plate of dodo and chicken, with a couple of sausages. I just smile at both of them while I wait for my food to come.

"Mum," Chinedu says. "Are you going to get married again?"

I didn't even see that question coming. I give him a small smile and nod. "Hopefully. By God's grace."

Chinedu beams. "Good. Are you going to go out with Uncle Segun then?"

I furrow my brows. "Uncle Segun? Why would you think that?"

Chinedu looks down. "I'm sorry. I heard you telling Uncle Victor

CHAPTER THIRTY - LIFE AFTER DEATH

that he said he loved you…"

"When?"

"After church, at Demilade's house."

Oh, wow. I didn't know he had been listening or was even that aware. "That was a private and adult conversation."

"I'm sorry, Mummy," he says, head bowed. Looking up again, the relentless kid asks, "Don't you like him?"

I look at my son, a little perplexed. Why is he talking about Segun all of a sudden? I look at Osinachi, and she returns my gaze.

"I do, actually. He seems nice," I say at last.

"I think you should go for it, Mum," Osinachi says, and Chinedu nods in agreement.

I look away from them, though I sense something mysterious going on again. *God, are You answering me through my children?*

"When God gives you a second chance, take it." The words Dotun spoke as he recounted his own mysterious experience replay in my mind. I'm encouraged that God has answered me once again.

"Okay, I will," I say with a smile.

I exhale. I'm ready to live again.

CHAPTER THIRTY-ONE - TRUE LOVE

ADAEZE

When we return home after breakfast, I go up to my room and sit on my bed. I bring out my phone and search for the Barrister's number. *Here goes nothing,* I think as I dial.

Segun picks up after three rings. "Hello, Adaeze."

I'm instantly filled with warmth at the sound of his voice. "Hi, Segun. How are you?"

"I'm great! What about you?"

"I'm in a better place."

I think I hear him beaming. It comes across when he says, "Really?"

I give a little chuckle. "Yeah, really."

"I'm really happy to hear that."

I smile and nod, then breathe. He doesn't say anything as we both appreciate the brief silence.

"I was thinking about going to see a movie tonight… But I don't want to go by myself," I say after a while.

"I'd love to go with you, if you're asking…"

"I'm asking."

He beams, and it carries in his voice. "Then it's a date."

"Okay."

"What time would you like to go?"

"What are you doing now?"

CHAPTER THIRTY-ONE - TRUE LOVE

"Oh, wow. Actually, nothing. We can catch an early movie then."

"Maybe have some lunch first?"

"Great! I'll pick you up at lunch time, Ada."

"Okay. See you then."

I fall back on the bed after our conversation. I can't believe I just did that! I turned a dinner date into a lunch date because I can't wait to see him again. I'm so happy he is available to see me today.

I clasp my hands together in front of me and shut my eyes as I say, "Thank You, Lord."

SEGUN

I drop to my knees in worship after Ada's call. God has worked another miracle in my life, and I'm overjoyed. She wants to be with me like I want to be with her, and it makes me feel amazing.

"Thank You, Father! Thank You for bringing her to this better place. Please guide me as I begin a relationship with Your daughter. You know my desire. You have kept me from sinning against You. Please hold me now so I don't run ahead of You and make a mess of this good thing You are working out between us. Thank You for trusting me with her heart. I love You!"

I rise and continue to praise Him in song as I prepare myself for my first date in years. It has been long since I have had any desire to ask any woman out. After my fiancée fell ill and died of cancer five years ago, I haven't been ready to enter another committed relationship, and I'm not one to date casually. I've been waiting for God to relight my fire, and it happened on the day I met Ada. It was like something ignited in me, and I loved her before I knew her.

I was afraid that I scared her away when I confessed my true feelings prematurely, and again when I denied her the comfort she desired at the prison, but God has shown Himself merciful and faithful once more.

I sing along as I play my new favourite Gospel song, "Been So Good," by Elevation Worship on my YouTube Music app.

I'm actually hungry, but I'll wait to see Ada before I eat.

ADAEZE

Segun looks more handsome than I remember when he comes to pick me up for our date. He is dressed simply in loose-fitting, blue jeans, a white, short-sleeved Polo with black lining on the base of the sleeves, where they grip his muscled arms, and black loafers on his feet. He presents me with a bouquet, which I collect, beaming.

As soon as he steps into my home, my mischievous munchkins rise to welcome him. I would have preferred that I got to know him and love him first, but it seems they are too ready for a man in their lives. They bombard him with questions as I go to the kitchen to find a vase for my flowers.

The bouquet of assorted flowers is an arrangement of white tulips - my favourite - purple orchids, red roses, with million stars all around. It looks beautiful and smells so fragrant. I sniff them before bringing them back out to place on the coffee table.

"So, how many bad guys have you put in prison?" Chinedu asks Segun.

He looks up at me helplessly. "Actually, I defend the accused. I don't prosecute."

"Oh... Does that mean you defend murderers?" Chinedu frowns.

"No... At least I try not to."

"Okay, kids! Please behave," I say.

"It's okay," Segun says, rising from his seat and walking towards me by the door. "It was lovely seeing you guys again."

"Mrs Abike!" My matron comes out of the laundry room with a basket of clean clothes. "I'll be out for a few hours. Please ensure they behave and eat well."

CHAPTER THIRTY-ONE - TRUE LOVE

"Yes, ma'am," she says to me, bearing the same mischievous smile on my kids' faces. I guess it's about time for me to date...even though my husband was just buried yesterday.

I look up at Segun, and he seems to notice what's going on as he smiles down at me. I feel a flutter in my stomach. I take a deep breath and lead the way out of the house.

When we get outside, and I shut the door, Segun takes my hand in his, and I marvel at how I have missed the feel of his hand on mine since he last held me at the prison. We walk to his car, and he opens the door for me before going around to enter at the driver's side.

When he starts the car, Gospel music starts playing through the speakers. Chris Tomlin is singing, "Good Good Father," and I listen to the lyrics appreciatively, smiling as the words resonate.

SEGUN

I take Ada to the House Lagos, one of my favourite food haunts. Knowing that we have a similar taste in food, I think she's going to enjoy it.

When I park, I'm eager to get to her because I can't wait to hold her hand again. I have been itching to hold it, even while driving. I don't know how something so simple can feel so amazing.

But it does as I take hold of her hand again, intertwining my fingers with hers.

We settle in our seats at the restaurant, and I send her the menu on WhatsApp because I already have it on my phone. She goes for the House Stir Fry Jollof, while I order the Peppered Turkey & Smoky Jollof. For drinks, she orders the Ginger Citrus Burst mocktail, and I go for the Passion Twist.

When the waiter leaves after taking our orders, I just admire Ada. She's wearing a white two piece with flared bottoms that makes it hard for me to ignore her lovely figure. She has really taken care of her body over the years, I think, swallowing.

She leans into me and smiles flirtatiously. "What are you looking at?"

"You're gorgeous..." I breathe.

She sits back and averts her eyes, as though my compliment makes her uncomfortable.

I reach out my hand to hold hers again. "You think it's another line?"

She looks at me and shakes her head. She swallows. "Wouldn't you rather be with someone younger?"

I'm taken aback for a second. "How do I say this without it sounding like a line...?"

She giggles.

"It is you my heart wants."

She meets my gaze. "To be honest, I'm not sure I can handle a younger man."

"Why?"

"Different life experiences, mindsets, maturity... I feel like we have a problem before we have even started our journey."

"I don't see it as a problem. I think I'm much more responsible than many men ten years older. I value you as a gift from God to me..." I exhale, and she just stares at me. "I haven't felt what I feel for you for anyone in years... I don't think that's a mistake."

"For years?"

I nod.

"Wow... But you don't even know me."

"That's why we are on a date, Ada," I beam. "Are you getting to let it happen?"

She swallows and nods. And I beam, lifting her hand to place a kiss on it. I'm so glad we've got that out of the way.

ADAEZE

CHAPTER THIRTY-ONE - TRUE LOVE

I am enjoying my date with Segun. He is so easy to be around. He's very observant, intelligent, passionate… Even the age-gap thing is an advantage because he is like a newer model of my ideal man. I smile as I listen to him talk about his family.

He has just one sister in her late 20s. Her name is Tayo, and she's a fashion designer. Both of them were miracle babies, with him opening his mother's womb after 10 years of marriage. His parents have had a long, happy marriage, and he learned how to abide and trust in God from their example of faithfulness over the years.

By now, he knows so much about my family, having met the whole lot of us, so I tell him about my childhood and how my parents almost broke up because of my dad's infidelity. I also tell him what my dad revealed the day I confronted him about it.

"He said my mum's prayers were what changed things for him," I say, looking into Segun's eyes. "It made me think about Nnamdi… Like, maybe things got worse because I didn't pray for him."

"Don't do that to yourself, Ada. Sometimes, despite our prayers, people still do evil," he said, reaching out to wipe a wayward tear from my cheek. "Now you know the power of prayer; you can use it daily. I pray every day for God to help me not to sin against Him." He swallows and looks at me intently. "Sometimes, I wonder why it took so long to find you, but then I think if I had met you while you were married, perhaps I would have fallen."

I gawk at him. *Are his feelings so strong?* I close my mouth and swallow my saliva. "Thank you."

He nods and smiles at me. The waiter comes with our lunch orders, and I breathe in deeply, thinking about all we have discussed even before the food arrived.

When she leaves, he reaches for my hand again. "If you're struggling to forgive, pray for God to help you forgive."

"Actually, I believe I have forgiven Nnamdi and even Nneka. But forgiving Rita has been a little bit harder. I now understand the sudden and gradual nature of the process of transformation that my dad spoke of," I say.

Segun nods. "Yeah, it will take time for you to heal completely."

"I guess I have no obligation to attend her funeral, unlike with Nnamdi. We weren't even friends when she died. It just hurts every time I get messages in our Alumni group about their plans to visit her family, attend the wake, and go for the burial because I know they all know what happened," I continue, feeling a need to unburden myself. "I keep wanting to leave the WhatsApp group, but I think God wants me to stay. All I've been able to do since is send in my RIP message."

"That's good. That's something."

I giggle. "Yeah. It got five 'heart' reactions!"

Segun giggles. "I'm proud of you. Just keep taking those little steps and listening to God's leading. This our walk is truly one day at a time. God is patient and faithful."

"I'm so glad I found you," I say what's been weighing on my heart.

He beams at me. "Me too." He exhales. "Ready to tuck in?"

I chuckle and nod before I face the scrumptious-looking food on my plate. It smells amazing.

Segun reaches out again to hold both my hands over the food. "Shall we pray?"

I nod. "Yes, let's."

"Father, I thank You for what You have started in us. I trust that You will nurture it to perfection. Thank You for this lovely day You made and this delicious food before us. We bless it in the name of Jesus, amen."

"Amen."

*****

Segun drops me at home in the evening after a two-hour lunch, two

CHAPTER THIRTY-ONE - TRUE LOVE

and a half-hour movie, and a three-hour dinner and drinks. We just didn't want the date to end. At my door, he hugs me tightly, and I long for more. I can't wait for our next date.

I know I like him a lot, and the realisation is scary. I can't help wondering if it is too soon for me to get involved with someone new. Do I really know him? Yes, he is a man of godly character, but is he really the one for me? What if he hurts me?

However, I feel God's peace come over me, and my fears dissipate. This time, God is going to guide me because, this time, I am going to seek His face and trust Him.

THE EPILOGUE - THE LAST WILL AND TESTAMENT OF NNAMDI GERALD UKWUEZE

To my beloved wife, Adaeze. Thank you for choosing me and loving me despite my many flaws. For all the pains I caused you in life, I leave to you, in death, my entire estate, less ten percent to be divided equally among my children. I would not have gotten it without you, Ada. You brought me so much joy and peace. I wish I could have given you what you really wanted. Please forgive me.

My children are:

Osinachi and Chinedu, born by Adaeze Ukwueze;

Demilade, Dapo, Seun, and Sade, born by Nneka Aregbesola;

Nomnso, Kelechi, and Idun, born by Cynthia Adesola;

Gloria and Anthony, born by Amarachi Chukwudi;

THE EPILOGUE - THE LAST WILL AND TESTAMENT OF NNAMDI GERALD...

Taiwo and Kehinde, born by Adenike Rogers;

Stephen, born by Susan Harrison;

Ariana, born by Tamara Irede.

This is the will and testament of Nnamdi Gerald Ukwueze as it was last updated on the 30th of October 2025.

BONUS CHAPTER - A WOMAN'S SECRET

TAMARA

The sound of my six-month-old baby crying rouses me from sleep. *What does she want again? I just fed her like an hour ago!*

"Huh, no," I grunt as I stir in bed. *Whatever possessed me to go and get pregnant?*

I feel my husband's hand on the small of my back. "Don't worry, baby. Sleep in. I'll take care of her."

"Uh... Thank you, baby," I mumble into my pillow and shut my eyes again. Just one more hour. Maybe two if God is merciful.

I'm glad when the crying stops. I don't wake up again until my Saturday morning alarm goes off on my phone at 9 am. I reach out and hit the dismiss button. I still haven't changed it from the days I was a childless wife. It serves as a memorial now, a reminder and a hope that I will soon be able to sleep in on Saturday mornings again.

I sit up and swing my legs over the bed. The doorbell rings, and I hear Nelson as he opens the door. I wonder who will be calling at this time.

I rise and head into my bathroom to freshen up before leaving my bedroom and going down to meet my family. Nelson is in the kitchen, sitting at the small dining table and feeding Ariana with one of the bottles I expressed yesterday. He is such a hands-on dad!

"Good morning, baby. Thank you for letting me sleep in," I say as I go over to him and kiss him on the lips.

"No problem. You have mail," he says, nodding in the direction on an envelope he left on top of the microwave.

"Oh, nice," I say as I go to pick it up. It's a DHL recorded delivery package, marked Private and Confidential. I can't imagine what it is. The sender appears to be a law firm in Lagos.

I open it and take a letter from the package. *All this just for a letter?* But it's not just any letter. It's a copy of Nnamdi's will that names my child as a beneficiary.

"What is it?" Nelson says, rising to come and look at it, our baby in his arms.

It's too late for me to prevent him from seeing it, but still I try. I move away so I can finish reading it, hoping he didn't see much.

"Is that what I think it is?" Nelson asks.

I swallow. "Umm… Baby… Please don't be mad."

"Can I see it?" he asks.

With a trembling hand, I hand him the letter, and he snatches it from me with his free hand, while the other hugs our baby to his chest. He reads the letter in its entirety.

Still, he asks, "What is this?"

"Baby… I can explain."

"Start talking."

*****

In August 2024, after two years of marriage, my husband and I found out that we couldn't get pregnant. We were both tested, and we discovered that the problem was with him. He wasn't producing enough sperm to achieve fertilisation.

The doctor told us about a way to overcome the challenge. All that was needed was for me to undergo Intrauterine Insemination (IUI), using my husband's sperm. He said it would increase our likelihood of getting pregnant. So, we agreed to the procedure.

But three months later, after three cycles, we were advised to try IVF, but the cost was significantly greater with no guarantees. The doctor said we could do three more cycles of IUI to see if it helps, and Nelson and I agreed to give that another shot before trying IVF.

When we got home, Nelson said he would prefer for us to adopt a child instead of doing the IVF treatment. He didn't think we needed to spend so much money trying to have a baby when we still need to have money to raise one.

"Six cycles of IUI have to be enough because this economy isn't smiling," he said.

Even though I nodded in agreement, I wasn't happy about his decision. I really wanted my own baby. After the fourth cycle failed also, I got an idea. It was crazy, but if it could work, it was worth trying, I thought.

I went to LionsGate Inc. and waited to see the CEO. Even as I waited, my hands shook. I had seen him a few times over the years, and we hadn't had much interaction, but I was aware of his reputation.

"Tamara…" he said when I walked into his office. He was leaning back in his executive chair and smiling up at me. I was honestly surprised he knew who I was. I usually dealt with his secretary, Amarachi. "What are you doing here?"

"Good morning, sir. Please, I need to speak with you about something."

"Take a seat." He indicated the right seat in front of his grand desk and sat up, putting his elbows on the desk and cradling his head in his hands. He looked at me expectantly, an amused smile on his lips.

I took the seat offered and then took a deep breath. "Please, sir. Don't be offended." I swallowed. "I know your reputation with women. I know you can give me what I want."

"What do you want, Tamara?"

"I need your sperm, sir."

His eyebrows shut up, and he sat back in his chair. "Wow! That's a first!"

"You see, my husband and I have been trying to get pregnant for more than two years now, and we have done four cycles of IUI. We have just two left, and well... I'm not so optimistic that I will be able to get pregnant with the remaining two."

Nnamdi chuckled. "Oh, wow. So, what are you asking? You want me to hand you my sperm in a tube?"

With my head bowed, I nodded.

"Why me? Can't you get some from a sperm bank?"

I swallow and look up at him. "They are a bit too anonymous. And I know you are a brilliant man. It's a quality I would like in my child."

Nnamdi beamed, appraising me for a moment. "I'm afraid I don't share my sperm."

"Please... I wouldn't ask if I wasn't desperate."

"Then let's do it the natural way. We might as well have some fun while we are at it."

"Please, I don't want to cheat on my husband... I just want a baby."

Nnamdi exhaled. "Don't you see you are cheating just by asking to swap his sperm for mine? I'm sorry; I can't help. I think you should continue with your treatment. If you change your mind, you know where I am."

I looked at him, and he returned my gaze, his eyes steady on my face. I nodded and rose to leave. "I'm sorry I bothered you."

I cried when I got home because I couldn't believe I had stooped so low. Nnamdi was right. Switching my husband's sperm would also be cheating. Was it so bad to agree to do it with him once? *Yes!* I knew it was. I decided I'd take my chance with the fifth cycle.

But after another 28 days, I lay in bed crying because I wasn't pregnant.

"Hey, baby," Nelson said, as he rubbed my arm, my back turned to him. "I'm sorry it didn't work. It's all my fault."

I just sobbed.

"I was thinking… If the last one doesn't work, we could try a sperm donor. I think that's cheaper than IVF."

I turned to him. "Really?"

He nodded. "If it means that much to you to carry a baby, I don't mind. It's a bit better than adoption because at least the baby will have your beautiful features." He stroked my face lovingly.

"Oh, darling! Thank you! I love you so much," I said to him, then kissed him.

Nelson returned my kiss with passion, turning me to lay on my back. "I love you," he said as he made love to me with vigour. It was amazing, the best we had ever had.

Later that night, as we lay in bed, I thought of what Nelson said. He didn't mind if he wasn't the biological father as long as I got my baby. I could hardly sleep as I weighed the options I had: to use a sperm donor or to have sex with Nnamdi Ukwueze. I was already on fertility drugs, so I was sure I would only need to sleep with him once. With my husband's arm around my waist, I decided I would return to Nnamdi's office the next day.

However, when I went to his office in the morning, I was told he was busy with meetings all day and couldn't see me. I returned to my office thinking I had blown my chance. But then Nnamdi called. He invited me to meet him at a hotel at lunchtime. He had booked us a room.

Nnamdi opened the door to me wearing the hotel's long, white bathrobe. He stepped aside for me to enter the deluxe suite he had booked. I looked at the king-sized bed, all made up with white sheets and a fluffy duvet, and I suddenly realised the gravity of what I was about to do. *Could I really do this?*

Nnamdi came to me and offered me a glass of champagne. "It will help with the nerves," he said.

I took it and sipped it. Then took a gulp.

Nnamdi came up behind me and began to kiss my shoulder. "I don't think I can do this," I said.

"Sure, you can," he muttered. "Just forget you are married for a second. If you keep it in your mind, you won't get the orgasm you need to conceive… Relax, let's have fun, and let's get you pregnant. Okay?"

I nodded, and he turned my head to the side and brought his lips to mine. I tried to do what he said, forget that I was married. When he kissed me, it wasn't hard to do. Nnamdi was such a good kisser. He was a master in the art of love making. I thought he would get to it within a minute, but he spent about 15 minutes just kissing me and touching me, until my body was yearning for him to take possession.

Still, he deferred the main event, making a detour to my lower regions, where he gave me pleasure like I had never experienced before. I was already having an orgasm when he finally decided to take me. It was incredible! I must have come three times that afternoon.

I lay in bed afterwards, ruined. Tears streamed down my face as I realised what I had done to my marriage. How was I going to ever sleep with Nelson again?

A couple of days later, Nnamdi invited me to his hotel room again. He didn't need to convince me that it was necessary to increase my chances of pregnancy. I went because I had been longing for him since the first time he claimed my body. I didn't want to stop. I couldn't stop.

I never took the sixth treatment, but a month later, in February 2025, when I took a pregnancy test, it was positive. I had gotten my baby.

Nelson was so happy that I was finally pregnant, he didn't even ask if I used a sperm donor. I think he assumed we had finally gotten lucky!

Nnamdi and I continued our affair until June 2025, when he went to the US for Ada's 44th birthday. When he got back in September, I had just delivered my baby. I still missed him and longed for him, but he never called for me again. I soon learnt of his relationship and engagement to Rita, but I was more devastated when I learnt that he had been murdered. Thankfully, his murderer was caught and was given the death sentence last week.

*****

"Baby, I'm so sorry!" I cry to Nelson after confessing my infidelity. "Please forgive me!"

I am on my knees before him in the living room, where he is sitting on the sofa. Ariana's asleep in her crib, where he placed her a few minutes ago.

"So, you are one of his prostitutes?!" Nelson cries.

"No, no, baby. It wasn't like that."

"I don't know who you are. I want a paternity test!"

I weep, as he rises from the sofa, sobbing as he goes to our bedroom. The next sound I hear is the door slamming.

*****

We are both seated at the doctor's office when he comes in with the results of the test for the paternity of my baby.

"It's positive," he says simply, looking between Nelson and me.

"What do you mean? The baby is mine?"

The doctor smiles. "Yes. Ariana is your biological child."

I am so shocked. Nelson looks at me, his eyes wet with tears. He rises up and leaves the doctor's office.

"Thank you, doctor," I say as I rise to follow my husband out.

I can't believe it's not Nnamdi's baby. My mind goes back to our love making the day before I went to see Nnamdi. Was I actually already pregnant then and didn't know it?

"Nelson, I'm sorry," I say when we get home. We had driven in silence the whole way. "Baby, please forgive me."

He turned to me, wiping his tears. "I would have done anything for you, Tamara. But I know now that I would have wasted my life. Not anymore."

I crumble to my knees and weep as my husband walks away from me. I gave up hope and ruined my marriage because I wanted to have a baby. *What have I done?!*

"May the God of hope fill you with all joy and peace as you trust in him, so that you may overflow with hope by the power of the Holy Spirit."
(Romans 15:13, NIV)

Acknowledgements

God, I thank You for enabling me to write this story, through the talent and boldness You gave me to address deep issues of life and sensitive matters of the heart. I wanted to shrink from the challenge, but You encouraged me and helped me!

To my Daddy, thank you for believing in my talent and supporting me the way you do. You are a treasure to me, and I love you so much. Uncle John and Aunty Pat, you've read all my stories and continually cheer me on. I am so encouraged to have your support and guidance too.

To my beta readers, Ijeoma Okonkwo, Chioma Oparadike, Christianah Omolade, Oruare Ojimadu, Gloria Elemide, and Temitope Adeniran. You guys were amazing! I would have submitted a half-baked story without your honest feedback.

To everyone who gave to help me print my first set of books, I pray God will send you help whenever you call. Thank you so much!

To my patrons and dedicated readers; I'm so glad I have you in my corner. You are the reason I stay encouraged to keep pushing and writing these stories. I always look forward to your feedback and reviews. May God bless you and send you encouragers and supporters to accomplish His will for your lives too. Amen!

About the Author

Ufuomaee is a writer, blogger, and Christian fiction author. She tells stories to help young people make the right choice before marriage and deal with challenges that often arise during and after. She loves to use parables and poetry to teach about God's love. When she's not writing or working, Ufuomaee loves to watch action movies and romcoms on Netflix. She also loves reading romantic and inspiring books by other amazing authors, which she reviews at www.ufuomaee.blog.

CONNECT WITH ME
BECOME A PATRON: www.patreon.com/ufuomaee
AMAZON: www.amazon.com/author/ufuomaee
GOODREADS: bit.ly/UfuomaeeGoodreads
FOLLOW ON FACEBOOK: @ufuomaeedotcom
TWITTER: @UfuomaeeB
INSTAGRAM: @ufuomaee
MEDIUM: @ufuomaee
WEBSITE: www.ufuomaee.com
BLOG: www.ufuomaee.blog
EMAIL: me@ufuomaee.com

OTHER TITLES BY UFUOMAEE
The Church Girl
An Emotional Affair
Broken
He Cheated!
A Small World - Season One
A Small World - Season Two
A Small World - Season Three
A Small World - Season Four
A Small World - Season Five
The House Girl
Perfect Love
Beauty and the Beast
The Atheist
The Naive Wife - Rachel's Choice
The Naive Wife - Rachel's Diary
The Naive Wife - Rachel's Hope
A Valentine Set-Up

**Check out my full catalogue of books at
www.ufuomaee.com/library**